The Third Circle

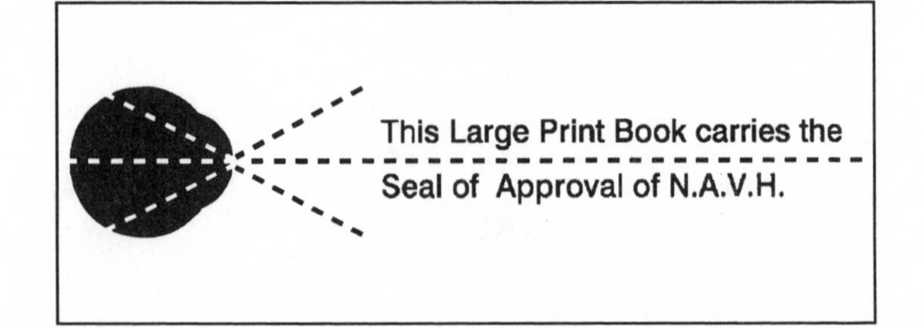
This Large Print Book carries the
Seal of Approval of N.A.V.H.

The Third Circle

Amanda Quick

THORNDIKE PRESS
A part of Gale, Cengage Learning

Detroit • New York • San Francisco • New Haven, Conn • Waterville, Maine • London

An Arcade Society Novel.
Thorndike Press, a part of Gale, Cengage Learning.

Thorndike Press® Large Print Basic.
The text of this Large Print edition is unabridged.
Other aspects of the book may vary from the original edition.
Set in 16 pt. Plantin.
Printed on permanent paper.

LIBRARY OF CONGRESS CATALOGING-IN-PUBLICATION DATA

Quick, Amanda.
The Third Circle / by Amanda Quick.
p. cm.
"An Arcade Society Novel."
ISBN-13: 978-1-4104-0474-9 (hardcover : alk. paper)
ISBN-10: 1-4104-0474-9 (hardcover : alk. paper)
1. Relics — Fiction. 2. Hypnotists —Fiction. 3. Secret societies — England — Fiction. 4. Large type books. I. Title.
PS3561.R44T49 2008b
813'.54—dc22

2007052089

Published in 2008 in arrangement with G.P. Putnam's Sons, a member of Penguin Group (USA) Inc.

Printed in the United States of America
1 2 3 4 5 6 7 12 11 10 09 08

FOR MICHELE CASTLE

With thanks for being a terrific sister-in-law.
Looking forward to the next family cruise!

1

Late in the reign of Queen Victoria . . .

The heavily shadowed gallery of the museum was filled with many strange and disturbing artifacts. None of the antiquities, however, was as shocking as the woman lying in a dark pool of blood on the cold marble floor.

The ominous figure looming over the body was that of a man. The wall sconces were turned down very low, but there was enough light to reveal the silhouette of his boot-length overcoat. The high collar was turned up around his neck, partially concealing his profile.

Leona Hewitt had only a split second to register the frightening scene. She had just rounded a massive stone statue of a mythical winged monster. Dressed as a male servant, her hair pinned beneath a masculine wig, she was moving swiftly, almost running in her frenzied effort to locate the crystal. Momentum carried her straight toward the man who stood over the body of the woman.

He turned toward her, his coat sweeping out like a great black wing.

She tried frantically to alter her course, but it was too late. He caught her as effortlessly as though she were a lover who had deliberately flown into his arms, a lover he had anticipated with great eagerness.

"Silence," he said, very softly, into her ear. *"Do not move."*

It was not the command that stilled her utterly but rather the sound of his voice. Energy pulsed through every word, flooding her senses like a great ocean wave. It was as if some mad doctor had forced an exotic drug straight into her veins, a potion that had the power to paralyze her. Yet the fear that had sluiced through her a moment ago vanished as if by magic.

"You will remain silent and motionless until I give you further instructions."

Her captor's voice was a chilling, oddly thrilling force of nature that swept her away into a strange dimension. The muffled sounds of drunken laughter and the music from the party taking place two floors below faded into the night. She was now in another place, a realm where nothing mattered but the voice.

The voice. It had forced her into this bizarre dream state. She knew all about dreams.

Comprehension flashed through her, disrupting the trance. Her captor was using some sort of paranormal power to control her. Why was she standing so still and passive? She should be fighting for her life. She *would* fight.

She summoned her will and her own senses the way she did when she channeled energy through a dream crystal. The wavering sense of unreality shattered into a million glittering fragments. She was suddenly free of the strange spell, but she was not free of the man who had her pinned against him. It was a lot like being chained to a rock.

"Bloody hell," he muttered. "You're a woman."

Reality, together with fear and the muted sounds of the party, returned in a startling rush. She started to struggle wildly. The wig slid forward over one eye, partially blinding her.

The man clamped his hand across her mouth and tightened his grip on her. "I don't know how you slipped out of the trance, but you had best keep silent if you want to survive this night."

His voice was different now. It was still infused with a deep and compelling quality, but his words no longer resonated with the electrifying energy that had briefly turned her into a statue. Evidently he had abandoned the attempt to employ his mental powers to control her. Instead, he was doing it the more traditional way: using the naturally superior physical strength nature had bestowed on the male of the species.

She tried to kick his shin, but her shoe skidded on some slick substance. *Oh, heavens, blood.* She missed her target, but her toe struck a small object on the floor beside the body. She heard the item skitter lightly across the stone tiles.

"Damnation, there is someone coming up the stairs," he whispered urgently into her ear. "Can't you hear the footsteps? If we are discovered, neither one of us will get out of here alive."

The grim certainty of his words made her suddenly uncertain.

"I'm not the one who killed the woman," he added very softly, as though he had read her thoughts. "The murderer, however, is likely still in this house. That may be him returning to clean up after his crime."

She realized that she believed him, and not because he had put her back into a trance. It came down to cold logic. If he were the killer, he would no doubt have slit her throat by now. She would be on the floor beside the dead woman, blood pooling around her. She stopped struggling.

"At last, signs of intelligence," he muttered.

She heard the footsteps then. Someone was, indeed, coming up the stairs into the gallery; if not the killer, one of the guests perhaps. Whoever he was, there was an excellent chance that he was quite drunk. Lord Delbridge was entertaining a large number of his male acquaintances this evening. His parties were notorious, not only for the unlimited quantities of fine wine and excellent food but also for the bevy of elegantly dressed prostitutes who were always invited to attend.

Cautiously, her captor removed his hand from her mouth. When she made no attempt to scream, he released her. She pushed the wig back into place so that she could see.

His fingers closed around her wrist like a manacle. The next thing she knew, he was drawing her away from the body and into the deep shadows cast by what appeared to be a large stone table set on a massive pedestal.

Halfway toward his goal, he leaned down just long enough to scoop up the small object she had kicked across the floor a moment earlier. He dropped whatever it was into his pocket before pushing her into the space between the heavy table and the wall.

When she brushed against one corner of the table, a tingle of unpleasant energy crackled through her. Reflexively, she pulled back, flinching a little. In the dim light she could see strange carvings in the stone. It was no ordinary table, she realized with a shudder, rather an ancient altar, one used for some unholy purposes. She had felt similar splashes of acid-dark energy from several of the other relics housed here in Lord Delbridge's private museum. The entire gallery reeked of troubling emanations that made her skin crawl.

The footsteps were closer now, moving from the top of the main staircase into the hushed gallery.

"Molly?" A man's voice, slurred with drink. "Where are you, my dear? Sorry I'm a bit late. Got delayed in the card room. But I haven't forgotten you."

Leona felt her companion's arm tighten around her. She realized that he had sensed her involuntary shudder. Unceremoniously, he pushed her down behind the shelter of the stone table.

Crouching beside her, he drew an object out of the pocket of his coat. She sincerely hoped that it was a pistol.

The footsteps came closer. In another moment the newcomer would surely see the dead woman.

"Molly?" The man's voice sharpened with annoyance. "Where the devil are you, you silly girl? I'm not in the mood for games tonight."

The dead woman had come up to the gallery to keep a tryst. Her lover was late, and now he was about to find her.

The footsteps halted.

"Molly?" The man sounded bewildered. "What are you doing on the floor? I'm sure we can find a more comfortable bed. I really don't . . . *bloody hell.*"

Leona heard a choked, horrified gasp followed by a flurry of footsteps. The would-be lover was running, fleeing back toward the main staircase. When he passed in front of one of the sconces, Leona saw his silhouette flicker on the wall like an image in a magic lantern show.

The man in the black coat was suddenly on his feet. For an instant Leona was dumbfounded. What on earth did he think he was doing? She tried to grab his hand to pull him back down beside her. But he was already moving, gliding out from behind the shelter of the dreadful altar. She realized that he meant to step directly into the path of the fleeing man.

He was mad, she thought. The fleeing lover would no doubt conclude that he was being confronted by the killer. He would scream, bringing Delbridge and the guests and the staff up into the gallery. She readied herself for a desperate flight to the servants' staircase. Belatedly another plan occurred to her. Maybe it would be better to wait and try to blend in with the crowd when it arrived.

She was still trying to decide on the best course of action when she heard the man in the black coat speak. He employed the same strange voice that had temporarily frozen her into complete immobility.

"Halt," he ordered in deep, rolling tones that resonated with invisible energy. *"Do not move."*

The command had an immediate effect on the running figure. The man scrambled to a stop and stood motionless.

Hypnosis, Leona thought, comprehending at last. The man in the black coat was a powerful mesmerist who somehow augmented his commands with psychical energy.

Until now, she had not paid much attention to the art of hypnosis. It was, generally speaking, the province of stage performers and quacks who claimed to be able to treat hysteria and other nervous disorders with their skills. Mesmerism was also a subject of much lurid speculation and anxious public concern. Dire warnings of the many fiendish ways in which hypnotists could employ their mysterious talents for criminal purposes appeared regularly in the press.

Regardless of the intentions of the hypnotist, the business was said to require a tranquil atmosphere and a quiet, willing subject. She had never heard of a practitioner of the art who could freeze a man in his tracks with only a few words.

"You are in a place of complete stillness," the hypnotist continued. *"You are asleep. You will remain asleep until the clock strikes three. When you awaken you will remember that you found Molly murdered, but you will not remember that you saw me or the woman who is with me. We had nothing to do with the murder of Molly. We are not important. Do you understand?"*

"Yes."

Leona glanced at the clock standing on a nearby table. In the light of an adjacent sconce she could just barely make out the time. Two-thirty. The hypnotist had bought them half an hour in which to make good their escape.

He turned away from the frozen man and

looked at her.

"Come," he said. "It is past time to leave this place. We must get out of here before someone else decides to wander up those stairs."

Automatically she put one hand on the surface of the altar to push herself to her feet. The instant her skin came in contact with the stone another unpleasant sensation, almost electrical in nature, swept through her. It was as though she had touched an old coffin, one in which the occupant did not lie in peace.

She snatched her hand away from the altar, rose and hurried out from behind the relic. She stared at the gentleman standing statue-still in the center of the gallery.

"This way," the hypnotist said. He went swiftly toward the door that opened onto the servants' stairs.

She jerked her attention away from the entranced man and followed the hypnotist down an aisle lined with strange statues and glass cases filled with mysterious objects. Her friend Carolyn had warned her that there were rumors about Lord Delbridge's collection. Even other collectors as obsessed and as eccentric as his lordship considered the artifacts in his private museum extremely odd. The moment she had arrived in the gallery, she had understood the reasons for the gossip.

It was not the design and shape of the artifacts that appeared peculiar. In the dim light she was able to discern that most were ordinary enough. The gallery was crammed with an assortment of ancient vases, urns, jewelry, weapons, and statuary — the sort of items that one expected to encounter in any large collection of antiquities. It was the faint but disturbing miasma of unwholesome energy swirling in the atmosphere that stirred the fine hair on the nape of her neck. It came from the relics.

"You feel it, too, don't you?" the hypnotist asked.

The soft question startled her. He sounded curious, she thought. No, he sounded intrigued. She knew what he was referring to. Given his own talents it was not surprising that he was as sensitive as she.

"Yes," she said. "I feel it. Quite unpleasant."

"I have been told that when you cram a sufficient number of paranormal relics into one room, the effects are noticeable even to those who do not possess our sort of sensitivity."

"These objects are all paranormal?" she asked, astonished.

"Perhaps it would be more accurate to say that each has a long history of having been associated with the paranormal. Over time they absorbed some of the energy that was generated when they were used by those with psychical abilities."

"Where did Delbridge find all these strange relics?"

"Can't speak for the entire collection, but I do know that a fair number were stolen. Stay close."

She did not need the command. She was as eager to get away from this place now as he was. She would have to return another time to find the crystal.

The hypnotist was moving so quickly she had to run to keep up with him. It was only her men's clothes that made that possible. She would never have been able to move so swiftly in a woman's gown, with its layers upon layers of heavy fabric and petticoats.

Her senses tingled. More energy. It came from one of the objects around her but the currents were decidedly different. She recognized them immediately. Crystal energy.

"Wait," she whispered, slowing to a halt. "There is something I must do."

"There is no time." The hypnotist stopped and turned to face her, black coat whipping around his boots. "We've got half an hour, less if someone else comes up those stairs."

She wriggled her fingers, trying to free her hand. "Go on without me, then. My safety is not your affair."

"Have you lost your senses? We have to get out of here."

"I came here to recover a certain relic. It is nearby. I am not leaving without it."

"You are a professional thief?"

He did not sound shocked. Most likely because he, too, was in the business of theft. It was the only logical explanation for his presence here in the gallery.

"Delbridge has a certain relic that belongs to me," she explained. "It was stolen from my family several years ago. I had given up hope of finding it tonight, but now that I know it is close at hand I cannot leave without looking for it."

The hypnotist went very still. "How do you know that the relic you seek is nearby?"

She hesitated, uncertain how much to tell him. "I cannot explain, but I am very sure."

"Where is it?"

She turned slightly, seeking the source of the small pulses of energy. A short distance away stood a large, elaborately carved wooden cabinet.

"There," she said.

She gave one last tug on her wrist. This time he let her go. She hurried to the cabinet and examined it closely. There were two doors secured by a lock.

"As I expected," she said.

She reached into her pocket, removed the lock pick that Adam Harrow had given her and went to work.

The process did not go nearly as smoothly as it had when Adam had supervised her practice sessions. The lock did not yield.

The hypnotist watched in silence for a moment.

Perspiration dampened her forehead. She angled the pick in a slightly different direction and tried again.

"Something tells me you haven't had a lot of experience at this sort of thing," the hypnotist said neutrally.

His condescension jolted her.

"On the contrary, I've had a great deal of practice," she said through her teeth.

"But evidently not in the dark. Stand aside. Let me see what I can do."

She wanted to argue but common sense prevailed. The truth was, her practice with the lock pick consisted of only a couple of days of hurried experimentation. She thought she had displayed considerable aptitude, but Adam had warned her that picking a lock when one was feeling pressured was a different matter entirely.

The ticking of the clock on the table was very loud in the quiet gallery. Time was running out. She glanced at the frozen figure waiting to come out of his trance.

Reluctantly she stepped back from the cabinet. Mutely she held out the pick.

"I brought my own," the hypnotist said.

He produced a small, slender strip of metal from the pocket of his coat, fitted it into the lock and went to work. Almost immediately Leona heard a faint snick.

"Got it," he whispered.

To Leona's ears, the squeak of the hinges was as loud as a train. Anxiously she looked back along the gallery toward the main staircase, but there was no shifting of the shadows at that end of the room; no footsteps reverberated along the gallery.

The hypnotist looked into the depths of the cabinet. "It appears that we both came here on the same errand tonight."

A new and different chill went through her. "You came here to steal my crystal?"

"I suggest we save the topic of the legal ownership of the stone for another time."

Outrage sparked, overriding her fear. "That crystal is mine."

She started forward, intending to retrieve

the crystal, but the hypnotist blocked her path. He reached into the cabinet.

It was difficult to make out his movements in the darkness, but she knew immediately when disaster struck. She heard his sudden, sharp exhalation followed by a low, muffled cough. Simultaneously she caught a faint whiff of some unfamiliar chemical.

"Get back," he ordered.

There was so much intensity in the command that she found herself obeying without stopping to think.

"What is it?" she asked, retreating a few steps. "What's wrong?"

He turned away from the cabinet. She was amazed to see that he was staggering a little, as though he was having trouble maintaining his balance. He held a black velvet pouch in one hand.

"Delbridge will most likely be very busy dealing with the police after the woman's body is discovered," he said quietly. "With luck it will be a while before he will be able to start searching for the stone. You will have time to escape."

A flat, grim quality laced the words.

"And so will you," she said quickly.

"No," he said.

A terrible dread welled up inside her. "What are you talking about? What's wrong?"

"Time just ran out." He seized her wrist again and hauled her toward the servants' stairs. "We cannot delay another second."

A moment ago she had been furious with him, but now panic was beating through her veins. Her heart pounded.

"What happened?" she demanded. "Are you all right?"

"Yes, but not for long."

"For heaven's sake, tell me what occurred when you took the crystal out of the cabinet."

He opened the door that led to the spiral staircase. "I triggered a trap."

"What sort of trap?" She peered closely at his hands. "Were you cut? Are you bleeding?"

"The crystal was inside a glass case. When I opened the case, I got a face full of some noxious vapor. I inhaled a quantity of it. I suspect it was a poison."

"Dear God. Are you certain?"

"There is no doubt." He struck a light and then gave her a firm shove that sent her plunging down the ancient stone steps. "I can already feel the effects."

She looked back over her shoulder. In the flaring light she saw him clearly for the first time. Jet-black hair, unfashionably long, swept straight back from his high forehead and fell behind his ears to brush the collar of his shirt. His features had been ruthlessly hewn by a sculptor who had cared more about portraying power than good looks. The hypnotist's face suited his mesmeric voice: haunting, mysterious and dangerously fascinating. If a woman looked too long into those fathomless green eyes, she risked falling under a spell from which she might never escape.

"We must get you to a doctor," she said.

"If the vapor is what I think it is, no doctor will know how to counteract it. There is no known cure."

"We must try."

"Listen closely," he said. "Your life will depend upon following my orders. In a very short period of time, perhaps fifteen minutes at most, I will become a madman."

She struggled to take in the terrible meaning of what he was saying. "Because of the poison?"

"Yes. The drug produces hellish hallucinations that overwhelm the victim's mind, causing him to believe that he is surrounded by demons and monsters. You must not be anywhere near me when the stuff takes control of my senses."

"But —"

"I will become a grave threat to you and

anyone else who happens to be nearby. Do you comprehend me?"

She swallowed hard and hurried down a few more steps. "Yes."

They were almost at the bottom of the staircase. She could see the crack of moonlight under the door that opened onto the gardens.

"How do you intend to leave this place?" the hypnotist asked.

"My companion is waiting for me with a carriage," she said.

"Once we are clear of the gardens you must get as far away as possible from me and this damned mansion. Here, take the crystal."

She paused on one of the worn stone steps, half turning. He held out the velvet pouch. Stunned, she took it from him, aware of the slight tingle of energy. The gesture told her more clearly than his words that he truly did not expect to survive the night.

"Thank you," she said, uncertainly. "I did not expect —"

"I have no choice but to give it to you now. I can no longer be responsible for it."

"Are you absolutely certain there is no remedy for the poison?"

"None that we know of. Pay close attention. I understand that you feel you have a claim on that damned crystal, but if you have any common sense, any care at all for your personal safety, you will return it to its true owner. I will give you his name and address."

"I appreciate your concern, but I assure you there is no way Delbridge will be able to find me. It is you who are in danger tonight. You said something about hallucinations. Please, tell me precisely what is happening to you."

He dashed the back of his sleeve across his eyes with an impatient movement and then shook his head as though to clear it. "I am starting to see things that are not there. At the moment I am still aware that the images are fantasies, but soon they will become real to me. That is when I will become a threat to you."

"How can you be so certain?"

"I believe that the vapor was used twice in the past two months. Both victims were elderly collectors. Neither was prone to violent outbursts, but under the influence of the drug they attacked others. One of them stabbed a loyal servant to death. The second tried to set his nephew afire. Now do you comprehend the danger you are in, madam?"

"Tell me more about these hallucinations you say you are starting to see."

He put out the dying light and opened the door at the bottom of the stairwell. Cold, damp air greeted them. Moonlight still illuminated the gardens, but rain was coming.

"If the reports are accurate," he said evenly, "I am about to be consumed by a waking nightmare. I will likely soon be dead. Both of the other victims died."

"How did they die?"

He stepped outside and drew her with him. "One threw himself out a window. The other suffered a heart attack. Enough chatter. I must get you safely away from here."

He spoke with a cool detachment that was almost as worrisome as the prediction. He had accepted his fate, she realized, yet he was making plans to save her. A thrill of astonished wonder came over her, leaving her breathless. He did not even know her name yet he was determined to help her escape. No one had ever done anything so heroic for her in her entire life.

"You will come with me, sir," she said. "I know something of nightmares."

He dismissed the promise of hope out of hand, not even bothering to respond.

"Keep your voice down and stay close," he said.

2

I'm a dead man, Thaddeus Ware thought.

It was odd how little effect the knowledge had on him. Perhaps he was already under the spell of the drug. He thought he was holding the nightmares at bay, but he could not be certain. The conviction that he was strong enough to resist the poison for a few more minutes might in itself be an illusion.

Nevertheless, in the desperate hope that he was, indeed, managing to control the bizarre images, he concentrated his attention on the woman and the need to see her to safety. It was now his only goal. It seemed to him that the bizarre images gathering at the edge of his awareness receded a little when he focused hard on saving his companion. Something to be said for all the years spent learning to control his hypnotic talents. He did not lack for raw willpower. He sensed the ability was all that stood between him and the coalescing dream world that would soon engulf him.

He led the way through the gardens, following the path he had taken earlier when he had entered the mansion. For once the lady obeyed, staying close beside him.

A long, high hedge loomed in their path. He reached out and caught hold of the woman, intending to steer her toward the gate, but when his hand closed around her arm, his concentration shattered like a fine china vase dropped on a marble floor. Without warning elation flooded his veins. He tightened his grip, savoring the heady rush of pleasure.

He heard a soft, startled gasp, but he paid no attention. He was suddenly intensely aware of the exquisite, supple roundness of the arm he held. The woman's scent was intoxicating, driving out all rational thought.

Demons and monsters crept out from under the hedge. They grinned, moonlight glinting on their fangs. *You can take her here, now. There is nothing to stop you. She is yours.*

The woman must realize how erotic she looked in men's clothes, he thought. It amused and pleased him to know that she had deliberately dressed that way in order to tempt him.

"You must get hold of yourself, sir," she

said urgently. "We are not far from the carriage. Only a few more minutes, and we will both be safe."

Safe. The word triggered an elusive memory. He concentrated, trying to recall something that was important, something he had to do before he claimed the woman. It came to him then, a wispy bit of knowledge tossed about by invisible winds. He seized hold of the little scrap of reality and held fast. He had to save the woman. Yes, that was it. She was in danger.

The demons and monsters wavered, becoming briefly transparent.

You're hallucinating, Ware. Pay attention or you'll get her killed. That realization struck with the impact of ice water. He pulled himself back from the brink.

"Be careful or you'll trip over him," he said.

"A demon?" she asked warily.

"No, the man under the hedge."

"What on earth?" Startled, she glanced down and gave another little gasp when she saw the booted foot poking out from beneath the thick foliage. "Is he — ?" She did not finish the sentence.

"I put him and the other guard into a trance on my way into the mansion," he explained, urging her toward the gate. "They will not awaken until dawn."

"Oh." There was a short pause. "I, uh, did not know that Delbridge employed guards."

"You might want to allow for that possibility the next time you undertake a spot of burglary."

"I entered the mansion in the guise of one of the many servants hired for the evening, but I was planning to escape through the gardens. I would have run straight into the guards if you had not already taken care of them. How fortuitous that we met up tonight."

"My luck definitely runneth over this evening, no doubt about it."

He did not bother to hide his sarcasm. Her positive attitude was almost as maddening as the damn hallucinations.

"You sound very tense," she whispered, hurrying along beside him. "Are the hallucinations coming on more strongly?"

He wanted to shout at her; he wanted to shake her until she understood the direness of the situation. The hallucinations were not coming on; they were lying in wait in dark corners, anticipating the moment when his will would falter again as it had a moment ago. The instant he lost control the nightmares would flood his brain. Most of all he wanted to kiss her before he fell into the nightmare.

But the simple truth was that he did not have time to do any of those things. He was doomed. The only thing he could do was try to save her. A few more minutes. That was all he needed to get the woman to her carriage and see her off. Just a few more minutes. He could hold on that long. He had to hold on for her sake.

He opened the heavy gate. The woman went through it quickly. He followed.

The Delbridge mansion was located a few miles outside of London. Beyond the high garden walls lay a thick stand of trees. The woods appeared impenetrable, but when he looked more closely he could see the monsters lurking in the deep shadows.

"The carriage is not far from here," the woman said.

He removed the pistol from the pocket of his coat. "Take this."

"Why would I want your gun?"

"Because the hallucinations are getting worse. A moment ago I was about to force myself on you. I do not know what I will do next."

"Nonsense." She sounded genuinely shocked. "I do not believe for one moment that you would have forced yourself on me, sir."

"Then you are not half as intelligent as I first thought."

She cleared her throat. "Nevertheless, under the circumstances, I understand your concerns."

She took the pistol gingerly, gripping it awkwardly in one hand. Turning, she led him down a narrow, rutted lane dimly lit by the moon.

"I don't suppose you know how to use that gun I just gave you," he said.

"No. But my friend is familiar with guns."

She had a friend, a *male* friend. The news hit him with the force of a blow. Outrage and an inexplicable possessiveness clawed his insides.

No, he was in the grip of the hallucinations again. In any event, in all likelihood he would be dead by dawn. He had no claim on the woman.

"Who is this friend?" he asked, nevertheless.

"You will meet him in a moment. He is waiting for me in the woods."

"What sort of male friend would allow you to take the risks you are taking tonight?"

"Adam and I concluded that it would be easier for one person rather than two to enter the mansion," she said. "In any event, someone had to watch the carriage and the horses."

"Your friend should have gone into the mansion and left you behind with the carriage."

"My friend is a man of many talents, but he does not possess the ability required to sense the crystal. I was the only one who had any hope of finding it."

"That damn crystal was not worth the risk you took tonight."

"Really, sir, this is hardly the time to administer a lecture."

She was right. The nightmarish images were crowding closer again. Ghouls hovered at the corner of his eye. Demons prowled at the edge of the lane. A large snake with glowing red eyes slithered through the overhanging branches of a nearby tree.

He stopped talking and went back to concentrating on the need to get the woman into her carriage so that her good friend Adam could take her away from this nightmare.

They rounded a curve in the rutted path. A small, closed, very fast-looking carriage loomed in the path. There was no one on the box. The two horses stood quietly, dozing.

Leona stopped, looking around somewhat anxiously.

"Adam?" she called softly. "Where are you?"

"I am here, Leona."

Excitement and an unfamiliar sense of wonder unfurled inside Thaddeus. At last he had a name for the woman: Leona. The ancients had believed that names had power. They were right. The name Leona infused him with strength.

You're hallucinating, Ware. Get hold of yourself.

A slender man enveloped in a coachman's heavily caped greatcoat stepped out of the trees. He had a cap pulled down low over his eyes. Moonlight glinted on the pistol in his hand.

"Who is this?"

The voice was that of a cultured young gentleman, not the rough accents of a coachman.

"A friend," Leona said. "He is in mortal danger and so are we. There is no time to explain. I have the stone. We must get out of here at once."

"I do not understand. How is it that you encountered an acquaintance inside Delbridge's mansion? One of the guests, perhaps?" Cold disapproval laced the last question.

"Please, Adam, not now." Leona hurried

forward and opened the carriage door. "I will explain everything later."

Adam was clearly unconvinced, but he evidently concluded that this was not the time to debate the matter.

"Very well." He pocketed the weapon and scrambled lightly up onto the box.

Leona stepped up into the unlit cab. Thaddeus watched her disappear into the intense darkness inside. Through the growing haze of his nightmares it suddenly occurred to him that he would never see this amazing woman again, never know her secrets. She was about to vanish, and he had never even held her in his arms.

He moved closer to the open door.

"Where will you go?" he asked, needing to hear her speak one last time.

"Back to London, of course. For heaven's sake, why are you standing there? Get into the carriage."

"I told you, I cannot come with you. The nightmares are closing in quickly."

"And I told you, I know something of nightmares."

Adam looked down at him. "You are putting all of us at risk," he snapped in low tones. "Get into the carriage, sir."

"Go without me," Thaddeus commanded quietly. "There is something I must do before the visions take control."

"What is that?" Adam asked.

"I must kill Delbridge."

"Huh." Adam sounded abruptly thoughtful. "Not a bad idea."

"No." Leona's face appeared in the opening. "You cannot risk going back to the mansion, sir, not in your condition."

"If I don't kill Delbridge, he will search for the crystal," Thaddeus explained.

"I told you, he will never find me," Leona assured him.

"Your new friend has a point," Adam said to her. "I suggest we follow his advice and leave him here. Where is the harm in letting him try to kill Delbridge? If he succeeds, we will have one less problem to worry about in the future."

"You don't understand," Leona insisted. "This man is in the grip of a terrible poison that is creating hallucinations. He does not comprehend what he is saying."

"All the more reason to leave him behind," Adam said. "The last thing we need tonight is a madman for a traveling companion."

Thaddeus looked hard at Leona, trying to catch one last glimpse of her face in the moonlight. "He is right. You must go on without me."

"Absolutely not." Leona reached out and

caught hold of his sleeve. "Trust me, sir, I give you my word, there is a very good chance I can help you. We are not leaving without you."

"Damnation," Adam muttered. But he sounded resigned. "You may as well get into the carriage, sir. It is difficult to win an argument with Leona when she is convinced she is right."

It wasn't Leona's stubbornness that was making him hesitate, Thaddeus realized; it was her conviction that she might be able to save him.

"Concentrate on the positive, sir," Leona ordered bracingly. "It is not as if there is anything to be gained by dwelling on the negative."

"She is also very keen on the powers of optimism and positive thinking," Adam grumbled. "It is an excessively annoying trait, to be sure."

Thaddeus looked longingly at the open door of the carriage, unable to extinguish the tiny flicker of hope Leona had ignited.

If she saved him he would be able to protect her from Delbridge and claim her as well.

That logic tipped the scales. He vaulted up into the carriage and dropped down onto the seat across from Leona.

The vehicle jolted forward immediately. The horses moved into a swift trot. In some vague, still rational place in his brain, Thaddeus realized that Adam had not turned up the outside lamps. He was using moonlight to guide the team along the curving lane. It was madness, but it was all of a piece with everything else that had occurred tonight.

Inside the cab he could barely make out Leona silhouetted against the dark cushions. He was fiercely aware of her, however. The very atmosphere seemed to shimmer with her feminine essence.

"What is your name, sir?" she asked.

"Thaddeus Ware."

How odd to think that although he had just shared a harrowing adventure with this woman, he had no clear vision of her looks. Thus far he had seen her only in the dimly lit museum gallery and the moonlit garden. If he were to meet her tomorrow in a London street he might not even recognize her.

Unless she spoke. The sound of her voice, low and warm and intriguingly sensual, was impressed on his memory for all time. He would know her scent, too, he thought, and something of the shape of her, as well. He had been vividly aware of her compelling curves when she was pressed against him. And there was something else, a faint whisper of seductive power that could only be coming from her aura.

Oh, yes, he would know her anywhere.

Because she is yours, one of the demons whispered.

Mine.

Without warning, the last of his defenses disintegrated. The monsters were freed. They leaped from the shadows of his mind straight into the carriage.

In the blink of a demonic eye, the interior of the cab was transformed into a dark dreamscape. A creature the size of a large dog perched on the seat beside him. But the monstrosity was no dog. Eight feathery legs projected from its glistening, bulbous body. Moonlight glinted darkly on soulless, multifaceted eyes. Poison dripped from its fangs.

A ghostly face appeared at the window. The eye sockets were empty black holes. The mouth opened on a silent shriek.

He caught a hint of movement to his left. He did not need to turn his head to know that what crouched there possessed scaly, clawed feet and antennae that writhed like tormented worms.

The windows of the carriage no longer looked out onto the night-darkened woods. Instead they revealed unearthly scenes from another dimension. Volcanic rivers flowed through trees fashioned of black ice. Strange birds with the heads of snakes perched on the frozen branches.

He possessed just enough awareness to know that he was a fool to believe that willpower alone could contain the nightmares. Delbridge's poison had been churning through his blood for at least fifteen minutes, doing its foul work. Now it was in full control.

The astonishing thing was that he no longer gave a damn.

"Mr. Ware?"

Leona's voice, the voice that he would know anywhere, came to him out of the darkness.

"Too late," he said, amused by her tone of concern. "Welcome to my nightmare. Things aren't so unpleasant here once you get used to the place."

"Mr. Ware, you must listen to me."

Hot lust surged through him. She was only inches away, his for the taking. He had never wanted a woman more, and there was nothing to stop him.

"I can help you fight the hallucinations," she said.

"But I do not wish to fight them," he said softly. "Indeed, I am enjoying them. And so will you."

Impatiently she yanked off the wig, reached inside her coat and removed an object. He could not see what it was, but a few seconds later moonlight glowed between her hands.

Now he saw her for the first time. Her dark hair was pinned into a tight coil on top of her hair, revealing features that could only be described as striking, although not in the way that was generally associated with great beauty. Instead he saw intelligence, determination and a certain delicate sensitivity in her face. Her mouth looked very soft. Eyes of molten amber gleamed with feminine power. Nothing was more seductive.

"Sorceress," he whispered, fascinated.

She flinched as though he had struck her. "What?"

He smiled. "Nothing." He looked down at the crystal, intrigued. "What is this? Another one of my hallucinations?"

"It is the aurora stone, Mr. Ware. I am going to walk through your dreams with you."

3

She had not held the aurora stone in her hands since her sixteenth summer, but it responded instantly to the energy she sent into its heart. No longer a dull, murky white, it glowed with the faint inner light that signaled it was now alive with power. She held it in the palm of her hand and gazed into its depths, focusing all of her senses. The stone brightened visibly.

She could not explain how she was able to access the energy of certain crystals. It was a talent passed down through the generations on the female side of her family. Her mother had possessed a gift for working crystal. So had her grandmother and the many great-grandmothers before her for at least two hundred years.

"Look deeply into the crystal, Mr. Ware," she said.

He ignored the instructions. A slow, sensual smile etched his mouth and raised every hair on the nape of her neck.

"I would rather look deeply into you," he said, employing the dark, irresistible voice he had used earlier to try to mesmerize her.

She shivered. The atmosphere had altered. A moment ago Thaddeus had been waging a savage battle to hold on to his sanity in the face of the rising tide of hallucinations, but now he seemed to be reveling in the fantastical dream in which he found himself.

She fought to regain control of the situation. "Tell me what you see in the crystal."

"Very well, I am in a mood to humor you tonight. At least for a time." He looked at the stone again. "I see moonlight. A clever trick, madam."

"The light you see is the crystal's natural energy. It is a very special power that resonates with the energy of dreams. All dreams spring from the paranormal side of our nature, even in those who do not believe that they possess any such sensitivity. If one alters the currents generated by the dreams, one can alter the nature of the dreams themselves."

"You sound like a scientist I know. His name is Caleb Jones. He is always going on about the scientific aspects of the paranormal. I have found that it makes for dull conversation."

"I will try not to bore you with the reasons why the crystal works," she said, stifling her growing unease. "Please pay attention. You are having a waking dream. We are going to diminish the force and power of that dream. We cannot erase it altogether, but we can weaken it to the point where it will no longer seem real or compelling. But you must cooperate, sir."

He smiled his slow, dangerous smile again. "I am not in the mood to play your crystal games. I prefer other entertainment this evening."

"Mr. Ware, I ask you to trust me, just as I trusted you earlier tonight."

In the light of the crystal she saw Ware's coldly brilliant eyes narrow faintly. He leaned forward and drew a fingertip along the underside of her jaw. The caress sent a small shiver through her.

"I saved you because you belong to me," he said. "I protect what is mine."

He was slipping deeper into the hallucinations.

"Mr. Ware," she said, "this is very important. Look into the moonlight and concentrate on your hallucinations. Describe them to me."

"Very well, if you insist." He looked into the crystal again. "Shall I start with the demon at the window? Perhaps the viper clinging to the door handle would be of more interest."

Power jumped in the heart of the stone, a great deal of it. The moonlight flared. He was finally focusing on the crystal as she had directed, but she had not allowed for the strength of his talent. She had to concentrate harder herself to keep the currents under control.

"None of the creatures that you see around you is real, Mr. Ware."

He reached out and ran his thumb across her lower lip. "You are real. That is all that matters tonight."

"I have not been acquainted with you long, sir, but it is obvious that you are possessed of a formidable will. You are not entirely lost to your nightmare, sir. Some part of you is still aware that you are hallucinating."

"Perhaps, but it no longer concerns me. You are all that interests me at the moment."

The light in the crystal faded. Thaddeus was no longer concentrating on it.

"I cannot do this without you, sir," she said firmly. "You must focus harder on the moonlight. Together we will use its energy to dissolve the fantasies in your mind."

"Your therapy will not work on me," he said, amused. "It appears to be a form of mesmerism, and, like you, I have a natural immunity to hypnosis."

"I am not attempting to hypnotize you, sir. The crystal is merely a tool that will allow us to tune the waves of your dream energy. At the moment, that energy is generating the hallucinations."

"You are wrong, Leona," he said softly. "The vipers and the demons are not hallucinations; they are real, and they are mine to command, my servants, bound to me by all the forces of hell. You are bound to me also. Soon you will comprehend that."

For the first time she began to fear that she might lose him. Anxiety flickered inside her, shattering her concentration. He looked down at the crystal and laughed.

The light in the stone abruptly darkened and changed color. Leona stared, shocked. A storm was brewing in the heart of the crystal. Instead of moonlight, strange dark currents swirled ominously. Thaddeus was pouring his own power into the crystal, overwhelming her carefully directed waves of energy.

The storm coalesced, gathering strength. She watched with gathering dread as the disturbing forces surged and flared. She had never encountered anyone who could do what Thaddeus Ware was doing. Because he was so completely in the grip of his dream, she doubted that he even realized what was happening.

A monstrous insect, its eyes composed of a thousand small mirrors, appeared on the seat beside Thaddeus. The creature's fangs glistened wetly.

She froze in horror. There was nowhere to run. Nowhere to hide. Her fingers and toes tingled painfully with prickles of fear. Perspiration dampened her shirt. She tried to scream, but the sound was locked in her throat.

"Calm yourself, my sweet," Thaddeus said. "It will not hurt you. It is my creature to summon. I will protect you."

Instinctively she reached for the door handle. She snatched her fingers back just before they closed around the head of a red-eyed viper.

"You see them now, don't you?" Thaddeus asked, pleased. "You have entered my world."

It dawned on her that he was somehow drawing power from the crystal to make his hallucinations visible, not just to himself but to her as well. If she had not witnessed the astonishing scene with her own eyes she would not have believed it possible for anyone to do such a thing.

Out of nowhere one of Uncle Edward's sayings came to her: *"Remember, Leona, you must control your audience from the moment you step on the stage. Never allow your audience to control you."*

She had to regain control of the crystal, or she would be sucked into the dreamscape along with Thaddeus Ware and they would both be lost.

Calling on every fragment of her willpower, she forced herself to look away from the terrifying insect and focused instead on the raging currents inside the crystal.

"Look into the stone, sir," she said, putting all the authority she could muster into the command. "It is your only hope. The hallucinations have taken control. You must fight them."

He smiled. "I would far rather you joined me here in my dream. Together we will rule our own little corner of hell."

Before she realized his intent, his hands closed around her shoulders. He drew her toward him.

"Release me at once, Mr. Ware." She fought to keep the fear out of her voice, but she knew that he sensed it.

"Now, why would I do that?" Thaddeus asked, voice roughening with a dangerous sensuality. "In this world you are mine. It is past time I tasted your power and let you feel my own."

She tried to pull free of his hands, but he tightened his grip. Instantly she stilled, her intuition warning her that resistance would only provoke him. Frantically she considered the few courses of action open to her. If she screamed for help, Adam would surely hear her and come to her assistance. But Adam's solution to the crisis would likely be to lodge a bullet in Thaddeus Ware's brain. That not only seemed somewhat excessive but extremely unfair, given the fact that Ware had likely saved her life earlier tonight by rendering the two guards unconscious.

It was her job to save him now. She must be strong for both of them.

"You will not force yourself on me, sir," she said with a calm she was far from feeling. "You saved me tonight. It is not in your nature to do violence to a woman."

He pulled her closer. In the light of the stone his eyes gleamed with a dark passion.

He studied her mouth as though it were some rare and exotic and very ripe fruit. "You know nothing of my nature. Not yet. But soon, my sweet, very soon, you will comprehend the bond that exists between us."

"I know that you will not hurt me because you are a man of honor," she said evenly.

He responded by unfastening the collar of her shirt. She was intensely aware of the way his fingers brushed against her throat.

"Honor is a complicated concept when it comes to this sort of thing," he said.

"There is nothing at all complicated about it, and well you know it," she whispered. "The forces of your nightmare are controlling you."

"No one and nothing controls me, not even you, my lovely Leona."

"I am not the one who is manipulating you. It is Delbridge who is doing that with his poison. Surely you will not allow him the victory."

Thaddeus hesitated, eyes narrowing. "Delbridge. If he ever discovers that you took his crystal he will stop at nothing to get it back."

She realized that somewhere in his dreamscape a door to rationality had just cracked open. She seized the opportunity.

"You are right, sir," she said gently. "I see now that Delbridge is a grave threat to my person. But you cannot deal with him while you are under the influence of the poison. You must recover your senses so that you will be able to protect me from him."

"I vow I will keep you safe from him and any other man who dares to try to take you from me." He drew one of the pins from her hair. "You are mine."

"Yes, indeed," she said briskly. "I am yours, and therefore you will fight Delbridge's poison tonight. For my sake, sir. You will not let him destroy your sanity because then you would be in no shape to guard me."

"For your sake," he repeated, as though taking an oath. "I would walk through the gates of hell to protect you, Leona."

Energy shimmered invisibly in the small confines of the carriage and not just inside the crystal. Her own senses were responding to his dark, drugging aura. The stuff drew her like an intoxicating scent. A fever began to build deep within her. Part of her suddenly yearned to enter into his dreamscape and share it with him.

He drew another pin from her hair. Then, very deliberately, as though staking a claim, he wrapped one hand around the nape of her neck and crushed her mouth beneath his own.

It was a kiss of possession and thrilling power. Her aura flared to meet his. Their energy currents clashed, merged and then began to resonate together. Through half-closed eyes she saw lightning flash inside the crystal.

Thaddeus drank from her as though she

offered him some rare nectar. She longed to follow him to wherever the currents of the dream might take them.

With a low, husky sound, Thaddeus raised his head and started to pull her down onto the seat.

"Mine," he whispered.

It was now or never. She had to act for both their sakes or all was lost. Another one of her uncle's sayings came to her: *"Always give the audience a show."*

She gripped the crystal in both hands.

"Look into the stone, Thaddeus," she whispered in the same voice that she would have used to invite him to her bed. "See how your energy has set fire to it."

He responded to the small seduction and looked down at the glowing stone.

She was waiting for him. The instant she sensed his attention was focused on the crystal, she pounced, slamming every ounce of her own power into the stone. There was no time to finesse the currents of her own energy as she would have done with any other client. She could not afford to be delicate or cautious about the business. Overwhelming Thaddeus's churning energy with her own raw power was the only hope.

The storm inside the crystal pulsed wildly one last time, and then it faded.

It was over in seconds. Thaddeus shuddered and sank back against the cushions.

"I am no longer in the nightmare," he said, dazed.

"No," she agreed.

"You saved my sanity and, no doubt, my life. I owe you my most profound thanks."

"We are even, sir. I owe you my gratitude for helping me escape Delbridge's house tonight."

"Delbridge. Right." With a weary gesture he turned up one of the lamps. "He is going to be a problem, Leona."

"There is no need to worry about Delbridge, Mr. Ware. Now you must rest."

"I do not think that I can do anything else." He picked up the wig she had worn and examined it as though he had never seen it before. "I cannot recall ever having felt so exhausted."

"You expended a great deal of energy tonight. You require sleep, a lot of it."

"You will be here when I wake up?"

"Mmm."

He tucked the wig into the pocket of his coat and smiled faintly. "You're lying."

"Really, sir, this is not the time to engage in an argument. You need rest."

"There is no point running from me, Leona. You and I are bound together now.

No matter where you go, I will find you."

"Go to sleep, Mr. Ware."

He did not argue. He settled deeper into the corner of the seat, legs outstretched so that his thighs brushed against hers. She watched him for a long time.

4

When she was satisfied that he was, indeed, sound asleep, she rose, kneeled on the cushions and pushed open the trap door to speak to Adam.

"How is your patient?" Adam asked, over his shoulder.

"Sleeping. The poison was very strong. For a time there I was afraid that I would not be able to save him."

A gust of cold wind carrying the first splatters of rain blew into the carriage.

"What sort of poison induces nightmares?" Adam asked.

"I don't know. Mr. Ware claimed that Delbridge used it to cause two men to go mad. Both victims died within hours."

Adam flicked the reins, urging the horses to a faster pace. "Delbridge is obviously more dangerous than we believed. He was supposed to be nothing more than an eccentric collector."

"It is worse than you know. I did not get a chance to tell you earlier, but there was a dead woman in the museum at the mansion. Her throat was slit open. It was . . . ghastly."

"Bloody hell." Adam was so shocked he hauled on the reins, throwing the horses off stride. Hastily he corrected the action. "Who was she?"

"I don't know. She must have been one of the women that Delbridge brought in to entertain his guests. Evidently she went to the gallery to meet a man. The killer got to her first."

"Please do not tell me that our passenger was the killer."

"No."

"How can you be certain?"

"Two reasons. First, he did not murder me when I came upon him standing over the body. If he was guilty I'm certain he would have wanted to get rid of a witness."

"Good lord above. You found him *standing over the body?*"

"The second reason I am convinced that he is not the murderer is because he did not kill the two guards patrolling Delbridge's gardens."

"What two guards are you talking about? There weren't supposed to be any guards there tonight."

"It appears that Mr. Pierce's information was wrong on several counts."

"Bloody hell," Adam repeated, this time very softly. "Leona, this is shaping up to be an unmitigated disaster."

"Nonsense. I admit there were a few complications, but they have all been sorted out."

"Trust you to think positive in a situation where any sane person would be contemplating the purchase of passage to America or some other conveniently distant place."

"Only consider the facts, Adam. We are safely away from the mansion, and there is no way Delbridge can ever discover who took the crystal."

"You are forgetting one major complication," Adam said darkly.

"What is that?"

"The one that is presently asleep in the carriage. What do you know about him?"

"Very little, aside from the fact that he is an incredibly powerful psychical hypnotist," she admitted.

"A *psychical hypnotist?*"

"He dealt with the two guards as well as one of Delbridge's guests by putting them into an instant trance. It was astonishing. I have never seen anyone do what he can do with mesmerism."

"And we are helping him return to London?" Adam was appalled. "You must be mad, Leona. Everyone knows that hypnotists, even those without paranormal powers, are dangerous. We have to get rid of him at once."

"Calm down, Adam. There is no need for panic. All will be well."

"I must warn you that Mr. Pierce is not fond of hypnotists, especially those with psychical talents, and neither am I," Adam said grimly.

"You encountered a hypnotist with paranormal abilities? Good heavens, I had no idea. What happened?"

"Suffice it to say that the hypnotist in question is dead. Suicide. Perhaps you read about it in the papers. Her name was Rosalind Fleming."

"Now that you mention it, I do seem to recall the name. But there was nothing in the papers concerning her mesmeric talents. She was a lady who moved in high society, was she not?"

"Before she manipulated her way into elevated social circles she made her living as a medium. She employed her skills to blackmail her clients."

"She jumped off a bridge, as I recall."

"Yes."

The perfectly neutral response set off warning bells. Leona knew it meant that the subject was closed. That, in turn, probably meant that the topic of conversation threatened to probe a little too deeply into the mysteries surrounding Adam's very good friend Mr. Pierce.

"The question now," Leona said, "is what are we to do with Mr. Ware?"

"You say he is asleep?" Adam asked.

"Yes."

"Is it a deep sleep?"

"Very deep," Leona said.

"In that case, I suggest that we leave him in the woods beside the road."

"You can't be serious. The man saved my life tonight. Besides, it is starting to rain. He would likely catch his death of cold."

"You cannot take him home with you as though he were another stray dog," Adam muttered, exasperated.

"Perhaps you could put him up for the night?"

"Absolutely not. Mr. Pierce would never approve. He had strong misgivings about our scheme from the outset, if you will recall. If he were to learn that I dragged home a hypnotist —"

"All right, let me think a moment."

"Why was Ware in Delbridge's museum tonight?"

Leona hesitated. "He went there to get the crystal."

"*Your* crystal?"

"Well, yes, as it happens."

"Damnation. In that case there is something else you should take into consideration while you are pondering what to do with your hypnotist."

"What?"

"You had best assume that when he awakens he will still want the damned stone."

Leona felt her usually resilient spirits plummet. Adam was right. If Thaddeus came looking for her it would only be because he wanted the stone, not because he wanted her. That electrifying kiss a short time ago was a product of his hallucinations, part of a nightmare. It was hardly the sort of encounter that would inspire desire in a gentleman's heart.

"From what little I saw of him earlier," Adam continued, "I suspect that he will not gracefully abandon his quest and allow you to claim the stone."

"You are correct," Leona said. "We must get rid of Mr. Ware. I have an idea."

5

The clock struck three.

Richard Saxilby awakened and looked around the gallery. Confusion struck first. What was he doing up here? He had accompanied the others on the tour that Delbridge had insisted upon conducting earlier in the evening, but he had not enjoyed the experience. He had little interest in antiquities and had fully expected to be bored. But boredom had not been the problem. Instead, the collection of relics displayed in the gallery had given him a distinctly unpleasant sensation.

Why had he come back?

Memory returned in a stomach-churning rush. He was here because of Molly. The saucy little baggage had suggested they meet here after the dancing began. She had told him that no one would think to look for them in this place.

But Molly was dead, savagely murdered.

He whirled around, heart pounding. No,

it had not been a dream. She was still lying there on the floor. So much blood, he thought. Her throat was sliced open. She had been slaughtered.

His guts rebelled. For a dreadful moment he thought he would be ill. He turned away from the sight of the body.

Someone should tell Delbridge so that the police could be summoned.

The police. Panic tightened his chest. He could not afford to be associated with murder. The investment scheme he had worked so hard to put together was at an extremely delicate point. Very important gentlemen were about to decide whether or not to finance the project. Gossip spread quickly in the clubs.

Worse yet, the police might think he was the one who had killed the pretty whore. How could he possibly explain his presence here in this damned gallery to the men from Scotland Yard? And then there was his shrew of a wife to consider. Helen would be furious if he dragged the family name into a murder investigation. She would be even angrier if she discovered that he had come here tonight to keep an assignation with a prostitute.

He had to get out of here before anyone else arrived. He would go back downstairs and mingle with the guests, make certain that everyone saw him dancing with some of the women Delbridge had supplied for the evening.

Let someone else find the body.

6

Two hours later . . .

Delbridge paced the long gallery, ignoring Molly Stubton's bloody body. She was the least of his problems at the moment. He was furious. He was also very worried.

"What the devil is wrong with the guards?" he said to Hulsey.

Dr. Basil Hulsey shook his head and fidgeted with his spectacles. There was no telling when his fringe of graying hair had last been washed, let alone cut. The ratty tufts stuck straight out in a disgusting halo as if he had touched an electricity machine. His perpetually rumpled coat and baggy trousers hung from his skeletal frame. Beneath the coat he wore a shirt that had no doubt once been white. Now, however, it was a grayish-brown, the result of years of noxious chemical stains.

All in all, Hulsey looked like what he was:

a brilliant, eccentric scientist who had been dragged from his laboratory — a laboratory that Delbridge had paid for — in the wee hours of the morning.

"I have no idea what ails the g–guards," Hulsey stammered nervously. "Mr. Lancing brought them into the k–kitchen as you ordered. We both tried to wake them. Threw a bucket of cold water on them. Neither so much as stirred."

"I would say that they both passed out after drinking too much gin," Lancing said. He sounded elegantly bored, his customary mood when he was not pursuing his favorite sport. "But neither reeks of drink."

Hulsey concentrated intently on cleaning his spectacles. He always appeared anxious when he was outside his laboratory but never more so than when he was obliged to be in the same room with Lancing. Delbridge did not blame him. It was like forcing a mouse to share a cage with a viper.

Delbridge contemplated the creature named Lancing, concealing his own wariness of the man. Unlike Hulsey, however, he knew better than to show fear. Or perhaps he was simply more adept at hiding the instinctive response.

He was simmering with rage, but he was well aware that he had to be careful. In the glary light cast by the nearby wall sconce, Lancing looked like an angel from a Renaissance painting. He was an exquisitely handsome man with eyes that were the blue of pale sapphires and golden hair so pale that it appeared almost white. Women were drawn to him like moths to a flame. But looks were most definitely deceiving in Lancing's case; the man was a cold-blooded killer. He lived for the hunt and the kill, and his favored prey was human, preferably female. He was frighteningly good at the business. Indeed, nature had endowed him with a talent for pursuing and bringing down his victims that could only be described as preternatural. When his paranormal hunting senses were aroused, he could detect the psychical spore of his victim.

His talents also endowed him with the ability to see clearly in the darkest night. When he attacked he could move much faster than even the most skilled soldier or boxer. His speed was that of a beast of prey, not that of a normal man.

Delbridge was a member of the Arcane Society, a secretive organization devoted to the study of the paranormal, the vast majority of whose members possessed at least some demonstrable talents. In recent years the Society had undertaken an organized effort to research, study and catalogue the various types of abilities that had been recognized thus far. Thanks to the growing catalog, there was now a name for those who exhibited Lancing's peculiar and extremely dangerous syndrome of skills: parahunters.

There were many within the Society, especially those who subscribed to Mr. Darwin's theories, who were convinced that psychically enhanced hunters were, in truth, primeval throwbacks. Delbridge was inclined to agree with them. Lancing, however, took another point of view. As far as the elegant viper was concerned, he was a superior, more highly evolved man. Either way, he had his uses.

Delbridge had tracked him down after accounts of a savage killer who preyed upon prostitutes began appearing in the sensation press. It had been easy enough to lure the Midnight Monster, as *The Flying Intelligencer* had labeled him, out of hiding. Molly Stubton, with her blonde hair and pretty face, had fit the description of the Monster's victims. She had posed as a poor streetwalker plying her trade in the part of town where the Monster was known to hunt. Delbridge had hovered close by in the shadows, two loaded pistols in his pocket and a vial filled with one of Hulsey's potions in his hand.

For years he had been frustrated by his own talent. It was gratifyingly strong but of extremely limited usefulness. He was able to sense very distinctly others who possessed strong paranormal talents. In addition, he could identify the nature of their particular powers. The ability had finally been put to good use the night he detected Lancing.

When the Midnight Monster had emerged from the fog one night, dressed like an elegant gentleman and smiling his angelic smile, even Molly, who possessed some extremely well-honed street instincts, was fooled.

Lancing's hunting senses were fully aroused, however, and Delbridge had immediately identified the nature of the disturbing aura that surrounded him. Even if there was no name for the Monster's talent, Delbridge would have recognized him for what he was: a killer.

He had offered the parahunter employment and something that he sensed intuitively would be vastly more important to him: admiration and acknowledgment of his extraordinary powers.

He had quickly learned that Lancing had a second weakness, one that he was forced to pander to in order to control the Monster. Lancing came from the streets but yearned to rub shoulders with his betters in a world that, because of the circumstances of his birth, had always been denied him. The bastard craved acceptance among the elite the way a starving man hungered for bread. Clearly it stuck in his craw that he, a *superior* sort of man, lacked the social status and connections required to be invited into exclusive circles.

Delbridge hated having been obliged to introduce the viper to his tailor, let alone invite him to an occasional social affair such as the party tonight, but there was no help for it. Allowing Lancing to hover on the fringes of his upper-class world was the price of doing business with the Midnight Monster.

Delbridge looked at him. "What went wrong here tonight? The plan to get rid of Miss Stubton was simple and straightforward. You were to escort her back to her town house after the party tonight and get rid of her there. Why the devil did you kill her right here in my house? Don't you realize the risk you took?"

Molly Stubton had been a strikingly beautiful woman. Her smoldering sensuality combined with her skills in the bedroom had made her useful as a seductress. Delbridge had employed her to learn the secrets of some of his rivals. She had performed her role brilliantly. Lately, however, she had become difficult. She had begun making annoying demands, even going so far as to hint at blackmail. The time had come to get rid of her but Lancing had bungled the business.

Lancing raised one shoulder in a graceful shrug. "For some reason she came up here. I suspect she planned to meet one of the guests. I followed her to see what she was about. When she saw me her fear was as thick as perfume." Lancing's mouth curved in a reminiscent smile. "She guessed what was to come. There was no way she would have agreed to let me escort her home. I had no choice but to silence her immediately."

"Even if you felt you had to act on the spot, there are neater methods," Delbridge pointed out. "Why the devil did you cut her throat and leave her here? What if one of the other guests had come into the gallery, discovered the body and rushed downstairs to sound the alarm? I would have had no choice but to summon the police."

"There was a great deal of blood," Lancing said, still smiling. "It utterly ruined my coat and splashed my trousers. I went to one of the bedrooms to clean up and change my clothes."

Suspicion surged through Delbridge. "You

brought a second set of clothes with you to-night?"

"Of course. I always carry a change of clothing when I know I will be amusing my-self with one of my little entertainments."

In other words he had planned all along to kill Molly here in the mansion, not in her town house. The beast had no doubt savored the thrill of getting away with murder in a house full of gentlemen who considered themselves his social superiors. Delbridge suppressed a sigh. Hulsey was right, Lancing was neither entirely sane nor entirely controllable. The thing was, he was extremely useful.

"How long did it take you to clean yourself and put your clothing to rights?" Delbridge asked, striving for patience.

Lancing gave another delicate shrug. "Twenty minutes perhaps."

Delbridge set his back teeth very tightly to-gether. "Yet you did not come to tell me that the crystal was gone and that the two guards were unconscious until three-thirty."

"Nancy Palgrave came looking for me." Lancing smirked. "When I left the bedroom, I found her on the first-floor landing. Natu-rally I invited her into one of the bedrooms. What else could a gentleman do under the circumstances?"

That probably ought to count as another

one of Lancing's weaknesses, Delbridge thought. The hunt and the kill aroused him sexually. Finding an attractive woman waiting for him would have been too much temptation for him to resist.

More time had been lost because it had been impossible to attend to the crisis until the last of the guests had departed. In addition it had been necessary to wait until the staff that had been hired for the evening had also left. He had then sent his housekeeper and her husband, the only two servants who actually lived in the mansion, to their beds. They had served him faithfully for years; both knew better than to question his orders.

A thought occurred to him. He paused in his pacing and frowned.

"Perhaps the stone was stolen earlier in the evening before you followed Miss Stubton up here," he suggested.

"Perhaps." Lancing was unconcerned, as usual, with minor details.

"Are you certain you can tell me nothing about the thief?" Delbridge asked for what must have been the third or fourth time.

Lancing went to stand in front of the cabinet that had held the crystal. "I've explained to you that I can only detect the spore left by intense emotions. Fear. Rage. Passion.

That sort of thing. I don't sense any of those here."

"But the thief must have experienced some very strong emotion when he removed the crystal and inhaled the vapor," Delbridge insisted. "Shock? Fear? *Something.*"

Lancing cradled the lock in one long-fingered hand. "I told you, this is too murky to read. A lot of people have touched it in recent days, including you." He paused, suddenly and uncharacteristically thoughtful. "But now that I concentrate I believe I can sense a fresh whisper of power clinging to it."

Delbridge felt the surge of energy around Lancing when the killer unleashed his paranormal senses to examine the lock. Although he was braced for the experience, it was nevertheless unnerving. A distinct chill went down his spine. Even Hulsey, whose talents lay in the scientific realm, must have sensed the killer's dark aura. He took a hasty step back.

"Not emotion?" Delbridge prodded.

"No, just a trace of energy," Lancing said. "Odd. I've never before picked up that sort of spore. Whoever he was, he must be very strong, indeed."

"Another hunter perhaps?"

"I don't know." Lancing appeared intrigued. "But where there is that much power, there is a capacity for violence. Whoever he is, he is dangerous."

"As dangerous as you?" Delbridge asked softly.

Lancing smiled his beatific smile. "No one is as dangerous as I am, Delbridge. You know that."

Hulsey cleared his throat. "Excuse me, your lordship, but there are a couple of logical explanations for the lack of the sort of spore that Mr. Lancing is sensitive to."

Delbridge and Lancing both looked at him.

"Well?" Delbridge prompted, impatient as always with the scientist.

"The vapor would have exploded in the thief's face at the instant he picked up the pouch that held the crystal," Hulsey said. "He might not have been touching the cabinet or the shelf at that point, if you see what I mean. Just the pouch."

Lancing nodded. "Makes sense. If he didn't have physical contact with the cabinet after he triggered the trap, he wouldn't have left his spore."

Delbridge frowned. "Regardless of whether or not he left any traces of his emotional state at the time of the theft, he would have succumbed to the effects of the vapor shortly thereafter. Ten minutes or fifteen minutes at most."

"Time enough to get out of the mansion," Lancing said.

"But he wouldn't have been able to travel far."

"Might have had some help," Lancing suggested. "A companion, perhaps, who was able to get him away from this place."

"Bloody hell," Delbridge muttered. The thought that there might have been a second man was extremely worrisome.

Hulsey coughed in a diffident sort of way. He looked at Delbridge. "If I might remind you, sir, once the drug took hold, the thief would have become a grave threat to a companion."

"Yes, yes, I understand," Delbridge said brusquely. "He likely would have attacked anyone who happened to be in the vicinity, just as Bloomfield and Ivington are reported to have done." He slapped a hand against a nearby statue, frustrated. "Bloody hell, he should be dead by now, just as the other two are. His body must be out there in the woods somewhere."

"If there was someone else with the thief," Lancing said, smiling again, "and if that other man had the presence of mind to kill his associate when the madness struck, it's entirely possible that he left the body in the woods and took the crystal."

Delbridge and Hulsey both stared at him.

Lancing swept out a hand in a small arc. "It is what I would have done, had I been the second man."

"No doubt," Delbridge said dryly.

"Hell," Lancing continued with an air of good cheer, "if I had been the second man, I probably would have killed my associate once we had the crystal, regardless of whether or not he showed signs of madness. Why share such a valuable item?"

Delbridge resisted the urge to pick up a vase and hurl it against the wall. He had to recover the damned crystal, and he had to do it quickly. He had already sent word to the leader of the Third Circle that he had found the relic. A demonstration of its power was scheduled to take place in a few days. If all went well when he presented the aurora stone to the members, he would be formally inducted into the Order. Without it, he would be denied admission.

He had to find the crystal. He had worked too hard, invested too much time and money, taken too many risks to fail now.

Lancing angled his sculpted chin at the body. "Shall I get rid of her?"

Delbridge frowned. "We don't have time

to dig a grave right now. In any event, it is pouring rain. The ground will be too muddy."

Hulsey looked troubled. "Surely you don't intend to leave the body there on the floor."

Delbridge swung around on his heel and studied his collection of stone sarcophagi. "We will put her in one of those. She will keep safely enough until we can bury her out in the woods. The servants know better than to enter this gallery unless they are instructed to do so by me."

In point of fact, the servants never entered the museum willingly. None of them possessed any measurable paranormal talents, but Delbridge knew that every individual was endowed with some degree of sensitivity, whether or not he or she was aware of it. That sensitivity manifested itself in the forms of dreams and intuition. The contents of the museum, massed together as they were, generated enough disturbing energy to affect even the most insensitive people to some degree. Earlier tonight it had amused him to watch his guests try to conceal their distaste for the relics.

There was a grinding, grating, stone-on-stone rumble when Lancing shoved aside the heavy lid of the sarcophagus. He looked at Hulsey and smiled.

"Give me a hand with the body," he said.

Hulsey started violently. Lancing rarely spoke to him directly. It unnerved him. He pushed his spectacles higher on his nose and then, with great reluctance, he stepped forward.

Lancing strolled toward the dead woman. His path took him near the ancient altar. Absently he reached out to touch it. Delbridge took note of the small action. He'd seen Lancing touch other relics in the gallery in that same affectionate manner, as though he were stroking a cat. Unlike most who entered the museum, the Monster relished the dark energy given off by the relics.

In that way, we are alike, Delbridge thought. It gave him an uncomfortable chill. He did not care for the notion that he had anything in common with such a low-born individual.

Lancing halted abruptly, his hand still resting on the altar.

"What is it?" Delbridge asked quickly. "Do you sense something?"

"Fear." Lancing mouthed the word as though it were the rarest of spices. "A woman's fear."

Delbridge scowled. "Molly's fear of you?"

"No. She tasted much different." Lancing moved his fingertips across the stone surface. "This woman was not in mindless, hysterical panic as Molly was. She was still in control. Nevertheless she was very frightened."

"You're certain the person was a female?" Delbridge asked sharply.

"Oh, yes." Lancing was practically crooning now. "This is a woman's sweet fear."

Delbridge hesitated. "Perhaps you sense one of the prostitutes who were in this house tonight. They accompanied my guests on the tour."

"So did I," Lancing reminded him. "None of the women were frightened, not as this woman was. Believe me when I assure you that I would most certainly have noticed."

"What the devil happened in here?" Delbridge asked, bewildered.

"Don't you understand?" Lancing asked, eyes heating with a feral lust. "There were, indeed, two thieves here tonight. The second one was a female."

"A woman came here to steal my crystal?" Delbridge was dumbfounded. "Surely no female would have the courage, let alone the skill, to risk breaking into my mansion."

Hulsey frowned again. "Do not forget, she had the assistance of a man."

"Why would he bring a woman along?" Delbridge demanded, baffled. "It makes no sense. She would only put him at greater risk of discovery."

Hulsey took off his spectacles and began to polish them, very thoughtful now. "Perhaps he needed her."

"For what purpose?" Delbridge shot back.

"According to my research into the subject, almost all those who have been known to possess a talent for accessing the power of crystals have been female," Hulsey said, falling into his lecturing tones. "It may have been that the man brought this particular woman with him tonight to help him find the stone."

"It was the man who left that fresh trace of energy on the cabinet," Lancing said, very certain. "Presumably he will now be either dead or trapped in the madness of a nightmare."

Hulsey put his spectacles back on his nose and adjusted them with his forefinger. He fixed Delbridge with a steady stare. "It appears you will be searching for a woman."

"But we know nothing about her," Delbridge said plaintively.

"That is not entirely true, sir." Hulsey knitted his bushy brows. "We know that it is quite likely that she can work crystal energy."

■ ■ ■ ■

A short time later Delbridge stood with Hulsey in the kitchen. It was still raining, but the heavy clouds were starting to lighten to a dull gray as dawn arrived.

He looked down at Paddon and Shuttle, the two guards he had hired for the evening. Both were sprawled on the canvas that covered the floor.

Delbridge had rarely had occasion to visit this particular room of the mansion. He was a gentleman; gentlemen did not concern themselves with the running of their households. This morning he was vaguely surprised by the amount of grease stains on the canvas. It made him wonder about the cleanliness of the food his housekeeper served him.

"The intruders must have drugged them," he said to Hulsey. "It is the only explanation."

Hulsey, noticeably calmer now that Lancing was no longer around, prodded one of the guards with the toe of his shoe. "Perhaps."

"We can only hope that the effects eventually wear off. If they die on us we may never get any answers. Hulsey, we must recover that crystal."

"I assure you, I am as concerned as you are, sir."

"As you damn well should be. It cost me a fortune to set you up in that laboratory. If I don't get that crystal back, I won't have any reason to continue financing your experiments, now will I?"

Hulsey flinched. Delbridge took some satisfaction from that reaction. Hulsey's weaknesses were as glaring as Lancing's. The only thing that mattered to the scientist was his research.

"We will find it, sir," Hulsey said quickly.

"We have only a few days until I will be required to deliver the stone to the leader of the Third Circle. If I fail in the task I will not be given a second chance to apply for membership. The leader was damnably clear about that."

"I understand, sir."

Frustration welled up inside Delbridge again. "I have come so far. Taken so many risks. Months of planning. Two high-ranking gentlemen dead. The crystal in my hands at last." He knotted his fingers into a fist. "And now it is gone."

Hulsey did not respond. He was studying the two men on the floor.

"I think Mr. Shuttle is stirring," he said.

Delbridge looked down. Sure enough,

Shuttle was moving, opening his eyes.

Paddon's eyes popped open too. He stared blankly at the ceiling.

"Interesting," Hulsey said. "I do not know of any drug that allows a sleeper to awaken quite like this. It is as if both men were instructed to open their eyes precisely at dawn."

Shuttle and Paddon sat up and looked around, taking in the sight of the large iron cooking range, wooden tub, zinc basin, long table and racks of knives as though they had never seen the like before.

"What the devil?" Paddon muttered.

"Get to your feet, both of you," Delbridge ordered.

Shuttle and Paddon climbed heavily to their feet. They looked like what they were, a pair of tough, violent men from the streets who made their living selling their services as bodyguards and enforcers. Neither was particularly intelligent. Delbridge had believed that to be an asset when he had employed them. Now he was having second thoughts.

"What in blazes happened out in the gardens?" he demanded.

"Nothing in particular, sir," Shuttle said, running one beefy hand through his hair. "Quiet night. No trouble at all." He frowned. "Don't remember coming in here, though."

"Must have popped in to ask the cook for coffee to help us stay awake," Paddon said. But he looked and sounded rattled.

"Neither of you walked into the kitchen of your own accord," Delbridge said. "We found both of you asleep at your posts. While you were napping, a pair of intruders made off with a particularly valuable artifact. You were hired to make sure that sort of thing did not happen while I was entertaining my guests. What do you have to say for yourselves?"

The two stared at him, dumbfounded. Then Paddon scowled.

"We just told you, yer lordship, nothing happened. Don't know what you're talking about, sir."

Delbridge looked at Hulsey for guidance.

Hulsey fixed his attention on Paddon. "What is the last thing you remember before you woke up a moment ago?"

Paddon shrugged. "I was walking through the garden, making my rounds. I remember thinking that we'd likely have rain before morning and then —" He stopped, shaking his head. "Then I woke up here."

Shuttle nodded. "It was the same way for me."

"Do you remember seeing anyone outside in the gardens?" Delbridge asked.

"A couple of guests came out onto the terrace for a few minutes but it was too cold for what they had in mind so they went back inside," Paddon offered.

"This is a waste of time," Delbridge said. "Leave, both of you."

Paddon and Shuttle exchanged glances.

"About our fees," Shuttle said. His voice had lost its deferential edge.

"You'll be paid, before you leave," Delbridge assured him impatiently.

The two men stalked out of the kitchen. Delbridge waited until he could no longer hear the heavy thuds of their boots.

"Do you think that they were in on the theft?" he asked.

"Perhaps," Hulsey said. "But I'm inclined to doubt it. Something about the calmness and speed with which they awakened just as dawn arrived makes me suspect another possibility."

"What is that?"

"I wonder if they were put into an hypnotic trance."

A chill shivered through Delbridge. "Mesmerism?"

"It would explain the condition in which we found them."

"Which of the thieves was the hypnotist?" Delbridge said. "The man or the woman?"

"If I am right in concluding that the woman was the crystal worker, then it follows that her companion was the hypnotist. As I'm sure you are aware, when it comes to the truly powerful paranormal talents, individuals get only a single type. A person might be a crystal worker or a hypnotist but not both."

"Whoever he is, he'll be dead within hours."

"Perhaps," Hulsey said.

Delbridge did not care for the expression on Hulsey's face. The scientist looked as if he were pondering other possibilities.

Lancing reported back an hour later. He was soaked and not in a pleasant frame of mind.

"No body," he said tersely.

"Damn it! Whoever he is, he cannot have escaped the effects of the vapor," Delbridge insisted.

Lancing gave one of his annoyingly elegant shrugs. "Then you had best assume that the woman somehow managed to take him away in a carriage."

"She would soon have found herself in the company of a violent madman," Hulsey pointed out. "Unless —"

Delbridge and Lancing looked at him.

"Unless what?" Delbridge demanded.

Hulsey removed a cloth from his pocket and began to polish his spectacles. "Unless she knew how to save him from the hallucinations."

"Impossible," Delbridge said.

Hulsey put the spectacles back on his nose. Behind the lenses his eyes gleamed. "Interesting, actually."

7

Thaddeus opened his eyes to the heavy gray light of a fog-bound day. For a moment he lay still, trying to orient himself. Nothing about the small room with its dingy green walls and grimy windowpanes was familiar.

From his position on the bed he could see his coat hanging on a wall peg. In one corner there was a rickety-looking washstand that stood next to a small, battered chest of drawers. The sheets on the bed did not smell fresh.

Memories returned in a rush: the fascinating woman with golden eyes, Delbridge's poisoned vapor, the headlong flight in the private carriage, the knowledge that he would probably not survive the night, at least not with his sanity intact.

Leona. Last night her name had been a talisman.

He remembered the crystal aglow with moonlight and the compelling certainty in her voice. *"I am going to walk through your dreams with you."*

He sat up slowly, pushing aside the ragged quilt. Cautiously he let himself recall the details of the struggle against the hellish world of dark fantasies that had threatened to engulf him. Mercifully the images were now no more than fading fragments, uncomfortably sharp in places, to be sure, but no worse than the memories of any other particularly vivid nightmare. He was no longer hallucinating.

The mysterious Leona had used the crystal to save him from descending into a hell from which he might never have returned.

Sorceress, he thought, smiling a little.

And he had repaid her by trying to force himself on her.

He stopped smiling. The shattering memory brought him to his feet. Perspiration dampened his brow. He had never before lost control the way he had last night. *Never.* The powers of self-mastery that he had perfected in order to deal with his hypnotic talents had served him well in all aspects of his life, including the realm of sexual desire. But last night the poison had induced in him a feverish lust that he had not been able to restrain.

Disgust swept through him. He had not

even tried to control his ravenous hunger. In the grip of the hallucinations he had told himself that he had every right to take her. He had convinced himself that she was his true mate, the only woman he had ever encountered whose power matched his own. The only woman who had learned the secret of his talent and did not fear him.

Thankfully, her own talent had saved her from his predatory desire. She had managed to stop him. Nevertheless, the realization of how close he had come to hurting her sickened him. He would have to live with that knowledge for the rest of his life.

Glancing down he saw that he was fully dressed except for his boots. He found them under the bed next to a badly chipped chamber pot.

He sat down on the edge of the bed and put on the boots. Where in blazes was he? He forced himself to think.

After the session with the crystal he had been overcome by an irresistible exhaustion. He had partially awakened when the carriage had halted, but he had been too groggy to take note of his surroundings. Leona and her companion had half carried, half dragged him out of the vehicle and into a room. There had been an unlit fireplace. He remembered that much. Also a man and a woman who looked as if they had been summoned from their beds. And a narrow flight of wooden steps.

It was when he had found his arms draped across not one but two sets of delicate shoulders that he had finally understood that Leona was not the only female dressed in men's clothes. Her friend, the coachman, was also a woman. What was the name she had used? Oh, yes, Adam.

He recalled what Adam had said as she and Leona hauled him through a doorway. *"Mark my words, we're going to regret this. Should have left him beside the road."*

You were right, Adam, he thought. Neither of you has seen the last of me.

A light, tentative knock on the door snapped him out of his brooding memories. It occurred to him that he had no notion of whom he might find standing in the hall outside.

He crossed the room to where his coat hung on the wall. He reached into one of the pockets without much optimism. There was an object inside, but it was not his gun. He pulled it out and saw that he was holding a lady's rouge pot. He remembered picking it up off the floor near the body.

Another knock sounded on the door.

He tried a different pocket. This time

he found the gun. When he removed the weapon he was further gratified to see that it was still loaded.

The gun was not the only thing inside the pocket. A brown-haired wig cut in a shaggy, unkempt masculine style was snagged around the barrel.

"Yes?" he called out.

"Cook thought ye might be awake and wanting some coffee and yer breakfast, sir." The voice was that of a young person.

He dropped the wig back into the coat pocket. Keeping the gun out of sight alongside one leg, he opened the door a couple of inches. A girl of about twelve stood in the hall. She wore a neat white cap and an apron over a simple gray dress. There was a heavily laden tray in her hands. The smell of coffee and the sight of a plate heaped high with eggs, toast and kippered salmon made him realize how hungry he was.

"Thank you," he said, opening the door wider. "Please set it on the table."

"Yes, sir."

The maid carried the tray into the room. When her back was turned he leaned out into the hall to make certain it was empty. Satisfied that no one lay in wait, he slipped the gun into the pocket of the coat.

The maid turned around and dropped a

small curtsy.

"Will there be anything else, sir?"

He smiled at her. "Would you mind answering a few questions? I confess my recollection of my arrival last night is somewhat vague."

"Aye, sir. Pa said you were as drunk as a lord. He had to help yer friend and his coachman take you up the stairs. Yer friend told him that when you woke up this morning you would probably be —" The girl paused, frowning a little in grave concentration. "— considerably confused. But he told Pa not to think for one moment that you were a lunatic. He said you were a very important person with friends in high places."

In other words, the crystal worker had warned the innkeeper not to try to take advantage of him.

"She was right about my confusion," he said mildly. "What is the address of this place?"

"Kilby Street, sir. Yer at the Blue Drake."

That answered the most pressing question. The two women had left him at an inn located in a decent but none-too-prosperous London neighborhood.

"One more thing," he said. "Did my friend happen to tell your pa where he and his coachman intended to go last night after they deposited me here?"

She shook her head. "I don't think so, sir."

Of course not, he thought. The pair had not wanted to provide any clues. They had planned to disappear.

"Thank you for the breakfast tray," he said. "It looks very appetizing."

The girl beamed. "Yer welcome, sir. Yer friend said to be sure to feed you right and proper this morning as you'd had a very hard night. Paid for the food and the room in advance, he did. Tipped Pa handsomely into the bargain."

That explained the overflowing plate on the tray.

"I don't suppose my very good friend left a message for me?" he asked.

"No, sir. He just said to tell you that he said good-bye and wished you well. Then he drove away in the carriage." The maid hesitated.

"What is it?" he prompted.

"Nothing important, sir. It is just that, well —"

"Well, what?"

She cleared her throat. "I heard Pa and Ma talking this morning. Pa said that yer friend seemed downcast when he left last night. Pa said you'd have thought that he was saying farewell forever, as if he never expected to see you again."

"If that was the case, my friend was wrong." He thought about the wig in his coat pocket. "We will most certainly meet again, just as soon as I can arrange it."

8

"You and Adam left Mr. Ware asleep in an inn?" Behind the lenses of her gold-rimmed spectacles, Carolyn Marrick's expressive eyes narrowed with sharp disapproval. "That was extremely risky, don't you think?"

"It is not as though we had a choice in the matter," Leona said. She removed a small stack of chemises from a drawer and put them carefully into a trunk. "We could hardly toss him out of the carriage and leave him by the side of the road."

Carolyn paused in her packing, looking quite blank. "Why ever not? That sounds as though it would have been an excellent way to get rid of him."

"I will admit that Adam did suggest that approach to the problem," Leona said. "I refused to go along with it. After all, he saved my life, Carolyn. What else could I do?"

The conversation was not going well. To ease her frustration, she paused on her way back to the chest of drawers to pat Fog. The big dog raised his head and grinned his wolfish smile.

It was early afternoon. The three of them were in Carolyn's bedroom. Two large traveling trunks, one filled with books and notebooks, the other with neatly folded clothes, stood open. Carolyn was preparing to set out on her honeymoon trip. In the morning she would marry George Kettering, a dashing Egyptologist who shared her passion for antiquities.

Neither the bride nor the groom possessed any close family, and neither wished to wait a moment longer than necessary to set out for Egypt. The ceremony was to be a small, private affair with only Leona and a friend of the groom's in attendance. The couple planned to leave on their journey directly afterward. It would be months before they returned, and when they did, Leona thought, things would not be the same.

She was thrilled for Carolyn, who literally glowed with love and excitement. Nevertheless, deep down, she had to squelch a pang of incipient loneliness. The truth was, she had never envisioned that her association with Carolyn would take this unexpected turn.

When they had met nearly two years ago,

a pair of impoverished spinsters alone in the world, it had seemed that they were destined to become close friends, each dedicated to her career, sharing a house and an abiding, lifelong friendship. But all that had changed when Carolyn had met George, a widower with a passion for Egyptian antiquities that matched her own.

Tomorrow night, Leona thought, things would be different. In truth, things already were different. Not wanting to alarm Carolyn any more than necessary, she had not told her all of the details of the night's adventure. Among other things, she had not mentioned the dead woman in the gallery. There was no point. Carolyn would have been horrified. The anxiety would likely have ruined her wedding day and the joy she felt as she embarked on her new life.

I'm keeping secrets again, Leona thought. *I'm already back in the habit of being alone.* Just like the old days after Uncle Edward left for America and never returned.

Enough of that nonsense. You are happy for Carolyn and you will not feel sorry for yourself. Remember Uncle Edward's advice: Never waste time dwelling on the negative. Where is the logic in that? Concentrate on the positive. You have a career, a roof over your head and a faithful dog. What is more, you are not entirely bereft of friends. There is Adam Harrow.

Well, yes, but Adam's first priority will always be Mr. Pierce.

What of it? You will make new friends.

Fog raised his head from his paws and looked at her intently with his fathomless eyes, his ears pricked. He was very sensitive to her moods. She reached down and gave him another pat, silently reassuring him.

"It seems to me you did more than enough when you saved Mr. Ware from the hallucinations brought on by that strange vapor," Carolyn said, busy with her brushes and combs. "Adam was right. You should have gotten rid of him as soon as possible. Everyone knows that hypnotists can be extremely dangerous."

Another secret, Leona thought. She had not told Carolyn that Ware's mesmeric abilities were of a paranormal nature.

"I admit that there have been a great many lurid reports in the papers concerning the dangers of mesmerism and how the talent can be used for criminal purposes, but they are all based on wild speculation," Leona said. "There is very little in the way of actual evidence."

She hardly needed to defend the mysterious Mr. Ware, but for some murky reason she felt compelled to do so.

"I read an article just the other day about a young man who stole a pair of silver candlesticks while under the influence of a hypnotist," Carolyn announced.

"Hypnosis sounds like a rather convenient excuse to pull out when one has been caught red-handed filching the silver."

"There have been actual scientific demonstrations of how a hypnotist can persuade someone to commit a crime."

"Most of those demonstrations took place on the Continent, primarily in France." Leona took a straw bonnet out of the wardrobe and put it in one of the trunks. "Everyone knows the doctors there have been feuding about mesmerism for years. I do not think we need to take their so-called experiments seriously."

"What about all the reports of women right here in London who were taken advantage of by hypnotists who claimed to be treating them for hysteria?" Carolyn shot back with an air of triumph. "Are you going to deny them, as well?"

Leona felt the heat rise in her cheeks as certain memories of the night returned in full force. "Really, Carolyn, I fear you spend far too much time reading the sensation press. You know as well as I do that such reports are highly suspect."

Carolyn raised her brows. "Some of those women treated for hysteria ended up pregnant."

"There are other explanations besides hypnosis that can account for that condition."

Carolyn pursed her lips, briefly defeated. "Well, yes, I suppose that's true. Nevertheless, you will admit that hypnotists, in general, are not well regarded by the medical establishment."

"Professional jealousy, no doubt."

"Let's be plain, here. You know nothing at all about this Mr. Ware except that he was after your crystal. That fact, alone, should have been sufficient to cause you to be extremely cautious."

"Adam and I did take precautions. Trust me, there is no way that Mr. Ware can find me."

"I would not depend on that, if I were you." Carolyn paused in front of the dressing table and looked at Leona in the mirror. "Now, in addition to worrying about Lord Delbridge, you must anticipate the possibility that Ware may also come looking for you. I said from the start that your plan might well lead to disaster, did I not?"

"Yes, you did," Leona agreed dryly. "And as I have mentioned on more than one occasion, your unwavering optimism has always been one of the things I admire most about you."

Carolyn made a face. "You can hardly blame me for pointing out the pitfalls of your scheme. I am an archaeologist by training. I take note of even the smallest details. Not that Mr. Ware sounds like a small detail, mind you."

Leona thought about the unyielding masculine strength she had felt when Thaddeus Ware had held her tightly against him. Definitely no small details there.

"Mmm," she said aloud.

In the mirror Carolyn's eyes narrowed. "I know why you wanted the crystal. But why do you think Mr. Ware wants it?"

"I don't know. There was no time to discuss the matter." But she had done a great deal of thinking about that very issue since leaving Ware at the inn. "I told you something of the crystal's history."

"You said that over the years it has been stolen many times, usually by someone connected to the secret society of eccentric paranormal researchers you mentioned."

"The Arcane Society. They are an obsessive, devious, untrustworthy lot. Some of the members, like Delbridge, will stop at nothing to acquire relics such as the crystal that they believe to have psychical value. And in the case of the aurora stone they seem to think that they have a claim on it based on an old and utterly ridiculous legend connected to the founder of the Society."

Carolyn frowned. "Do you think your Mr. Ware is a member of the Society?"

My Mr. Ware. Leona paused, savoring that little fantasy for a few seconds. Then she pushed it aside. Thaddeus Ware was not her Mr. Ware, and he never would be.

"No matter where you go I will find you." She pushed the memory of Thaddeus's vow from her mind. Personal issues aside, Carolyn's question was a very good one.

"I don't know," she said. "I suppose it's possible he is affiliated with the Society, but it doesn't matter because I will never see him again."

Carolyn's jaw tightened. "Thank goodness Mr. Pierce suggested that you wear servant's clothes last night. At least if Mr. Ware does decide to search for you he will not realize that he is looking for a woman."

"Mmm," Leona said. Yet another secret. She did not mention that Ware had penetrated her disguise, because she knew that fact would further alarm Carolyn. "I thought you did not approve of Mr. Pierce."

"I do not. I think it is clear that Pierce has connections to the criminal underworld."

"Those were the very connections that helped him locate the crystal for me," Leona pointed out.

Mr. Pierce was received in respectable social circles, but there was no getting around the fact that he lived a very mysterious life. Among other things, he seemed to know a great many secrets — damning secrets — of the rich and powerful.

Pierce had a few secrets of his own, as well, secrets that Leona had never revealed to Carolyn. Like his lover, Adam Harrow, Pierce was, in reality, a woman living life as a man. The pair moved in a strange netherworld inhabited by other females who had chosen a similar masquerade.

"Carolyn, you must not worry about me; I will be fine. Tomorrow you are marrying the man you love and leaving for Egypt. Concentrate on your future."

"My lifelong dream," Carolyn whispered. Wonder and happiness lightened her expression. She turned suddenly. "But I will miss you, Leona."

Leona tried and failed to blink back the tears. She crossed the room to hug Carolyn. "I will miss you, too. Promise you will write to me."

"Of course." Carolyn's voice was choked with sudden emotion. "Are you sure you will be all right here alone?"

"But I'm not alone. I have Mrs. Cleeves and Fog."

"A housekeeper and a dog are not much in the way of companions."

"I have my career." Leona gave her a reassuring smile. "You know how satisfying that is for me. It is my passion, just as your Egyptian antiquities are for you. You must not worry about me."

"My marriage won't change our friendship," Carolyn promised.

"No," Leona said.

But of course it would.

Think positive.

9

"She insisted that the aurora stone belonged to her," Thaddeus said. He looked at his cousin down the length of the long laboratory workbench. "Leona thinks that she has a legitimate claim to the crystal. After what I witnessed last night, I'm inclined to agree with her."

"There is no question but that the stone is the property of the Society." Caleb Jones closed the old, leather-bound volume he had been perusing and rested his hand on the cover. "Furthermore, it is dangerous. It belongs in the Society's museum at Arcane House, where access to it can be tightly controlled."

In the glare of the gas lamps that lit his laboratory and the vast library, Caleb's stern, dour face was rendered even more grim than usual. He was not noted for his charm or sociability. He had little patience with drawing-room conversation and the niceties of polite society. He much preferred the solitude of his laboratory and library. Here, in this place filled with scientific apparatus of every description, shelves crammed with books, ancient and modern, and the journals and records of the founder of the Arcane Society, he was free to indulge his unique abilities.

Caleb possessed a paranormal talent for detecting patterns and meanings where others saw only chaos.

There were those in the Society who whispered that he was nothing more than a wild-eyed conspiracy theorist of the first order and that his talent was actually an indication of mental instability.

Thaddeus did not have any difficulty accepting his cousin's unusual abilities or the brusque temperament that accompanied them. He understood as few others did. When it came to disturbing talents, none — not even Caleb's — had quite the same unsettling effect on others as did his own powers of psychical hypnotism.

He was well aware that most who knew of his talent secretly feared him. Who could blame them? Few wanted to take the risk of getting close to a man who was endowed with such a potentially predatory power. For that reason he, like Caleb, had few close friends.

His talent was also the reason he had not yet married, much to his family's chagrin. No woman of his acquaintance relished the prospect of being wed to a man who wielded his kind of power. For his part, he refused to conceal the truth from a prospective bride.

He and Caleb were cousins of the new Master of the Arcane Society, Gabriel Jones. They were all three descended from the founder of the Society, the alchemist Sylvester Jones. Sylvester had possessed a powerful gift for what in the late seventeenth century was known as alchemy.

Thaddeus sometimes wondered if, had the founder lived in the modern era, he would have been perceived as a brilliant scientist. One thing was certain: There was little doubt but that he would have been considered extremely eccentric in any era. In addition to manifesting a prodigious paranormal talent, he had been paranoid, reclusive and obsessed with his research. That obsession had taken him down a very dangerous path.

Those traits, however, had not stopped him from fathering two sons with two different women, both of whom also possessed psychical talents of their own. It was not lust or love that had prompted Sylvester to produce offspring. His goal, according to his own notes, was to discover whether his talents would be passed down to his children.

Sylvester's experiments were successful, although not in the way he had envisioned. What he had not anticipated was the variety of abilities that appeared in his descendants. In his hubris, he had expected that they would all develop his own paranormal aptitude for alchemical intuition.

But over the course of two centuries two things became evident: The first was that, while raw power could be and frequently was inherited by one's offspring, the particular forms the talent took were unpredictable.

The second outcome, which the arrogant alchemist acknowledged in his journal had come as a startling shock, was that the talented women he had chosen as his mates for the experiments had played just as big a role in the results as he had. Sylvester was flabbergasted to discover that the mothers of his children had bequeathed their own paranormal inheritances to future generations of Joneses.

"I do not think that Leona will give up her claim to the crystal easily," Thaddeus warned.

"Offer her money," Caleb said. "A lot of it. In my experience that is invariably effective."

Thaddeus thought about the way Leona's eyes had glowed with a feminine heat that could only be described as passion when she had channeled power through the aurora stone. Working the crystal had thrilled her in the way another woman might be thrilled by desire. The blood burned in his veins at the memory. Something deep inside him stirred.

"I would not count on money achieving the results you want this time," he said.

"Then you will have to find another way to get the crystal from her," Caleb said, flat and unequivocal. "This is the first time it has surfaced in over forty years. Gabe wants it back in the hands of the Society as soon as possible. If it disappears again, the way it did last time, it could be decades before we hear of it again."

"I know," Thaddeus said patiently. "I'm merely saying that the new owner will probably not want to give it up."

The aurora stone had a long and intriguing history within the Arcane Society. According to the legend, it had been stolen from Sylvester's laboratory by a woman he had named Sybil the Virgin Sorceress. The question of her virginity aside, the truth of the matter was that Sybil was a rival alchemist. The founder had not tolerated competition well; a *female* rival had enraged him. In his journal he had refused to dignify Sybil with the title of alchemist and had labeled her a sorceress instead in order to demean and deride her talents and skills in the laboratory.

The old bastard might have been brilliant, Thaddeus thought, but he was not what anyone would call a modern-thinking man.

"If money won't work, you'll have to find another way to take the stone from the woman," Caleb said. "Given your particular talent, I should not think that would be too difficult. Damn it, you could mesmerize her into handing over the crystal and then cause her to forget that she ever possessed it. I do not see why you are stalling here."

"She's immune to my talent."

That stopped Caleb cold. His eyes gleamed with the detached curiosity of the scientist.

"Huh," he said. "Interesting."

Why was he stalling? Thaddeus wondered. He was going to have to take the crystal away from Leona. He already knew that. Nevertheless, he found himself wanting to defend her right to it.

He wandered over to a nearby bench to examine a prism. "Do you really think that the crystal is another dark, dangerous Arcane Society secret like the founder's formula? I saw no evidence of that last night. Its powers appeared to be of a healing nature, not destructive."

Caleb folded his arms and gave the question some serious thought. "I will allow that the crystal is not as potentially harmful as the formula could be in the wrong hands. But I believe that is primarily because the talent for working it is extremely rare."

Thaddeus watched the light passing through the prism shatter and reform into a dazzling rainbow. "Leona worked the crystal quite easily last night. I assume that means she possesses this extremely rare ability?"

Caleb frowned. "Are you certain she worked it? You said yourself you were hallucinating. Perhaps, while you were under the influence of the drug, you imagined her to be channeling power through the stone."

Thaddeus looked up from the prism. "The power she employed was real. I have never seen any crystal worker do what she did last night."

Caleb grunted. "Most likely because the vast majority of crystal workers are frauds. London does not lack for charlatans who claim to be able to tap the energy of crystals. They are almost as common on the ground as mediums who promise to contact the spirit world. And some of those frauds,

I regret to say, are capable of deceiving even members of the Arcane Society. Remember the infamous Dr. Pipewell and his niece, whom he claimed could work crystal?"

"I am unlikely to ever forget," Thaddeus said dryly. "It has been two years since Pipewell disappeared with the investors' money. My uncle still fumes about how much he lost in that fraudulent scheme."

"I doubt that any of the other wealthy members of the Society who were taken in by Pipewell's promise of untold riches have forgotten, either."

"What of the niece?"

Caleb shrugged. "She disappeared at about the same time. I suspect they are both living well in Paris or New York or San Francisco by now. My point is that most who claim to work crystal are frauds."

"True. But Leona is no charlatan."

Caleb frowned. "Can you be sure that it wasn't your will alone that suppressed the hallucinations? Willpower is your stock-in-trade, as it were."

"I was a man drowning in a well of night," Thaddeus said quietly. "She threw me the lifeline I needed to climb back out."

"A colorful metaphor, but there is no need to waste such fanciful flights of the imagination on me. I prefer hard facts."

"I suppose you had to be there to grasp the full impact of the imagery."

Caleb exhaled slowly. "Then, yes, we will assume that she has the talent to work the stone." His jaw hardened. "All the more reason why we must take it away from her as quickly as possible. Who knows what she might do with it?"

"What, precisely, could she do with it?" Thaddeus asked.

Caleb unfolded his arms and opened the leather-bound book again. He drew his finger down a page of close, cramped, coded writing until he found the passage he wanted.

"Here is what Sylvester wrote," he said. " 'The stone is a fearful crystal, unlike any other I have ever studied. The sorceress possesses the strange and awful ability to make it destroy a man's most vital powers.' "

Thaddeus raised his brows. "Don't tell me Sylvester was afraid that Sybil the Virgin might render him impotent with the aurora stone."

"He wasn't talking about his sexual powers. He was referring to the destruction of something he prized even more, his psychical powers."

"Leona did nothing like that last night. I assure you, my senses are all intact today."

"I will be the first to admit that our eccentric ancestor had his character flaws, but he was never wrong when he set down a warning. If he wrote that the crystal is dangerous, rest assured that it is. It is a relic of power. All power is potentially dangerous."

Thaddeus shrugged. "I will not argue the point any longer. As it happens, I agree with you."

Caleb's brows shot up. "About time."

"The crystal is dangerous, but perhaps not in the way you believe. I am convinced that Leona is at risk as long as it is in her possession. Delbridge murdered two men in order to obtain it. He won't stop at anything to recover it. If he was to find Leona, he would not hesitate to harm her in order to take the stone."

Caleb looked satisfied. "It is settled then. Now, on to the other matter: the dead woman you discovered in Delbridge's house. Any possibility that he killed her?"

"I doubt it. He seems to favor murder by poisonous vapor. This killing was decidedly messy. Could just as well have been one of the guests." Thaddeus rested a hand on a gleaming telescope. "What is bothering me is that she died the same way the victims of the Midnight Monster died. Her throat was sliced open."

"Huh." Caleb contemplated that for a moment. "Any other similarities to the Monster's work?"

"None I found obvious. The woman who died in that gallery was clearly not a poor streetwalker. The very fact that she was at Delbridge's party indicates that she was a fashionable courtesan who catered to wealthy gentlemen. Until now the Monster has taken his victims from among the lowest class of prostitutes and done his work in disreputable neighborhoods, not fine mansions."

"Perhaps he is growing more proud and confident," Caleb mused. "If he is a rogue hunter, as we suspect, he may be seeking to draw more attention to his prowess."

The hunt for the Midnight Monster had begun two months earlier after two women had died gruesome deaths. Jeremiah Spellar, a detective at Scotland Yard who possessed a paranormal degree of intuition and who was also a member of the Arcane Society, had concluded that the killer might well be a parahunter. Unbeknownst to his superiors, who were unaware of his abilities, he had contacted Gabriel Jones and warned him of the problem.

Gabriel, inundated with his new duties as Master, had assigned the task of investigating the killings to Caleb, who had in turn called upon Thaddeus for assistance.

The investigation, however, had not gone well, because of the lack of clues. Thankfully, no more bodies had been discovered. But rumors of two prostitutes who had mysteriously vanished from the streets in recent weeks were now circulating in London's underworld. Nevertheless, it was as if the Monster had vanished.

Until last night, Thaddeus thought.

"It is difficult to see any connection between Delbridge and the Midnight Monster," he said. "Whatever else one can say about his lordship, he is a man of wealth and privilege who takes his status in the social world very seriously. Difficult to envision him associating with a man who murders prostitutes."

Caleb drummed his fingers on the journal. "Delbridge might not be aware of his associate's evening hobby."

"True," Thaddeus agreed.

"And I would point out at least one obvious connection between the two."

Thaddeus looked at him. "The fact that both possess some degree of talent?"

"Delbridge is a member of the Arcane Society. According to the records he has the ability to detect the nature of paranormal powers in others. He would recognize a hunter talent the moment he encountered one."

Thaddeus considered that briefly. "And if his lordship happened to be in need of a hunter to arrange the deaths of two high-ranking gentlemen, he might have found it useful to employ the Midnight Monster."

"It is not beyond the realm of possibility."

"No," Thaddeus agreed. "Assuming the Monster was open to an offer of employment."

"First things first," Caleb said. "Your priority at the moment is the recovery of the crystal. Once it is safely under the control of the Society we can concentrate once again on the Monster. And if it turns out that there is a link between Delbridge and the killer, the pursuit of one investigation will bring us closer to solving the other crimes."

"I agree," Thaddeus said. He peered into a microscope. The monstrous, faceted eye of an insect stared back, reminding him of the hallucinations. He straightened abruptly and found Caleb studying him as if he were a specimen under the microscope. He raised a brow. "What is it?"

"I was thinking that in order to discover that Delbridge had the crystal, this Leona of yours must have some interesting underworld connections of her own."

Interesting was one of Caleb's favorite words.

"That occurred to me also," Thaddeus said.

"How do you intend to start the search for her?"

Thaddeus reached into his pocket and brought out the wig. "I'm hoping this will lead me to her. The name of the shop where it was sold is inside."

Caleb took the wig and examined it intently. "This is excellent workmanship and the hair is genuine. I'm surprised she would make such an expensive investment in a disguise that was only intended to last for one night."

"I suspect that the wig may have been purchased originally for long-term wear and simply given to Leona to use last night."

"What makes you think that?"

"Leona's companion was a woman who was also disguised as a man, but, unlike Leona, he or rather she seemed quite comfortable with the disguise. I suspect she lives much of her life as a man. Either that or she is an actress who plays the parts of boys and young males on the stage."

Caleb went still. "The Janus Club."

"What?"

"Gabe told me about it after the affair of the stolen formula. It is a secret club whose members are all females who go about dressed as men."

"Sounds like a good place to begin my inquiries."

"I fear it will not be that easy. You will not be allowed inside the front door. No, you will have to take a more subtle approach."

Thaddeus shrugged. "The wig."

"Yes." Caleb tossed the wig back to him. "Notify me as soon as you recover the crystal."

"I will." Thaddeus dropped the wig into his pocket.

"One more thing."

Thaddeus paused at the door. "Yes?"

Caleb contemplated him with a curious expression. "I have never seen you this intrigued by a woman. What is it about this Leona that compels you so?"

"Let's just say I find her *interesting.*"

"She is attractive?"

"She is —" Thaddeus groped for the right word. "Fascinating. But that is not the reason I must find her again."

"What is the reason?"

Thaddeus smiled faintly. "She is the only woman I have ever met outside my family who learned the truth about me and was not afraid of me."

Sudden and complete understanding flashed in Caleb's eyes.

"An irresistible lure," he said.

10

The lean, handsome man with the pale blond hair and the equally pale eyes looked as innocent as a choirboy, but there was something about him that rang faint alarm bells somewhere inside Dr. Chester Goodhew. He could not explain his reaction with logic, however, so he chose to disregard it. After all, the fobs on the gentleman's watch were gold, the onyx ring looked real and there was no question but that his coat and trousers had been cut by an expensive tailor. In short, Mr. Smith, as he called himself, appeared to be an ideal client.

"I have heard that you can refer me to a woman skilled at explaining troubling dreams." Mr. Smith smiled his angelic smile, hitched up his fine wool trousers and crossed his legs. "I am quite desperate. Haven't slept in months because of the nightmares."

He appeared surprisingly well rested for a man who suffered from chronic insomnia, but what was the point in making that observation, Goodhew thought. This was a business.

"I may be able to assist you." Goodhew lounged back in his chair, propped his elbows on the arms and tapped his fingertips together. Smith appeared to be a candidate for the new services he was selling.

"May I inquire as to who recommended you to me?" he asked.

Smith wrinkled his nose in pained disgust. "A quack in Crewton Street. Calls himself Dr. Bayswater. Tried to convince me to buy some of his patent medicine. I was not about to touch the stuff. One never knows what is in those tonics and elixirs men like him sell."

They both glanced somewhat reflexively at the array of bottles on the shelf next to Goodhew's desk. The sign on the front door read: DR. GOODHEW'S NATURAL REMEDIES. The framed posters on the wall advertised the various nostrums sold on the premises: DR. GOODHEW'S HERBAL TONIC FOR LADIES, DR. GOODHEW'S STOMACH BITTERS, DR. GOODHEW'S COUGH SYRUP, DR. GOODHEW'S VITAL ELIXIR FOR MEN, DR. GOODHEW'S SLEEPING AID.

"The effectiveness of a medicine is directly connected to the expertise of the doctor who prepares it," Goodhew said smoothly. "You were wise to be wary of Bayswater's cheap concoctions. Sugar and water for the most part, with a little gin or sherry tossed in to give it some flavor. I assure you my medicines are of the highest quality and contain the most efficacious ingredients."

"I do not doubt that, Dr. Goodhew. But as I made clear to Bayswater and several other doctors today, I am seeking a cure that does not rely on any sort of unnatural chemical."

"I use only natural ingredients." Goodhew cleared his throat. "I must say, I'm surprised Bayswater sent you to me. He and I are not what anyone would call close."

Smith smiled benignly. "He did try to talk me out of my desire to consult with someone who employed crystals. Told me that all crystal workers were frauds. But I insisted. I made it worth his while to suggest another practitioner."

"I see." Goodhew tapped his fingers together again. "Well, if you're certain that you don't want to try a scientific remedy such as my sleeping tonic —"

"Quite certain."

"Then, I will be happy to make an appointment for you with Mrs. Ravenglass."

Smith's long-fingered hand tightened around the carved head of his walking stick.

A disturbing air of anticipation emanated from him.

"Mrs. Ravenglass is the name of the woman who works crystals?" he asked.

"Yes." Goodhew sat forward and reached for his leather-bound appointment book. "Would Thursday afternoon at three be convenient?"

"Thursday is three days away. Is there anything available today?"

"I'm afraid not. Wednesday afternoon, perhaps?"

A curious stillness came over Smith. Nothing changed in his expression, and he made no move, yet for some inexplicable reason an icy chill went down Goodhew's spine.

In the next moment, Smith appeared to relax. He smiled his engaging smile.

"Wednesday afternoon will be fine," he said. "What is her address?"

"She has consulting rooms in Marigold Lane." Goodhew cleared his throat. "You may be interested to know that I have concluded that the cause of disturbing dreams in men is a congestion of the masculine fluids."

Smith's brows rose. "I see."

"Scientifically proven," Goodhew assured him. "As it happens, for an additional fee Mrs. Ravenglass can be persuaded to provide a special therapy of a very *personal* nature in a private and very *intimate* setting that is guaranteed to cure that sort of problem."

"You don't say."

Goodhew leaned forward and picked up his pen. "Shall I put you down for the special therapy?"

"What the hell," Smith said. "Why not?"

11

Thaddeus found the woman who went by the name Adam Harrow in an art gallery examining a series of framed photographs.

Adam was still in men's clothes but she no longer wore the guise of a coachman. Today she was an elegant man-about-town, attired in well-cut coat and trousers. The wing-collared shirt and the four-in-hand tie were in the latest style. A knee-length overcoat swung from her discreetly padded shoulders. She had removed her hat, revealing light brown hair trimmed quite short and sleeked straight back from her forehead with pomade. It was a style perfectly suited to a gentleman of fashion.

Thaddeus stood quietly at the back of the gallery for a moment, studying his quarry from a distance. If he had met Adam Harrow socially and not known that she was a woman, he would never have guessed the truth. If one knew to look for it, there was a certain delicacy about the face and hands, but he had met many young men who presented an equally refined appearance. Judging by the ease with which she toyed with a handsome walking stick, her gracefully arrogant stance and exquisite air of ennui, Adam Harrow carried off the masculine persona with aplomb.

Thaddeus thought about the cool manner with which she had handled a pistol and a team of horses. She had clearly had a great deal of experience in the role she had created for herself. He wondered why an obviously accomplished and educated young woman would choose to live her life as a man. It was an interesting question, but not the one that he had come here to answer.

Sensing that she was being watched, Adam turned away from the photograph and looked in his direction. He knew the precise instant when she saw and recognized him. She covered her reaction almost immediately, hesitating for only a fraction of a second before concealing her shock beneath an expression of cool boredom.

She walked toward him with long, confident strides, as though she intended to go straight past him and out the door.

He stepped in front of her, forcing her to halt.

"Mr. Harrow," he said, keeping his voice very low. "I believe I have something that belongs to you. Allow me to return it."

He drew the wig out of his pocket.

Adam's mouth tightened. "Bloody hell. I told Leona that we should have got rid of you in a more permanent fashion."

"I'm glad that you mentioned Leona. She is the reason I am here."

"You actually expect me to tell you how to find her so that you can take the crystal from her?" Adam regarded him with scornful amusement. "Think again, Mr. Ware."

"Delbridge will be looking for her. If he finds her, he will very likely kill her."

Adam's fine brows rose. "What of yourself, sir? You appear to want the stone as badly as Delbridge did. That makes you equally dangerous."

"Not to Leona. I will take the stone from her because she is in serious jeopardy every moment that it is in her possession. But I will not hurt her."

"So you say."

"She saved my life. I have no reason to harm her. All I want is the crystal."

Adam eased one hand into the pocket of her overcoat. "Leona told me that you were a powerful hypnotist. Do you intend to use your talent on me to force me to give you her address?"

He considered telling her that if mesmerizing her had been part of his plan, he would have been on his way to Leona's address by now and she would be looking at photographs on the wall with no memory of the conversation. But, willingly or not, Adam had helped save his life last night. She deserved better, a reassuring lie at the very least.

"Calm yourself," he said. "I can see that you do not know a great deal about hypnotism. Allow me to assure you that no hypnotist, regardless of his powers, can put an unwilling person into a trance."

Adam seemed to relax a bit at that, but she remained suspicious. "I would have you know that I am armed, sir."

"I do not think you will shoot me dead here in public. It would make for a great many questions from the authorities, and something tells me that you would rather avoid that sort of close scrutiny."

"I admit I would prefer to avoid any and all conversations with the police. However, if you do attempt to employ your powers of mesmerism on me, I will not hesitate to use my pistol. I would rather have an awkward conversation with the authorities than betray a friend."

Thaddeus inclined his head. "I respect

your sense of loyalty. But if you care about Leona you will give me her address. She is in grave danger from Delbridge."

Adam hesitated uneasily. "Leona told me about the dead woman you found. Do you think Delbridge murdered her?"

"I do not know, but he is most certainly capable of cold-blooded murder. He has killed twice already to acquire the crystal. He will not stop now."

"What of your own intentions? Do you want the crystal for your own collection?"

Thaddeus felt his patience start to fray. "You must believe me when I tell you that I am not looking for Leona because I want that damn rock for my personal collection of antiquities. The crystal is the rightful property of a group devoted to research and study of the paranormal. I am here as an agent for that society."

Adam blinked, startled. "What is the name of the society you represent?"

Thaddeus hesitated and then decided there was no reason not to tell her.

"The Arcane Society. I doubt that you have heard of it."

Adam groaned. "I should have guessed."

Thaddeus frowned. "You know it?"

"I count the wife of the new Master of the Arcane Society as one of my friends."

It was Thaddeus's turn to be caught off guard. "You are acquainted with Mrs. Venetia Jones?"

"Indeed. I am a great admirer of her photographs." Adam waved languidly at the framed pictures displayed on the walls of the gallery. "As it happens, I came here today to examine her latest portraits."

"If you know Mrs. Jones, then you know that you can easily verify that what I am telling you is true. Will you give me Leona's address?"

"Probably." Adam stepped around him and started once more toward the door. "But first there is someone you must meet. He will make the final decision."

Thaddeus fell into step beside her. "Who is this person?"

"His name is Mr. Pierce. And I suggest very strongly that you avoid employing your mesmeric talents on him. He would be most annoyed. People who annoy Mr. Pierce live to regret it."

12

The day was clear and warm. The leaves in the tiny scrap of a park were that perfect shade of green that was the banner of early spring. Lancing much preferred the physical sensations of the night and the promise of the hunt that came with them, but he was quite capable of enjoying the heat of the sun and the scent of new growth. His talents were those of the hunter and a hunter was, by nature, always in touch with his surroundings.

He stood beneath one of the newly leafed trees and studied the front door of Number 7 Vine Street. An hour ago he had followed the mysterious Mrs. Ravenglass home from her consulting rooms in Marigold Lane. She had disappeared inside the house long enough to eat a light meal and refresh herself and then had reemerged to walk back toward her business premises.

His first plan was to wait until night and

then enter the house to search for the crystal. With his talents, it would be no trick at all to break into Number 7 without raising an alarm. It was how he had administered the vapor to Bloomfield and Ivington. Neither man had even awakened until he held the poison-soaked cloths over their mouths and noses. By the time they had opened their eyes, of course, it was too late.

Delbridge had specified that there was to be no killing when he recovered the crystal today for fear of drawing the attention of the police. But Lancing took that to mean no *unnecessary* killing. It would not be his fault if Mrs. Ravenglass or her housekeeper, the only occupants of the house at Number 7, were to awaken while he was inside. He would have no choice but to cut a throat or two. In fact, he anticipated using the threat to force the crystal worker to give up the stone. And afterward he would be forced to kill her. Couldn't leave any witnesses, now, could he?

But as soon as he had seen the dog greet Mrs. Ravenglass at her door he had changed his plans for a midnight burglary. His paranormal talents made him faster than the average man and heightened his natural senses. Nevertheless, he was still a creature of nature — albeit a highly evolved one —

not some magical or supernatural being. His speed and reflexes were far superior to those of others of his own kind, but he was no faster or better equipped to bring down prey than any of nature's other superior predators: a wolf, for example.

Mrs. Ravenglass's dog looked as if it had descended from wolves.

He did not fancy his chances against another such beast of prey. The dog would sense him the moment he entered the house. Lancing was not certain that his weapon of choice, a knife, would be effective against all those teeth and primeval reflexes. Even if he managed to kill the dog, the creature might well alarm the entire street with his barking before he died.

But large dogs required plenty of vigorous exercise, certainly more than could be provided in the tiny garden behind Number 7 or in the little park. Sooner or later someone inside the house would have to take the animal for a long walk.

As he watched, the front door of the house opened. The housekeeper appeared. She wore a gray gown, sensible shoes and a bonnet. In one hand she held the end of a leash. The wolf-dog was at the other end of the long strip of leather.

When the housekeeper and the dog reached

the bottom of the front steps, the beast halted abruptly and looked directly across the street into the park, ears sharpened. He stared hard at Lancing. There was an intent, unnerving steadiness about the animal's gaze. The housekeeper turned to see what had attracted his attention.

Lancing angled his hat over the side of his face, shielding his features, and started quickly away toward the far end of the street.

"Come along, Fog." The housekeeper tugged on the leash.

Reluctantly the dog trotted after her.

Lancing exhaled slowly, but he did not stop walking until he reached the far end of the park. Then he allowed himself to turn around. The housekeeper and the dog had both disappeared around the corner.

A short time later, Lancing made his way into the tiny garden at the back of Number 7. He took out his lock pick. He had the house to himself and plenty of time to search for the crystal.

13

"The dreams are becoming increasingly vivid, Mrs. Ravenglass." Harold Morton leaned a little farther across the table. In the light of the glowing green crystal, his eyes glittered with excitement. "Dr. Goodhew explained that they are due to a congestion of masculine fluids."

Leona looked at him through the heavy black veil she always wore for her consultations. It had been Uncle Edward's idea for her to dress as a widow when she worked crystal. At the start of her career the veil and the serious black gown had concealed her youth. She had been sixteen when she had begun working crystals professionally. Edward had explained that few clients would have trusted the experience and talents of such a young woman.

But as she grew older he insisted that she continue the pose. *"Adds an air of mystery and intrigue to the whole thing,"* Edward said.

"The clients want a bit of theater, whether they know it or not."

"Dr. Goodhew told you that your dreams were due to congestion?" she said warily to Morton.

"Yes, precisely." Morton's head bobbed up and down several times. "He explained everything and assured me that you could apply certain therapies designed to relieve that congestion."

Harold Morton was a lecherous cad, and she was trapped with him in the small consulting room. What on earth had Dr. Goodhew been thinking when he referred him to her?

With his slightly balding pate, well-trimmed whiskers and conservatively cut coat, Morton appeared to be every inch the respectable accountant he purported to be. But she had realized the moment she turned down the lamp and activated the emerald crystal that, regardless of his reasons for making the appointment, he was no longer interested in help for the disturbing dreams with which he claimed to be afflicted. He now had other things on his mind.

"I regret I will not be able to help you, Mr. Morton," she said briskly. Simultaneously she stopped channeling her own psychical energy into the crystal. The green glow began to fade.

"What's this?" Morton straightened angrily. "See here. Dr. Goodhew assured me that you used an exclusive therapy in an *intimate* setting."

"I'm afraid you were misinformed as to the nature of my therapy, sir."

"Come now, no need to be coy, Mrs. Ravenglass." Morton winked. "I paid Goodhew quite handsomely for the opportunity to consult with you in an *intimate* setting."

She froze. "You paid *extra* for the special therapy?"

"I most certainly did."

"I regret to say that crystal work will not help your problem. Perhaps you should try one of Dr. Goodhew's tonics to improve manly vigor."

"Nothing wrong with my manly vigor, I assure you, Mrs. Ravenglass," Morton said quickly. "That's why I'm here. An excess of manly vigor, that's the problem. I need a release, just like the woman in my dreams. We need each other, Mrs. Ravenglass. Desperately."

"I have no idea what you are talking about."

"Nonsense." Morton leaned forward again. His aura of flushed excitement grew stronger. "Let me describe my most recent dream. I have had it several times during the past fortnight and it is very vivid."

". . . Remember, Leona, you must control the audience from the moment you take the stage. Never allow your audience to control you . . ."

"I do not want to hear about your dreams, sir," she said sharply. "I cannot help you."

Morton ignored her. "The lady in my dream is a woman who was widowed on her wedding night. Her husband died before the marriage could be consummated, and she has been forced to live for years without ever having known the gratification of normal, healthy marital relations."

"That will be all for today, Mr. Morton." She made to rise from the table, intending to turn up the lamp.

"The poor, virginal widow endures the most debilitating bouts of hysteria. Everyone knows that widows and spinsters often suffer greatly from the condition because they are deprived of normal marital relations."

The green crystal was still glowing, albeit faintly. It should have gone dark. Halfway to her feet, Leona sat down suddenly, shocked. Harold Morton was activating the crystal, although he seemed unaware of it.

"I believe you are the lady of my dreams, Mrs. Ravenglass." Morton's voice thickened with lust. "I see now that fate has brought us together so that I can relieve your tension and prevent an attack of hysteria. That treatment will also relieve my congestion. We can satisfy each other, madam."

"Fate had nothing to do with our meeting, sir," she told him coldly.

She would have a few words to say to Dr. Goodhew. How dare he imply to male clients that she was a prostitute?

The crystal was glowing more brightly but not in a healthy, therapeutic fashion. Morton still gave no indication that he knew that he was the one stirring the energy of the stone. Nevertheless, it was obvious that he possessed more energy than the average client and he was somehow channeling it into the green crystal.

Everyone possessed some degree of paranormal ability. The vast majority of people lived out their entire lives unaware of it or unwilling to acknowledge it. Only in their dreams did they actively tap into that side of their natures. When they awoke, their conscious minds usually shrugged off the experience.

But dreams were not the only way in which an individual's latent energy surfaced. The intense emotions associated with sexual arousal could also release it. That was what was happening now. It was just bad luck that

Morton had been focusing intently on the crystal when he had been overcome with his lewd urges.

Although he was unconsciously pouring dark energy into the stone, he had no natural talent for controlling the crystal. As a result the paranormal currents generated from his own mind were rebounding on him, no doubt intensifying his sensation of arousal.

"I know that you lie awake at night, yearning for the touch of a man, Mrs. Ravenglass," he assured her. "I can bring you relief. Allow me to help you. No one need ever know. It will be our little secret."

She scooped up the illuminated crystal and got to her feet. "I assure you, I do not need your remedy, sir."

She channeled energy into the stone to defuse Morton's pulses. The green crystal quickly grew cloudy and then darkened altogether.

Morton's chair scraped on the floor. He shot to his feet, outraged. "See here, I paid well for my therapy."

She wished Fog was with her this afternoon. Until recently he had always accompanied her to her consultations, spending his time dozing in the reception room or lying at her feet beneath the table. But lately she left him at home because Dr. Goodhew claimed that some of the clients complained about the presence of a large, dangerous-looking dog in the consulting rooms.

She made a mental note to notify Goodhew that in future she would refuse all clients who professed a fear of dogs.

"You must leave now, sir," she said. "I have another client waiting."

That was not true. Morton was the last client with an appointment this afternoon, but there was no way he could know that.

"I cannot leave you in your terrible condition, Mrs. Ravenglass." Morton lurched to his feet. "I know how you suffer. Rest assured I will see to it that the great tension inside you is released in the most therapeutic fashion. I will bring you to a fever pitch of the most intense emotion. You will enjoy a truly cathartic release."

"No, thank you." She headed toward the door.

She had easily suppressed the energy in the crystal, but it was clear that Morton's sexual excitement had not been dampened. He rounded the table, reaching for her with a large, beefy hand.

"You must not leave, Mrs. Ravenglass. I will show you how desperately you need the catharsis I can give you."

She dodged his groping fingers. "I'm afraid

that your case is highly unusual, Mr. Morton. Quite beyond my poor abilities. The fee you paid will be fully refunded, of course."

He managed to grab her upper arm. When he hauled her close she discovered that his breath smelled of sausage.

"Never fear, madam. I will not breathe a word of what transpires between us here in this room," he assured her. "As I said, it will be our secret."

She smiled very sweetly. "Yes, it will. Look into the crystal, sir. Let us be transported together into the realm of the metaphysical."

"What?" He blinked again and automatically glanced at the stone, unconsciously pouring more energy into it.

It glowed bright green.

This time she did not merely dampen the currents of his energy, she swamped them. Then she used the stone's focusing power to send the tide straight into Morton's mind.

The energy she projected, enhanced by the crystal, struck all of Morton's senses with enough force to cause sudden, jolting pain.

The green crystal, like the others, with the exception of the aurora stone, was not strong enough to do any permanent damage, but it could certainly stop a man in his tracks for a moment or two.

With a groan of startled anguish, Morton released her arm and reeled back. He clapped both hands to his temples.

"My *head.*"

"I fear our time is up for today," she announced.

She rushed back to the door, yanked it open and dashed out into the reception room.

Thaddeus Ware caught her with one arm and scooped her close against him.

"We really must stop meeting like this," he said.

"What on earth?" Stunned, she stared at him, unable to believe her eyes.

Thaddeus ignored her to fix Morton with a cold, dangerous look.

"What is going on here?" he asked in a voice that could easily have frozen the fires of hell.

Morton jerked in reaction. His mouth opened and closed several times before any words came out.

"Now see here, sir," he sputtered. "You'll have to wait your turn. I paid for an hour-long session. I have a good thirty minutes left."

"You will leave now," Thaddeus said, infusing the command with just enough energy to create a deadly soft voice of doom.

Morton jerked violently, blanched and hurried toward the door.

His footsteps thudded heavily on the stairs. A moment later the outer door slammed shut behind him.

As if he had suddenly remembered that he was holding her, Thaddeus released Leona. She stepped back quickly, shaking out her skirts. It dawned on her that her veil was hanging at an awkward angle. She crumpled the black netting up onto the brim of the hat and then discovered that the hat, itself, had tilted sideways and was precariously perched over one ear.

Thaddeus reached up, removed a few pins and plucked the hat from her head. He handed it to her with an air of grave politeness.

"Do many of your consultations end in such an energetic fashion?" he asked without inflection.

"Really, sir, I hardly think —" She broke off when she saw Adam Harrow standing quietly to one side. "*Adam.* What are you doing here?"

"Are you all right, Leona?" Adam asked, frowning.

"Yes, of course," Leona said automatically. "What is going on? Why did you bring Mr. Ware with you?"

"I'm afraid the answer to that is somewhat complicated," Adam said apologetically.

"There is nothing complicated about it." Thaddeus turned his riveting eyes on Leona. "I told you that I would find you again, Miss Hewitt. You will learn that I always keep my promises."

14

"I realize I am no expert in the business of working crystals," Thaddeus said in chillingly neutral tones, "but a single woman closeted alone in a darkened room with a strange man would appear to be a recipe for disaster."

"One small, admittedly unfortunate, incident does not constitute a disaster," Leona said stiffly.

They were in the small parlor of the little house on Vine Street. Adam had left a few minutes earlier, after apologizing quietly for the second time. Leona had assured her that she did not blame her. It had been Mr. Pierce's decision to give Thaddeus the address of Leona's consulting rooms. It was understood that Adam's first loyalty was to Pierce.

In any event, Leona thought, her feelings at the moment were too muddled to allow for any clear sense of blame. Deep down, some part of her had hoped Thaddeus would come looking for her. In spite of everything, the irrepressible, optimistic side of her nature was convinced that the passion that had leaped between them during that dark journey back to London had not been generated solely by the hallucinatory vapors.

But now she knew that her secret fantasies were no more than the stuff of dreams. Thaddeus's fascinating eyes were certainly not blazing with passion today. There was a cold, hard, implacable aura about him that extinguished the tiny flames of hope that had burned within her.

All in all it had been a rather trying day. She had started out feeling a little low after spending her first night alone in the house following Carolyn's joyous leave-taking the day before. Then came the unpleasant encounter with Harold Morton. And now this: The man of her dreams had magically appeared on her doorstep only to make it clear that the only thing he wanted from her was the aurora stone.

Sensing her tension, Fog had taken up a protective stance next to her chair. She rested a hand on top of his head. He leaned into her skirts, his pricked ears and attentive gaze fixed on Thaddeus.

Thaddeus stood facing her, his back to

the window. He had said very little during the short carriage ride from the consulting rooms, leaving it to Adam to make the explanations.

By the end of the journey, Leona was forced to accept the fact that Mr. Pierce had betrayed her to Thaddeus Ware because he had genuinely believed she was in danger. There were few things more annoying than having someone act in what he perceived to be one's best interests, she reflected.

"What would you have done if Mr. Harrow and I had not arrived when we did?" Thaddeus asked.

Leona glowered at him. "I was in no danger. I had the situation under control."

"It did not appear that way," Thaddeus said evenly.

"It really is none of your business, sir."

"Probably not." He raised his brows. "But for some reason I find myself unable to ignore the matter."

"Concentrate a little harder. I'm sure that if you work at it you will manage to summon the willpower required to put the issue aside and move on to other things."

"I disagree. Wouldn't be surprised if I have a few unpleasant dreams tonight because of what I witnessed today."

"Don't come to me for crystal therapy if

that proves to be the case." Leona fixed him with a frosty glare. "Let us get to the heart of the matter," she said. "You are here for the aurora stone."

"I did warn you that it was extremely dangerous to possess," he said, a little gentler now.

"I don't believe you."

"Leona, be reasonable. If I found you so easily, Delbridge may do the same."

She frowned. "Delbridge does not know about Adam. Nor does he have a wig to use as a clue."

"No, but there are other ways of finding people, even in a city this size."

"How?" she demanded.

He shrugged. "If I were in his shoes, with nothing else to go on, I would start by tracking down every crystal reader in London. I'd ask questions, and I'd pay bribes until I collected some rumors and clues. It might take a great deal of time and effort, but sooner or later one of your competitors would point a finger toward you." He paused for emphasis. "It is even possible that I would get lucky immediately."

She stared at him, transfixed. "Good heavens. I never thought of that approach to the problem."

"Something told me that it might have escaped your notice."

She beetled her brows. "There is no need for sarcasm, sir."

"Leona, I thought that we had made it clear that Delbridge has murdered at least twice in order to get his hands on the crystal. You may be his next victim if you don't —"

"One moment, sir." Leona studied him closely, more suspicious than ever. "I was under the impression that you wanted the crystal for yourself. Who do you refer to when you say *we?*"

"I am acting on behalf of a society of psychical researchers."

"There are any number of such societies, most of which are composed of gullible fools and doddering eccentrics who know nothing of the paranormal."

"I am well aware of that," Thaddeus said. "And I will admit that the Arcane Society possesses more than its fair share of doddering eccentrics."

The shock of the name caused Leona to suck in her breath on a sharp gasp.

"I can see that I was mistaken," Thaddeus said, very thoughtful now. "You do know of the Arcane Society."

She cleared her throat. "I believe I may have heard some vague mention of it, yes.

You say you represent it? You were *engaged* by the organization to pursue the crystal?"

"I was asked to investigate, yes. But I am also a member."

She sighed. So much for that faint hope. "I see."

"I like to believe that I am not yet one of the doddering eccentrics in the Society," he continued. "But I may be deluding myself."

"If you meant that in jest, sir, I must tell you it was not amusing."

"My apologies." He paused, regarding her with a cool, assessing expression. "I must admit I am surprised to learn that you are aware of the Society. It has always taken great pains to avoid the attention of the press."

"Mmm."

"The members take their paranormal research seriously. They have no wish to be associated with the innumerable frauds, quacks and charlatans who create sensations with their demonstrations of levitation and spirit summonings."

She decided to try logic. "You say the Arcane Society feels it has a claim to my crystal."

"Yes. It was originally the property of the founder, Sylvester Jones."

Rubbish, she thought, but she managed

to keep her tone smooth. "And when did he lose it?"

"It was stolen from him some two hundred years ago."

"Two hundred years?" She managed an airy chuckle. "You must admit that it would be difficult if not impossible to prove theft after the passage of two centuries, sir."

"The members of the Arcane Society have long memories," Thaddeus said.

"Forgive me, but I think it more likely that certain members, the doddering eccentrics, perhaps, prefer to cling to their silly legends."

"I did not come here to argue with you about the ownership of the crystal," he said calmly. "I understand that you believe it is yours. We must agree to disagree on that point."

"But that isn't going to stop you from taking it, is it?" she asked. "And I, a frail, weak, helpless female, can hardly stop you should you try to take it by force."

His mouth twitched a little at the corner. "*Frail, weak* and *helpless* are not the words that spring immediately to mind when I think of you, Miss Hewitt."

"So much for appealing to your gentlemanly instincts. I should have known better."

For some reason that small shot across the bow seemed to strike home. To her amazement Thaddeus turned to stone before her very eyes.

"Yes," he said quietly. "You of all people should have known better than to credit me with the instincts of a gentleman."

What in the world was he talking about now? she wondered, going quite blank. She had only meant to make him feel some smattering of guilt for trying to force her to give up the stone. She wanted an apology from him, at the very least. Instead, he had reacted as though she were a judge who had condemned him to prison for the remainder of his life.

She gave him her most repressive glare. "Tell me, sir, why were you the one chosen to track down my crystal?"

He shrugged, coming out of that very still, quiet place where her comment about his lack of gentlemanly instincts had sent him a moment ago.

"Conducting investigations is what I do," he said.

She froze. "You are a police detective?"

He smiled, amused by her horrified start. "No. I make private enquiries on behalf of individuals or, in this case, a group of individuals, who, for whatever reason, do not wish to contact the police."

She relaxed a little at that reassurance. Her curiosity surfaced. "This is your business?"

He hesitated, as though uncertain how to answer that. "I do not do it for the money," he said finally.

"Then why do you do it?" she demanded.

"It . . . satisfies something in me."

She pondered that for a moment. "I understand. That is one of the two reasons I do what I do with crystals. I find it satisfies something inside me."

He cocked a brow. "What is the second reason?"

She gave him a cool smile. "Unlike you, sir, I do need the money."

She braced herself for some indication of disdain. He was a gentleman and apparently a wealthy one at that. Those who moved in elevated circles looked down on people who were obliged to work for a living. Within the Arcane Society there was an added degree of disapproval for any individual who worked crystals. In the social hierarchy of those who possessed paranormal abilities, crystal workers ranked at or near the bottom.

But Thaddeus merely inclined his head as though her answer had not fazed him in the least. Most likely because he had already guessed the truth, she thought.

"I am curious to know how you came to be acquainted with Adam Harrow and Mr. Pierce," he said.

"Mr. Pierce came to me on a number of occasions as a client. Whenever he arrived for an appointment, he was accompanied by Mr. Harrow. Over a period of several weekly visits, Adam and I became friends. He was very grateful to me for my work with Mr. Pierce. Pierce was also quite pleased with the results of my crystal work."

"Pierce suffers from nightmares?" Thaddeus asked. Intense curiosity sharpened the edge of the question.

She gave him a cool smile. He was not the only one who could keep secrets.

"I do not discuss the nature of my clients' complaints with others unless the client specifically approves," she said.

Thaddeus's jaw tightened. He did not like being thwarted, she thought. But he inclined his head in a short, brusque nod.

"I understand," he said. "I assume it was Pierce who informed you that Delbridge had stolen the crystal?"

"Yes. After receiving several consultations from me, he was convinced of my skill with crystals. One afternoon he asked very casually if I had ever heard of the aurora stone, as there were rumors going around that it had been stolen. I was stunned to hear that the crystal had surfaced after all this time."

Thaddeus frowned. "What do you mean by the term *surfaced?*"

"It was stolen from my mother when I was sixteen years old." Her hand stilled on Fog's head. "In fact, I have always believed that she was murdered for it."

"I see."

"I had given up all hope of finding it. Needless to say, I was thrilled when Mr. Pierce mentioned the rumors. When he realized how important it was to me, he made further inquiries and learned that Delbridge was the likely thief. I immediately began making plans."

"To steal the crystal?"

"To recover my stolen property," she said coldly. "When Mr. Pierce and Adam realized that I was determined to enter Delbridge's mansion to look for it, they both insisted that Adam accompany me."

Thaddeus frowned. "I'm surprised that Pierce, with all of his connections, didn't offer to steal the stone for you."

"He did. But I explained to him that I was the only one who could identify the real aurora stone. In any event, Mr. Pierce did not believe Delbridge to be nearly as dangerous as he apparently is. Delbridge's reputation is that of an eccentric collector. Who would have thought that he was actually an evil chemist capable of concocting drugs that can drive one mad."

Thaddeus looked out the window at the quiet little park across the street. "That is one of the strangest aspects of this business. Until now no one had any reason to believe that Delbridge was anything more than an obsessive collector of paranormal antiquities. I doubt very much that he knew how to brew up that hallucinatory vapor on his own."

"Do you think he has an associate?"

"It seems the only logical explanation. Perhaps more than one. I suspect that he has also employed a highly skilled killer, one who has practiced his craft on at least two prostitutes. Both died in the same manner as that woman we found in Delbridge's mansion."

Shock rolled through her. "Do you refer to that fiend the press is calling the Midnight Monster?"

"Yes. Miss Hewitt, do you begin to comprehend just how much danger you are in?"

Staggered, she could only stare at him for a moment. Eventually she found her tongue.

"Yes," she whispered. "Yes, I do take your point. To think that the Midnight Monster might be in the employ of Lord Delbridge. It is almost impossible to believe."

"The only reasonable thing to do is to give the crystal to me so that I can hand it over to the Arcane Society for safekeeping until matters are satisfactorily resolved. I promise you that when this matter is concluded, I will make certain that you have an opportunity to put forward your claim on the stone to the Master of the Society, himself."

Fat lot of good that would do, she thought glumly. "Thank you," she managed politely.

"I might also point out that by holding on to the crystal it is not just yourself you are putting at risk," Thaddeus said quietly. "As long as the stone is in your possession, your Mrs. Cleeves is in danger."

She stiffened at that. "What do you mean?"

"If his lordship has employed a killer, as I suspect, I doubt very much the villain would think twice about murdering your housekeeper."

Enough, Leona thought. She was unlikely to ever recover the crystal once it was back in the hands of the Arcane Society, but there was not much choice now. She could not put Mrs. Cleeves in jeopardy.

"Very well," she said. Resigned to the inevitable, she got to her feet, absently shaking out the tiered and draped folds of her black gown. "It's upstairs. If you give me a moment I will go and get it."

Thaddeus glanced at the sack that contained the three crystals she had brought back from the rooms in Marigold Lane. "You did not take it with you to your consultations in Marigold Lane today?"

"No." She went toward the door. "It is an extremely powerful stone with some unique properties. I was taught that it was only to be used in the most extreme circumstances."

"I know something of its power," he said, meeting her eyes. "And yours as well."

She could have sworn that he was trying to convey something important, a gesture of respect, perhaps. It warmed her a little.

"Thank you," she said.

He moved to open the door, watching her with an unreadable expression as she swept past him.

"You are making a wise decision," he said.

"That remains to be seen, doesn't it?"

She went out into the hall and up the stairs, Fog at her heels.

At the door of her bedroom, Fog sniffed the floor with sudden interest. When she opened the door he trotted straight toward the large trunk where she had stored the aurora stone and whined softly.

"What do you find so intriguing?" she asked. "Surely you know all the scents in this household."

She eased him aside, removed the key from the chatelaine she wore at her waist and inserted it into the lock.

The contents of the trunk were in disarray. Her mother's journal and the leather-bound box that contained the old notebooks and papers were tumbled together with a pair of walking boots, an old bonnet, a spare quilt and the other things stored inside.

Frantically she dug down to the bottom of the trunk.

The black velvet pouch containing the aurora stone was gone.

15

He had expected many things from her today, including anger and disgust. Lord knew she had every right to those emotions given what he had almost done to her. But he had not expected her to lie to him.

"Stolen?" Thaddeus repeated evenly. "What a very convenient excuse. A little too convenient. Do you really think to deter me with that flimsy story?"

Leona's mouth tightened. She paced the floor of the parlor, black skirts fluttering around her stylish, high-heeled boots. Her aura of outrage and alarm were genuine, Thaddeus decided.

"You are free to conclude whatever you wish, of course," she said. "But I am telling you that the crystal is gone." She waved a hand toward the parlor door. "Feel free to search the house, sir. When you are satisfied that the crystal is not on the premises, kindly take your leave. I'm sure you will want to continue your inquiries elsewhere."

He contemplated Fog. The dog was stretched out in front of the small sofa, head up, watching Leona's every move.

"When do you think the thief broke in?" Thaddeus asked, keeping his voice neutral.

"Who knows?" Leona stopped at the far end of the small room, swung around and stalked back toward the door. "Most burglars do their work at night." She shuddered. "Good heavens, to think that an intruder was prowling through this house while Mrs. Cleeves and I were asleep last night. It is quite terrifying."

He watched her sweep past him, aware that, even now, annoyed and worried about her safety as he was, his senses nevertheless savored the exciting energy that swirled around her. He and Leona were engaged in a full-blown quarrel yet he was aroused, physically and psychically.

"I doubt that this particular burglar came at night," he said dryly.

Leona stopped pacing and whirled around, glaring. "Why do you insist on that?"

He angled his head toward Fog. "Your dog. He does not look as though he would sleep while an intruder prowled into your bedroom."

She followed his gaze, bewildered at first.

Then comprehension and relief lit her face. "Oh. Right. Of course not. Fog is very protective. No one could have entered the house last night. He would have sounded the alarm and attacked the intruder." She frowned. "But if not last night, when did the villain steal the crystal?"

Two could play at this game.

"Did you take your dog for a walk this morning?"

"Yes, but we only went across the street and into the park for a short time because I had an early appointment with a client. We were never out of sight of the house. In any event, Mrs. Cleeves was here."

"I suggest we talk to Mrs. Cleeves."

"Mrs. Cleeves." Leona's eyes widened. "Yes, of course. She would have taken Fog out in the afternoon. I asked her to give him a nice, long walk as I'd cut his morning stroll short."

She hurried to the door, got it open and leaned out into the hall.

"Mrs. Cleeves?" she called.

A plump, pleasant-faced woman in a white apron appeared. There was flour on her hands.

"Did you take Fog for his afternoon walk today?"

"Certainly, ma'am. Just as you instructed."

She looked past Leona at Thaddeus and then back at Leona. "Is there something wrong, ma'am?"

This could not be a well-rehearsed play that he was witnessing, Thaddeus decided. He had seen Leona's shock earlier when she had rushed out of the consulting room into his arms. She had not been expecting him. There had been no opportunity for her and the housekeeper to have practiced this little scene.

He shuttered his expression so that the housekeeper would not see his unease and went to stand behind Leona.

"What time did you go out, Mrs. Cleeves?" he asked.

She frowned briefly in thought. Then her brow cleared. "It would have been about two o'clock, right after Miss Hewitt returned to Marigold Lane for her afternoon appointment."

"How long were you gone?" he asked.

"Somewhere above an hour, I suppose. I stopped to have a cup of tea with my sister in Perg Lane. She likes Fog, and the dog is fond of her because she gives him treats."

Leona gripped the doorknob very tightly. "Thank God, neither of you came home while the burglar was still here. There's no telling what he might have done if he had been interrupted in his search."

"What's this about a burglar?" Mrs. Cleeves's face flushed with anxiety. "See here, none of the silver is missing. I'd have noticed."

"It's all right, Mrs. Cleeves," Leona said hastily. "One of my crystals was stolen, that's all."

Mrs. Cleeves rolled her eyes. "Why would anyone want one of those ugly stones?"

"An excellent question, Mrs. Cleeves," Thaddeus said. "Did you see anyone hanging about on the street or in the park when you left the house?"

"No," she said automatically. Then her brows puckered. "Wait, come to think of it, there was a gentleman. He came out of the park and walked off down the street. But he could not have been a villain."

"What makes you so certain of that?" Leona asked quickly.

Mrs. Cleeves was clearly perplexed by the question. "Why, because he was dressed like a gentleman, of course."

"Do you recall anything else about him?" Thaddeus asked.

"No, not really. I barely glanced at him, to tell you the truth." Mrs. Cleeves frowned. "Wouldn't have noticed him at all if Fog hadn't seemed interested in him. Is it important?"

"It might be," Thaddeus said. "Mrs. Cleeves, are you familiar with the art of hypnosis?"

The housekeeper brightened with enthusiasm. "Oh my, yes. My sister and I went to a demonstration a few months ago. Very amazing it was. The hypnotist, Dr. Miller, selected a young girl out of the crowd and put her into a trance. She'd had no fancy education at all, mind you, but once Dr. Miller had mesmerized her she was able to recite whole scenes from Shakespeare. Very impressive, it was."

"More likely very fraudulent," Thaddeus said. "Would you allow me to put you into a brief trance to see if perhaps you can recall any other details about the gentleman you saw outside this house today?"

Mrs. Cleeves glanced doubtfully at Leona.

"It will be perfectly safe, Mrs. Cleeves," Leona said. "I will be right here the whole time. I will make certain that nothing occurs that you might find objectionable."

"Very well, then." Mrs. Cleeves was clearly intrigued. "But I doubt if you can put me into a trance, sir. I'm much too strong-minded."

"I do not doubt the strength of your mind for a moment," Thaddeus said. He opened his senses, focusing on the aura that Mrs. Cleeves, like every other living being, generated. He found the wavelengths he wanted and started speaking quietly.

"You are recalling the events of this afternoon. You are about to take the dog for a walk. Do you understand?"

With the aid of his natural talent and long practice, he used his voice to focus his own energy, neutralizing certain wavelengths in the housekeeper's aura. She went very still. Her face was suddenly expressionless.

"I understand," Mrs. Cleeves said tonelessly. She gazed straight ahead into the middle distance.

"You open the front door and go down the steps. Where is Fog?"

"He is with me on a leash."

"Do you see anyone?"

"There is a gentleman on the other side of the street."

"What is he doing?"

"He looks at me and then he walks off toward the corner."

"Describe him to me."

"He is very elegant."

"Can you see his face?"

"Only a little. His head is turned away

from me. He tilts his hat slightly. I can see the edge of his jaw."

"Is he young or old?"

"He is a young man in his prime."

"How do you know this?"

"By the way he moves."

"Can you see his hair?"

"Yes. There is some showing beneath his hat."

"What color is it?"

"Very pale blond, almost white."

"Can you describe his clothes?"

"His coat is gray. So are his trousers."

"Does he carry anything in his hands?"

"Yes."

"What?"

"A walking stick."

"You will awaken now, Mrs. Cleeves."

Mrs. Cleeves blinked and looked at him expectantly. "When will you be wanting to try to hypnotize me, sir?"

"I have changed my mind," Thaddeus said. "I have concluded that you are indeed too strong-minded to be put into a trance. You may go now. Thank you for your assistance in this matter."

"You're welcome, sir."

Looking rather disappointed at not having been able to display her strength of mind, Mrs. Cleeves went back down the hall toward the kitchen.

Thaddeus closed the door and turned to find Leona watching him with great interest.

"That was quite astonishing, Mr. Ware," she said.

"Unfortunately, it did not gain us much in the way of information. The gentleman Mrs. Cleeves saw on the street may or may not have been the person who stole the crystal. I think we can assume, however, that the thief entered this house while your housekeeper and the dog were out."

"A chilling thought."

"Yes, it is."

She went to stand at the window. "How dare he?" she whispered in a low, tight voice. "After all these years and all I went through in order to recover that crystal. How dare the bastard steal it?"

Sensing her distress, Fog got to his feet and went to her side. Thaddeus watched Leona reach down to touch him. She was reassuring herself as much as the dog, he thought.

"Miss Hewitt," he said, "do you live here alone?"

"No." She did not take her eyes off the view outside the window. "As you can see, I have Mrs. Cleeves and Fog."

"Forgive me, but is there anyone else with

whom you can stay? Any family?"

"No," she said softly. "Not any more."

"Friends?"

She flinched a little, as though taking an unseen blow. Then, very deliberately she squared her shoulders. "Until yesterday, my friend Carolyn shared this house with me," she said, voice strengthening. "But she is married now and on her way to Egypt."

"I see. Then you are alone?"

"No, sir, I am not alone." She gave the dog a brisk pat and turned around to face him. "I told you, I have Mrs. Cleeves and Fog. What is the point of all these personal questions?"

He exhaled slowly, trying to think of how best to say what had to be said.

"It is clear that Delbridge has found you. I want you to come and stay with me until I have recovered the crystal."

Predictably, she was speechless.

"There will be nothing improper about the arrangement," he assured her. "You will be a guest in my parents' household. They are traveling in America on business for the Arcane Society, but my great-aunt, who lives with them, is there."

"Why," she demanded, "would I even think of doing such a thing?"

He looked at her, willing her to understand

the dangers of the situation. "According to the old records, the crystal is useless unless it is activated by someone with a very rare sort of talent. Sooner or later it may occur to Delbridge that the most likely reason why you, a crystal worker, took such a risk to get the aurora stone is because you possess just such a talent. If that happens, you will not be safe."

16

The stress of trying to make polite conversation at the long dinner table had taken its toll. Leona thought she had held up rather well during the artichoke soup and fried trout, but by the time the roasted chicken and vegetables arrived, she was feeling the strain.

Thaddeus, seated at the far end of the table, did little to help. Ever since bringing her into the house, he seemed to have sunk deep inside himself. Leona supposed he was preoccupied with plans for the recovery of the crystal.

The only other person present at the table was Thaddeus's formidable great-aunt, Victoria, Lady Milden. From the first moment they were introduced, it seemed to Leona that the austere older woman had viewed her with undisguised suspicion and disapproval.

Victoria's reaction came as no great surprise. Leona was prepared for it. Victoria, like everyone else in the Ware family, was a member of the Arcane Society after all and no doubt held a very low opinion of crystal workers. The legend of Sybil the Virgin Sorceress had a lot to answer for. Victoria was clearly appalled by the prospect of having to entertain a female she considered no better than a carnival fortune teller.

The only one who appeared well pleased by the move to the large Ware family mansion was Fog. He had been instantly enthralled by the extensive gardens.

Victoria looked at Leona across the top of a high silver dish filled with dried fruits. "You say you arrived in London a year and a half ago, Miss Hewitt?"

"Yes," Leona said politely.

"Where did you live before that?"

"A small seaside town. Little Tickton. I doubt you've heard of it."

"You pursued your career there in Little Tickton?"

"That is correct, Lady Milden."

"For how long?"

The questions were moving into dangerous territory. Time to shade the truth a little, Leona decided.

"I have worked crystals professionally since the age of sixteen," she said politely.

"In Little Tickton," Victoria pressed.

"Mmm." Leona ate a bite of potato. She was under no obligation to tell the truth, she thought. She had a right to her privacy.

"I've heard that those with a talent for crystals are inclined to move around with some frequency," Victoria observed.

"Mmm." Leona concentrated on a carrot.

"If your career was going so well in Little Tickton for so many years, why did you feel compelled to move to London?"

"I thought business might be better here."

"And is it?"

Leona gave her a brilliant smile. "Oh, yes, without a doubt."

Victoria's eyes tightened at the corners. She had not liked the smile, Leona thought.

"Your dog is most unusual," Victoria said. "Rather startling, actually. Looks a bit like a wolf."

"He's not a wolf," Leona assured her, rising instantly to Fog's defense. It was one thing to insult her. She was not about to allow Victoria to insult her dog. "He is very well behaved and exceedingly intelligent. You will be quite safe with him."

"Where on earth did you acquire a dog like that?"

"In Little Tickton. He showed up at my back door one day. It was as if he materialized out of the mist. I fed him. The next thing I knew, I had a dog."

"Does he bite?"

Leona gave her another dazzling smile. "He would only attack someone whom he deemed to be a threat to me."

Victoria frowned and looked at Thaddeus. "Perhaps the dog should be kept on a chain outside in the gardens."

Leona did not wait for Thaddeus to respond.

"There will be no chain," she said coolly. "And Fog sleeps in my room. If that is not acceptable we will return to our own house on Vine Street."

Thaddeus shrugged and picked up his wineglass. "The dog appears to be well trained," he said to his aunt. "He'll be fine indoors."

"As you wish," Victoria said. She rumpled her napkin in a tight, tense manner. "If you both will excuse me, I believe I will go to my room and read for the rest of the evening."

The rudeness was breathtaking. Victoria had as good as announced that she did not intend to play the hostess to a lowly crystal worker. Thaddeus got to his feet to help her with her chair. With a swish of her expensive silver-gray skirts, Victoria swept from the dining room.

Thaddeus looked at Leona, his mesmeric eyes dark and somber. "I apologize on behalf of my aunt. She lost her husband, my uncle, a couple of years ago and suffers much from his absence. When my parents realized how depressed she was they insisted that she come here to stay in their house. They asked me to move in to keep an eye on her while they are away in America."

"I see." Leona softened at once. She was only too well aware of what it was like to lose the people you loved. "I'm sorry for your aunt's loss."

He hesitated. "Aunt Victoria has always been inclined to periodic bouts of melancholia, but the tendency has certainly grown worse since my uncle died. I think my mother secretly fears that she will sink into a deeper depression and do some harm to herself."

"I understand. But it is obvious that my presence here is upsetting her. Perhaps Fog and I should go back to Vine Street."

"You are not going anywhere," he said quietly. "Except, perhaps, out to the conservatory."

"What?"

"Would you accompany me on a tour of the conservatory, Miss Hewitt? There are some things of a personal nature that I must say to you and I would prefer to speak to you in a place where we are unlikely to be interrupted."

"If you are planning another lecture on that unfortunate situation in my consulting rooms today —"

"No," he said tersely. "I will undoubtedly lay awake for some time tonight torturing myself with what might have happened if Adam and I had not arrived when we did, but I promise you that there will be no more lectures."

"Very well, then."

When she put aside her napkin she realized that her pulse was suddenly beating a little too fast. Thaddeus held her chair. She rose, very conscious of his standing so close. When he offered her his arm, a thrill of sensual awareness tingled through her. In spite of everything, she could not resist responding to him, she thought.

She glanced at him out of the corner of her eye, but she could not tell whether touching her had any effect on him. His powers of self-mastery could be quite daunting. Then again, perhaps she did not really want to know the truth. Perhaps he felt nothing at all.

Yet she could have sworn that there was energy in the air around them, just as there had been the other night when they had fought the demons in the carriage. Something strange and wondrous happened when she was with Thaddeus, something that she had never experienced with any other man, not even William Trover, the man she had planned to marry.

Out in the hall Fog appeared as if by magic. He padded along behind them, looking hopeful. When Thaddeus opened the garden door, he trotted eagerly outside and disappeared immediately into the shadows.

Thaddeus drew Leona onto a terrace and along a short, graveled path. The gracefully arched glass walls of the conservatory gleamed opaquely in the moonlight. The gaslight streaming through the tall library windows revealed Fog snuffling at some nearby shrubbery.

"My dog is certainly enjoying your hospitality," Leona said, striving to strike a neutral note.

"I am well aware that you are not."

She winced. "I said nothing to indicate anything of the sort."

"You hardly needed to voice your opinion of my suggestion that you stay here. Your sentiments are obvious."

She cleared her throat. "It was not, as I recall, a suggestion. More in the nature of a command, I believe."

"Damnation."

The muttered oath told her more clearly than any words that he was gripped with tension, just as she was. For some reason that realization caused her spirits to lift. *Think positive. He feels the energy, too.*

"I brought you here because I could not come up with any other plan to ensure your safety," he added quietly.

"I understand, sir. And I do appreciate your interest in my welfare. Forgive my irritation earlier today. It has been a somewhat trying afternoon."

"I cannot imagine why you would say that, Miss Hewitt. By my reckoning there was not much out of the ordinary going on today. One of your clients clearly misunderstood the sort of therapeutic consultation you were offering and tried to assault you. I showed up unexpectedly on your doorstep after you had no doubt assured yourself that you were safely rid of me. And last but not least you discovered that an intruder had invaded the sanctity of your home and stolen the aurora stone."

In the light from the window she could see that his mouth was curved in a grim smile.

"Quite correct, sir," she said bracingly. "When you put it like that it becomes plain that I am indeed overreacting to events."

"You are not the only one, Miss Hewitt. I confess that today's activities have been hard on my nerves as well."

"Rubbish. You have nerves of steel, Mr. Ware."

"Not when it comes to you, madam."

He opened the door of the conservatory and ushered her into the scented darkness. The warm, humid atmosphere enveloped them. He paused to turn up a gas lamp. The low, glary light revealed a shadowy jungle.

She looked around with a sense of delight. Exotic palms and tropical plants of all descriptions spread broad leaves over a vast forest of ferns and unusual blooms.

"What a beautiful slice of Eden," she said, awed. "It is magnificent."

Thaddeus followed her gaze. "As a rule, the members of my family pursue their passions with great energy. This conservatory is my parents' passion. They both possess strong talents for all things botanical. I vow, they could grow roses on a stone."

She glanced at a nearby workbench that was covered with an assortment of gardening tools. A heavy sheet of canvas, folded into a neat square, rested at the far end.

"Your passion is your work as an investigator?" she asked, turning toward him.

He stood motionless, his back to the low

light. She could see nothing of his expression. "Yes."

There was a long pause.

"Not everyone comprehends that," he added after a moment.

She gave a tiny shrug. "Not everyone has a passion. Those who lack one probably have difficulty understanding those of us who do."

He nodded, very serious. "I suspect you are right."

There was another long, heavy silence.

She pulled her composure around her like a shawl. "Well, then, sir, you said there was something of a personal nature you wished to discuss."

"Yes."

She wrinkled her nose. "If you wish to tell me that you did not care for that little inn where Adam and I left you the other night, I apologize. I realize the establishment was not up to your standards, but it appeared reasonably clean."

"This is not about the damn inn," he cut in roughly. "It is about what happened in the carriage before you and Adam took me to the Blue Drake."

"I see." She frowned, not seeing anything at all. "You refer to my talents? Trust me, I am well aware that no one in the Arcane

Society thinks much of those with my sort of abilities. However, I really don't —"

"Trust me when I tell you that parahypnotists are not particularly popular within the Society, either."

"Oh." That gave her pause. "I had not realized —"

"What I wish to speak to you about concerns my behavior the other night."

"What of it?" she asked, going quite blank.

"This is not easy for me to say, Miss Hewitt. I am a man who prides himself on his powers of self-mastery. In addition, I was raised a gentleman."

"I don't doubt that for a moment, sir," she said, still baffled. "What *is* this about?"

"I am well aware that an apology is hardly adequate under the circumstances, but it is all that I have in my power to give."

"Whatever are you talking about, sir?"

His jaw went rigid. "I understand. You want me to acknowledge the true depths of my offense. I assure you, I do. I have never before tried to force myself on a woman. Do you want to know why I was so furious this afternoon when I found you fleeing from your client? It was because the scene made me fully aware that the other night I had behaved no differently."

She felt her jaw drop. "Mr. Ware."

"I realize that you will not be able to forgive me, but I hope to convince you that you can trust me not to repeat the experience."

Aghast, she took an impulsive step forward and covered his mouth with her fingertips.

"That is quite enough," she said. Abruptly aware of the intriguing feel of his lips against her palm, she hastily lowered her hand. "I do not want to hear another word of your apology. It is quite unnecessary. I do not blame you for what happened in the carriage. How could you possibly think that? I knew very well that you were under the influence of that noxious drug."

"That is not an excuse. You see, even though I was strongly affected by the drug, I knew what I was doing." His voice darkened. "I regret to say I did it quite deliberately."

A shiver of excitement tingled through her. She tried to suppress it. She was a professional, she reminded herself. It was not as if she had not had experience dealing with a client's most intimate dreams.

"You were hallucinating, sir," she said briskly. "It was a form of dreaming. Granted, it was a very intense version of the experience, nevertheless —"

"I was in the midst of a nightmare. But you, Miss Hewitt, were not one of the dark fantasies of my dream. You were, in fact, the only thing inside that carriage that I knew for certain was real, the only vision I could trust."

"Really?"

"I focused every scrap of will I could summon on you in an effort to avoid being overwhelmed completely by the phantasms."

"I see," she whispered, beginning to comprehend at last. Once again the tiny flame of hope inside her was blown out by the gusts of reality. "You must have employed a great deal of energy to keep yourself from sinking deeper into the nightmare."

"I did. And I regret to say that the power I drew on came from the most primal aspect of my nature. It was the energy generated by raw, untrammeled lust, Miss Hewitt."

She felt the heat rise inside her until she was certain it infused her entire body from head to toe. She hoped devoutly that the shadows concealed her blush. Clearing her throat she assumed what she hoped was a professional tone.

"There is no need to say anything more. Having worked with crystals for many years, I am well aware that in addition to the dream state, there are other aspects of our nature that can generate considerable energy. When stirred to great levels of excitement, as it were, all of the elemental emotions, such as sexual passion, produce strong currents, even in those who are unaware of their paranormal senses."

"I regret to say that desire was the only force powerful enough to counteract some of the effects of that damned drug."

"Actually, no, it wasn't," she said.

He frowned. "What the devil do you mean by that?"

"Given what I learned of your nature when I channeled your energy in the crystal, I can assure you that you could have summoned power from another source."

He gave her a searching look. "What other source?"

"One can draw enormous energy from the violent aspect of one's nature."

His jaw tightened. "Yes, of course."

"We all possess a capacity for violence," she said gently. "Part of what defines us as civilized beings is our capacity to control it. I assure you, you were very much in control of that element of yourself the other night. I knew that at the time. It was why I was not afraid of you."

His eyes narrowed. "I felt your fear. Do not pretend that you were not afraid of me."

"Listen to me closely, Mr. Ware." She touched the side of his face and fixed him with all the steady determination at her command. "What you felt was my fear that I might not be able to save you."

He said nothing, just stood there in the shadows, regarding her as though he had never seen her before in his life.

Suddenly conscious of the warmth of his skin beneath her fingers, she dropped her hand, drew herself up and straightened her shoulders. "I would remind you that I am a professional, sir. I am well aware that my particular expertise is not highly regarded within the Arcane Society. Nevertheless, when it comes to crystals, I am the expert."

"If you had not gained control of the crystal, matters would have ended very differently."

"I will allow that the situation was somewhat precarious for a short time," she said. "You are the most powerful client I have ever channeled. For a few minutes there in the carriage, we were both trapped by the crystal because the currents of your energy were so strong. But I can assure you that had you lost control completely and become the sort of beast you believe yourself to be, the resulting chaos would have had devastating effects. It is quite possible that neither of us would have survived the experience, at least not with our sanity intact."

"Are you certain of that?"

"Trust me when I tell you that the only reason I was able to control the forces we unleashed together in that carriage was that you still had some of your powers of self-mastery."

"You think I was in control of my desire for you?" he asked without inflection.

She might be immune to his hypnotic talents, she thought, but every time he employed the word *desire,* she was in danger of becoming entranced.

"I suggest we change the subject," she said lightly. "There is absolutely no reason to spend another moment discussing what occurred between us in the carriage. There is certainly no need for an apology on your part, and you must not feel any guilt in the matter. It is not as if I were some innocent young lady who sustained a violent shock to her sensibilities."

"I see."

She thought she detected an odd note in his voice, but she could not be certain. He sounded as though he might be trying to suppress some strong emotion. Evidently his sense of guilt was quite overwhelming. She tried to think of some other reassuring words.

"As I keep telling you, I am a professional,"

she said smoothly.

"I see," he repeated.

"In addition I have had some experience with desire."

"Indeed?"

"Two years ago I was engaged to be married. I'm sure I need say no more about the matter other than to assure you that I am a woman of the world when it comes to that sort of thing." She waved one hand. "You may believe me when I tell you that I never for one moment took your passions personally, as it were. I am well aware that you merely required a focus to help control the hallucinations. It just so happened that I and my crystal were available."

"I appreciate your assurances, Madam Professional," he said.

For the first time in several minutes, he moved, closing what little distance remained between them. The light angled across his hard face. She saw that he was smiling. So much for being overwhelmed by guilt, she thought, chagrined. An awkward embarrassment swept through her.

"Well, now that we have dealt with the issue, perhaps we should return to the house," she said gruffly.

He caught her chin with the tip of his finger and tipped her head up a little. "There is one remaining problem between us to be discussed."

It was hard to breathe normally when she was near him. She had to swallow a couple of times before she could find words.

"What is it?" she asked warily.

"I have been free of the effects of the poison for some time now, but I find that my primal desires still appear to be focused entirely on you."

She froze. Breathing was suddenly the least of her problems. She could no longer even think.

She moistened her lips with the tip of her tongue.

"Focused on me, you say," she managed with what she hoped was a professional air.

"Yes, Miss Hewitt, on you."

17

"Furthermore," Thaddeus continued, in a voice as seductive as moonlight on dark water, "you should know that the reason I found you so perfectly suited to serve as a focus the other night was because I was already attracted to you."

"But we had only just met," she gasped.

"When it comes to desire, time is not a factor, at least not for a man. I knew I wanted you before we even got out of that damned museum. My greatest regret at that moment was that I might not live long enough to make love to you."

A thrilling excitement sparkled through her.

"Really?" she whispered.

He examined her face in the pale glow of the gas lamp. "What of you, Leona? Did you feel anything between us?"

"Yes. Yes, I did," she said quickly, then hesitated. "But later I told myself that the currents that flowed between us were most likely produced by the danger of the moment. Danger arouses all sorts of dark energy."

"I know I was certainly aroused," he said dryly.

"I'm sure that the events that we went through together would have induced extreme excitement in even the calmest and most cool-headed individuals."

"Individuals like us?"

She moistened her lips. "Yes."

"I suggest we conduct a scientific test to verify your theory."

"A test?"

"Neither of us is facing extreme peril at the moment," he said. "It strikes me that this would be an excellent time to see if the emotions we both experienced the other night were unique to that situation."

"Oh." She hesitated. "How do you propose to conduct such a test?"

"I am going to kiss you, Miss Hewitt. If you find that a repulsive thought, tell me now and I will halt the test immediately."

"What will your test prove?"

"If you return my kiss with enthusiasm, we must conclude that some sort of energy exists between us that has nothing to do with facing danger, the effects of Delbridge's drug or your crystal. In short, Miss Hewitt, if we both enjoy the kiss we will be able to say with certainty that we are attracted to each other."

"And if one of us does not enjoy the kiss?" *You, for example,* she added silently.

He smiled. "That night when we fled Delbridge's mansion I seem to recall you insisting on the virtue of positive thinking. I am going to take that advice now."

His mouth came down on hers, hot and intoxicating. Her senses sizzled as irresistible currents of sensual energy crackled through her. She was suddenly shivering with sensation, weightless. Desire unfurled within her, sweeping her up into a thrilling vortex. She heard a soft, urgent little sound that was laced with both hunger and demand and knew that it emanated from her own throat.

Thaddeus uttered a heavy, urgent groan — as though he, too, had been caught off guard by the flashing, flaring energy.

"I knew it was no hallucination," he said against her mouth. His lips moved on hers, drugging her. "Tell me you feel the power that flows between us."

"Yes." She closed her fingers very tightly around his broad shoulders, savoring the strength in him. "Oh, *yes.*"

He trapped her head in the crook of his

other arm and leaned into her, deepening the kiss, forcing her head back.

There were no words to describe the myriad hues and shades of the currents of light that pulsed in the atmosphere around them. Unlike that last time, when she had engaged in a battle to save Thaddeus from the effects of the poison, tonight there was no need to resist the power of desire. Here in this glass-enclosed jungle she was free to abandon herself to the elemental thrill of passion.

One by one Thaddeus undid the small hooks that secured the snug bodice of her gown. She wore no corset. When the dress fell open, only the fine lawn of her thin chemise covered her breasts. She might as well have been naked. He lifted his head and looked down.

"Beautiful," he breathed.

His fingers brushed one nipple. Sensations cascaded through her. A deep, delicious, aching tension built.

Emboldened by the hot, sultry atmosphere of sensuality that enveloped them, she tried to unfasten his coat with eager, trembling fingers. After a few moments of awkward fumbling on her part, he gently captured her fingers.

"I think I'd better be the one to handle

this," he said, sounding both amused and impatient.

He broke free of the embrace long enough to shrug out of the garment. When he came back to her she fitted her hands to his waist, savoring the intimacy of the moment. Through the fine linen of his shirt she could feel the heat and sinewy strength of his body. The sense of urgency flowering deep inside her grew more demanding.

Maintaining his hold on her with one hand, he reached out and turned down the lamp. Now there was only the faint glow of the moon filtering through the leafy canopy to light the tropical world.

Thaddeus pushed the gown over her hips and down until it pooled around her feet. Then he removed the chemise. The pale light gleamed briefly on the white ruffles of her petticoat. He untied that garment too and let it fall away.

"I want to see all of you," he said softly.

He unfastened her drawers. They landed in a soft heap on top of all of the other discarded clothing.

For a moment, reality came crashing back. She was nude in front of a man for the first time in her entire life. True, it was very dark, and she doubted that he could see her any better than she could see him. Nevertheless, it was a shocking adventure for which nothing could have fully prepared her. She was about to take a highly significant, possibly quite dangerous step into the unknown.

The uncertainty that seized her had nothing to do with any maidenly trepidation or hesitation concerning the pleasures of illicit love. She intended to enjoy every moment of that particular aspect of the experience. But there was something else going on, something she did not fully comprehend. Her intuition warned her that, once she had gone down this road with Thaddeus, there would be no turning back.

"Thaddeus?"

But he was crouched on one knee in front of her, unbuttoning her high-heeled boots. He removed each with great care. When he was finished he closed his hands around her thighs and kissed the bare skin just above the dark triangle.

She shivered and shut her eyes against the force of such exquisite intimacy.

By the time he got back to his feet, she could no longer concentrate on what her intuition was trying to tell her.

She managed to get his shirt open with trembling fingers. When she splayed her fingers across his bare chest she could feel the crisp hair there. He pulled her tightly to him, crushing her gently against what felt like a solid wall of muscle.

This time his kiss was slow and intense. She could literally feel him willing her to respond. As if she could do anything else, she thought, curving her arms around his neck.

When Thaddeus raised his head she could hear his harsh, ragged breathing. He cradled her face in his hands.

"Tell me again that you are not afraid of me," he demanded roughly.

"I do not fear you, Thaddeus," she said softly. "I have never feared you. Well, perhaps for a moment or two back in Delbridge's gallery when I saw you standing over the body of that poor woman. But I soon realized that you were not the killer. I hardly think that tiny moment of concern matters, do you?"

He half laughed, half groaned and silenced her with another scorching kiss.

"Not at all, my sweet," he said when he finally lifted his mouth from hers. "I understand why you might have had a few doubts about me at that point. As it happens, I had a few momentary qualms about you, too."

"You did?"

"When I first caught sight of you in your gentleman's attire, it crossed my mind that you might have been the killer."

She was thunderstruck. "Good heavens.

Me? You thought I might have killed that woman?"

"It was just a passing thought."

"Good heavens," she said again. "I had no idea."

"Must we talk about this now? I fear a conversation about murder might spoil the romantic atmosphere."

"Sorry," she said quickly.

His soft laughter flowed around her, ruffling her senses in the most delightful way. She heard the rustle of heavy cloth. When she looked down she saw that he had removed the folded canvas from the workbench and spread it out on the floor.

"Not a bed of roses," he said, tugging off his boots. "But it is all I have to offer tonight."

"It will do nicely," she said.

She stepped onto the canvas sheet. He met her in the middle, barefoot, his shirt hanging open over his trousers. Gently he reached out and cradled in his hand the small crystal pendant she wore. Moonlight glinted darkly on the stone.

"Who gave you this?" he asked.

"It was a gift from my mother."

"Is it a stone of power, or is it purely decorative?"

"It has power, but I rarely use it."

"I understand," Thaddeus said. "It is a keepsake."

"Yes."

He took her into his arms.

Together they sank down, down, down, until she was lying flat on her back beneath him.

He loomed over her in the darkness. He stroked her slowly, not just learning the feel of her body but, in some manner she could not explain, laying claim to her. Compelled to respond in kind, she slid her hands under the edge of his shirt and explored the contours of his back. His skin was hot to the touch and slick with perspiration. His scent filled her head and clouded her mind.

He kissed her throat and found the aching core of sensation between her legs. The shock of his touch there was almost too much for her overwrought senses. She opened her mouth on a small shriek. He silenced her quickly with a kiss and then raised his head.

"Sound carries in the night," he warned.

She could hear the wicked amusement in his voice and was mortified at the thought of bringing the servants running from the house.

But before she could fret about that possibility, he began to work her gently, reverently, forcing the strange tension inside her to the breaking point.

Without warning, she shattered in his hands, twisting against him as the release swept through her. She would have screamed this time, heedless of alarming the household. But he was prepared. His mouth closed over hers again, drowning the cry.

He moved before the tremors had ceased, settling on top of her, guiding himself to her with one hand. He pushed into her, hard and relentless.

The shock of the invasion brought her back to reality with a jarring thud. He froze, buried deep within her, and looked down at her, braced on his elbows.

"Why the devil didn't you tell me that you've never done this before?" he demanded. The words sounded half-strangled in his throat.

She flexed her fingers into his shoulders and adjusted herself cautiously. "Would it have made any difference?"

He hesitated a few seconds, every muscle as hard as stone. Then, with a low groan, he lowered his head and kissed her throat.

"No," he said. "It wouldn't have made any difference. But I would have gone about things a bit differently."

"I was under the impression that things

were going along quite nicely. I suggest you save your complaints until later."

"Excellent advice," he got out between his teeth.

She held him as he increased the force and tempo of his thrusts. His shoulders got slicker and his breathing harsher. A moment later he sank himself to the hilt one last time, his back curved like a tautly strung bow, and gave himself up to the climax. In the moonlight she caught the flash of his bared teeth and tightly closed eyes. Sparks ignited the tropical atmosphere.

When it was over he collapsed on top of her, sated and unmoving. She lay quietly beneath him for a long time, looking up into the darkness and listening as his breathing gradually returned to normal.

Now at last she understood what her intuition had tried to tell her earlier. There was no going back after making love with Thaddeus because in some way she could not explain she was now bound to him — and not merely by the physical bonds generated by passion. Those, with time and willpower, could probably be severed, or at least dramatically reduced. Passion, by all accounts, was a strong but transient force.

No, the chains that bound her to Thaddeus were of a psychical nature. The basis for the links between them had been established the other night when they had worked the crystal together. Somehow, the physical act of lovemaking had enhanced and strengthened those bonds.

She did not fully comprehend, but she now knew that, come what may, she would never be free of the connection that bound her to him.

18

The handsome, elegant gentleman was in the alley again tonight, watching her from the fog-shrouded shadows. He thought she hadn't noticed him. Annie smiled to herself. She had news for him: When you made your living on the streets, you took note of even the smallest details. At least you did if you were smart. The girls who did not learn that lesson early on in their careers did not survive for long.

She prided herself on being a survivor. Not only that, but, unlike a lot of other girls who abandoned their futures to the gin bottle or an opium pipe, she had plans. Hers were not the impossible dreams that so many of those in her profession clung to: silly fantasies that usually involved some fine gentleman setting a girl up as his mistress and showering her with jewels, fancy gowns and a house of her own.

She knew better than that. A wealthy

gentleman might occasionally amuse himself with a street whore, but he would never choose one for his mistress. Mistresses were expensive. When a man spent money on a woman, he expected her to be as fashionable as his carriage or his club: an actress, perhaps, or one of the refined, educated, respectable ladies of the middle or even upper classes who, owing to a bankruptcy or the death of a husband, was forced to sell herself. And as for those silly girls who hoped that such a gentleman might actually marry them, well, they were simply deluded fools.

No, her dreams were of a far more practical nature. She had a talent for making lovely hats. Give her a few hours, and she could create a bonnet out of discarded scraps of fabric and a few cheap artificial flowers that would stand comparison with the finest creations in the windows of the most exclusive milliner shops.

Absently she touched the broad brim of her new green felt hat. She had finished it yesterday. The ostrich feather tucked into the green ribbon band was real. She had found it on the street in front of a theater earlier that week. It had evidently fallen off a lady's evening toque. It had proved to be the perfect finishing touch for the green felt.

One day she was going to disappear forever from the streets. She was saving every penny so that she would be able to rent a small shop and set herself up in business. None of her fashionable clients would ever know that she had once been obliged to make her living as a prostitute.

She stopped beneath the street lamp and glanced ever so casually toward the mouth of the alley. The silhouette of the elegant stranger was not much more than a shadow, but she could tell that he was still there. Apparently he was one of those nervous gentlemen who had to work up his courage to approach a girl.

She started walking slowly toward him, watching him from beneath the tilted brim of the green felt hat. She didn't want to frighten him off. There were not a lot of high-class clients like him about in this part of town, not on a foggy night like this.

"Good evening, sir," she said. "Would you be interested in a bit of sport tonight?"

The shadow drifted out of the alley and came toward her. As he drew closer she saw that he moved very gracefully for a man. His long, pacing strides made her think of a big cat.

"It's cold and damp out here," she said in her most inviting tones. "Why don't you come upstairs to my room? I'll soon have you warm."

The man moved at last into the circle of glary light cast by the street lamp. She could see now that she was right in her estimation of him. His clothes looked expensive. So did the walking stick he carried. In addition he was one of the most handsome men she had ever seen. The neatly trimmed hair that showed beneath his hat was palest gold.

"I would be delighted to accept your invitation, Annie," he said, smiling a little.

That stopped her cold. "How do you know my name?"

"I've been watching you for a while. I heard one of your friends call you Annie."

He was very close now, no more than a few steps away. For some reason a shiver of dread went through her. *Like someone walked across my grave.* She hesitated. She'd experienced these sensations with clients occasionally in the past. Generally speaking, she paid attention to such inexplicable feelings and turned down the business. A girl had to be careful these days, what with all the rumors about the fiend they called the Midnight Monster.

But in this case there seemed to be no logical foundation for the little chills. The elegant gentleman looked like an angel, a *clean* angel. More to the point, he looked like the type who would be happy to tip extra for special services.

"I've noticed you hanging about on this street a time or two during the past week," she said lightly. "I'm glad you spoke to me tonight."

To her surprise, that annoyed him.

"You did not see me until tonight," he said, his voice roughening with anger. "Your imagination is playing tricks on you."

The last thing she wanted to do was lose such a fine client over a nonsensical argument.

"I'm sure you're right, sir," she said, smiling coyly at him from beneath the brim of her hat. "After all, you're the sort of gentleman a girl dreams about on a night like this. So handsome and elegant."

He relaxed and smiled again. "I look forward to visiting your room, Annie."

Another icy finger touched her spine. She ignored it with an effort of will.

"It's above the tavern, sir," she said.

He nodded, looking toward the alley where he had loitered earlier. "I expect there's an entrance around back."

"No need to go in through the kitchens," she assured him. "I have an arrangement with the proprietor. Jed doesn't mind me taking my visitors through the main entrance."

In exchange for the occasional free tumble and a small cut of her profits, Jed rented her a room above the tavern. As a rule, she brought her customers in through the front door, but if they were shy, she used the kitchen entrance. Either way, Jed got a look at the men she took upstairs. If one caused trouble or became violent, she signaled him by kicking the wall a few times. He always came to the rescue.

"If we cannot go to your room unseen, I must decline your kind invitation," the elegant man said regretfully. "I am presently courting a wealthy young lady whose papa would reject my offer out of hand if word got around that I had been seen with a girl in your profession."

That explained his shyness, she thought. Courtship and marriage were a serious business for gentlemen of his class. A lot of money was no doubt at stake. He would not want to risk losing an heiress bride just for the sake of a quick tumble with a whore. A man in his delicate position had to be cautious, at least until after the wedding.

"I understand, sir," she said. "Very well, then, we'll go through the alley and around to the kitchens. No one will notice you with me."

"Thank you, Annie." He smiled his angelic smile. "I knew the first time I saw you that you were just the girl I've been looking for."

19

The atmosphere inside the conservatory had grown colder in the past few minutes. His front half was pleasantly warm and comfortable because he was sprawled on top of Leona, but Thaddeus was aware of a definite chill on his backside.

Reluctantly, he untangled himself and rolled to his feet. A narrow shaft of moonlight crossed Leona's face when she sat up on the sheet of canvas. There was something new in her expression, something that made him uneasy. He reached down to assist her to her feet.

"Are you all right?" he asked, letting his palms glide over the satin-smooth skin of her bare shoulders and soft upper arms. He had been well and truly satisfied, he reflected. Indeed, the experience had been unlike any other encounter he'd ever had. So how did it come to pass that the hunger was unfurling inside him again so soon?

"Yes, of course I'm all right." She fumbled briefly with her hair and then abruptly turned away to pick up her chemise. "Why wouldn't I be?"

He watched her for a moment, uncertain of her strange mood. "Perhaps because you have never before had a lover?"

She got the chemise on and scrambled to pull the white petticoat up over her hips. "Nonsense. I had a lover. I told you, I was engaged for a time."

He captured her face between his hands. "Yes, you did make it clear that, what with your work with crystals and your unfortunate affair of the heart, you were no innocent. But it seems I took your words a little too literally."

She stepped back, smiling coolly. "As you said a short time ago, it hardly signifies."

"No, I did not say that. I said it wouldn't have changed the outcome. There's a difference."

She concentrated very hard on getting into her gown. "Really, sir, are all men so chatty after this sort of thing?"

"I can't speak for other men." He grabbed his trousers off the workbench. "But as for myself, no, I'm not usually this inclined toward a lot of conversation." He got the trousers on and fastened and scooped up his shirt. "But this was all new to me, too. You're not the only innocent here."

She paused in the act of fastening the hooks of her gown. "I beg your pardon?"

"Trust me when I tell you that what happened between us tonight was not typical of the experience."

She watched him, her eyes deep and — he could think of no other word for it — *haunted.*

"The energy," she whispered. "You felt it, too?"

He smiled, relaxing a little now that he knew what was bothering her. "It would have been impossible to avoid feeling it."

"But what was it? What happened between us?"

"Damned if I know." He pulled on his shirt, too relaxed and satisfied to worry about her bewilderment. The aura that had enveloped them a short time ago had felt very, very good. He saw no reason to question it. "Probably a variation on what happened to us the other night when the currents of our energy collided in that aurora stone."

"Yes, there was something familiar about it," she said, still very serious. "But Thaddeus, I have worked crystals many, many times, including the aurora stone when I was young. I must tell you that I have never experienced anything like the sensations that were generated tonight."

He searched for his tie, quite certain that it had landed somewhere on the workbench. "The fact that they were unique does not seem to me to be a great cause for concern. This is not the first time I have heard that when two people of power engage in an act of passion, an unusual kind of energy is generated between them."

"I have never heard that."

He hid a smile. "There have always been those in the Arcane Society who have maintained that various types of links can be forged between two people, especially if both parties possess a significant degree of talent."

"Such links are common?" she asked, even more uneasy now.

"No. They are brought into existence by some strong emotion or dramatic event that resonates with both individuals."

"Can any type of strong emotion produce those sorts of links?"

He shrugged. "Theoretically, I imagine. But in reality only the strongest emotions, such as passion, are capable of generating enough power to effect a bond."

"Passion." She repeated the word as though she had never heard it before in her life.

"That is usually a very temporary condition, is it not?"

A temporary condition? Was that how she expected this bond between them to be? His good mood vanished in a heartbeat. He forced himself to speak in the calm, unemotional tones of a scientific lecturer.

"Passion can certainly be transient," he agreed. "Or it can become very powerful."

She frowned. "Like an obsession?"

He slung the tie around his neck and knotted it with quick, practiced hands. "Or it can grow into love." He waited a few seconds but she did not respond. "Tell me about your previous lover."

She eyed him suspiciously. "Why do you want to know about him?"

"I suppose because I am curious about you."

"Oh." She digested that briefly while she pinned her hair. "Well, his name was William Trover. I met him when he came to me as a client in Little Tickton. His father is a wealthy investor."

"Why did Trover seek out your services?"

"He suffered from dreams that made him extremely anxious."

He reached for his trousers. "What sort of dreams?"

"They involved his father. In William's

dreams he always found himself in situations where he was desperately trying to please his parent. He invariably failed."

"I think I can hazard a guess as to why matters between you and young Trover did not end well."

"Yes, I'm sure you can." She finished with her hair and shook out her skirts. "When William's father found out that his only son and heir had become secretly engaged to one of those *fraudulent practitioners of psychical nonsense,* he ordered William to terminate the association immediately and forbade him to see me again."

"And young William, naturally, obeyed his father."

"It was not as if he had a choice. Mr. Trover threatened to cut him off entirely." She sighed. "Under normal circumstances, it would not have been the end of the world. It was not public knowledge that William and I had formed an attachment. Ending the engagement, therefore, should not have created a scandal, as is generally the case."

A respectable woman's reputation could be ruined by a broken engagement, he reflected. Such a situation was never viewed as less than a great humiliation. There was always gossip and speculation concerning the reasons *why* the gentleman had felt obliged to reject the lady. Had he discovered that her moral standards were not of the highest order? Or — horror of horrors — had she misrepresented her financial status?

"What went wrong?" he asked quietly.

"I suppose I should have known things would not go smoothly, but I was in love, you see. And William loved me."

"You allowed yourself to be guided by your natural optimism and forceful nature."

"I suppose so," she admitted. "In any event, William came to see me for the last time. We said our farewells. But William's father was evidently concerned that his son might weaken and decide to defy him. So he took steps to ensure that would not happen."

"He destroyed you and your business."

"Trover put it about that I was little more than a common prostitute who engaged in sex with her male clients." She wrinkled her nose. "I will say that business was brisk for a few days in the wake of the gossip. There was a great influx of new clients."

"All male, I'll wager."

"Yes. But very shortly the gentlemen's wives heard the rumors, and my business fell off quite dramatically. It was a small town. I could not even walk down the street without being subjected to the most outrageous remarks. I had no choice but to pack my bags and move to London."

He regarded her for a long moment, thinking of the fierce currents of passionate energy that had electrified the atmosphere in the conservatory. Even now his senses still resonated with the echoes of the exhilarating storm.

He knew what it all meant, even if she did not. His parents shared such a bond. It was rumored that the Master of the Society shared a similar connection with his new bride. But his intuition warned him that Leona was not yet ready to deal with the reality of what had just happened. She did not yet fully comprehend. She needed time to adjust to their new association, time to realize that they were now irrevocably bound together.

"Both Trovers, the elder and the younger, deserve to be horsewhipped," he said. "But I must admit, I am very glad that you found your way to London."

He drew her back into his arms. The fragrant night closed in around them. He unfastened the hooks of her gown for the second time that night.

Some time later they made their way back into the house. Fog was waiting for them, curled up in front of the kitchen door. He rose and trotted into the back hall with them.

Leona dreaded encountering Victoria again. She was certain that she was blushing from head to toe and quite disheveled. Mercifully, it appeared that the older woman had not returned downstairs.

The lights were turned down very low, and the house seemed unnaturally quiet. It struck her as a little odd that all of the servants had retired ahead of their master and his guest, but she was too distracted to pay much attention to that small detail.

Thaddeus kissed her good night with lazy satisfaction at the foot of the stairs.

"Dream of me," he said softly. "Because I'm going to be dreaming of you." He gave her a slow, intimate smile. "Assuming I sleep at all, that is."

She felt herself grow hot all over again and was grateful for the low light. She reminded herself that she was a woman of the world now and should not be flummoxed by a gentleman's seductive talk.

"In my experience, one cannot place an order for a dream the way one would order buttered eggs at breakfast," she said. "And oddly enough, dreams are rarely of a pleasant nature. Indeed, it is astonishing how many dreams contain not only a bizarre quality but a measure of anxiety and unease as well. In fact, I have often wondered —"

He silenced her with a quick, ruthless kiss. When he raised his head she knew that he was laughing at her, albeit silently. He drew his thumb along the underside of her jaw, sending little shivers through her.

"Dream of me," he ordered in his spell-casting mesmeric voice.

The words scattered her senses to the four winds. It was all she could do not to throw herself on him and drag him down onto the floor.

Evidently satisfied, he stepped back.

"Good night," he repeated.

She whirled and fled up the stairs, Fog at her heels. At the landing she stopped and turned around. Thaddeus was still standing in the shadows at the foot of the staircase, one hand resting on the curved newel post. He smiled — an intimate, knowing smile that stole her breath. Then, he turned and walked off toward the library.

She tiptoed quickly toward her own room at the end of the hall. Fog prowled behind her. She got a nervous jolt when she noticed that the light was still on beneath Victoria's door. She hurried past, half expecting Victoria to yank open the door and administer a lecture on the low morals of crystal readers.

Victoria's door stayed firmly shut.

The silence of the household weighed heavily on Leona. Something was not right. An ominous sensation came over her. Just how late was it?

She paused beneath a wall sconce and examined the chatelaine watch attached to the waist of her skirt. Two o'clock in the morning.

She stifled a little shriek of horror. No wonder everyone else was asleep. She and Thaddeus had been out in the conservatory for *hours.* How could they have lost all track of time like that? Victoria and every member of the staff must have known that they had not spent half the night admiring rare plants.

Another thought followed, adding to her discomfort. Good grief, she would have to face the servants and Victoria at breakfast, knowing that they all knew what had occurred out there in the conservatory.

She took a deep breath and straightened her shoulders. This was the sort of thing one had to learn to deal with when one became a woman of the world. So what if she had lost her virginity tonight? It was about time. She was nearly thirty, after all. Furthermore, she was quite certain that very few women managed the feat in such a glorious fashion. For the rest of her life she would remember this night, a night of passion in a tropical garden.

She reached the safety of her room and hurried inside. After turning up the lamp she sat down on the edge of the bed to compose herself. Fog yawned, made a few circles on the rug and then settled down.

She was suddenly conscious of feeling a little sore, as though certain portions of her anatomy were gently bruised. She got up, undressed and bathed at the washstand.

She put on her nightgown and then, concluding that the room was quite cold, her robe and slippers.

After a while she realized she was not going to be able to sleep, at least not for some time. She went to the trunk that she had brought with her from Vine Street, opened the lid and picked up her mother's journal.

She needed to take her mind off what had happened between herself and Thaddeus. It was time to do some research on the aurora stone.

20

Shortly before breakfast the following morning, Thaddeus sensed a presence hovering in the doorway of the library. He looked up from the notes he was making. Victoria stood in the opening. She wore a dangerously resolute expression.

Until that moment he had been feeling in remarkably good spirits, considering the fact that he had a missing crystal and a few unsolved murders on his hands. The day appeared to be starting out very fine. The sun was actually shining in the garden. He was beginning to wonder if perhaps there was something to the business of positive thinking.

He had a feeling, however, that Victoria was about to change his newfound sense of optimism.

He got to his feet. "Good morning, Aunt Vicky. You are up early today."

"I am always up early." She marched into

the room and sat down in front of the desk. "You know I suffer from insomnia and unpleasant dreams."

"You might want to talk to Miss Hewitt about that problem. She is quite skilled at dealing with such matters."

"As it happens, it is Miss Hewitt that brings me here this morning."

He sat down and folded his hands on the surface of the desk. "I was afraid of that. I trust this won't take long. I don't wish to appear rude, but I was just about to eat breakfast and afterward I have a number of things to accomplish today."

"Breakfast," she said coldly, "is the reason I am here, sir."

"There is something wrong with breakfast?"

"Miss Hewitt requested the maid to bring hers to her on a tray this morning."

Victoria clearly expected that news to shatter him. He considered it closely for a moment, searching for the trap. He knew it was there, but damned if he could find it.

"I see," he said. It was, he had long ago discovered, the most useful statement one could make when one was utterly baffled. "Perhaps Miss Hewitt prefers privacy in the mornings."

Victoria's shoulders were rigid. "I'm certain she is seeking privacy."

A flicker of alarm shot through him. "Are you saying she is not feeling well? She was in the best of health last night. Does she have a fever? I shall send for the doctor immediately."

"There is no need for a doctor," Victoria said sharply.

Damnation. It must be one of those female complaints associated with a certain time of the month. But if that was the case, why was Victoria going on about it to him? Women did not discuss that sort of thing with men. Indeed the entire subject was a great mystery to those of his gender. The only reason he had some grasp of the subject was because, at roughly the age of thirteen, he'd developed an insatiable curiosity about the female form. One day his father had found him in his bedroom poring over an ancient medical text and two manuals devoted to the art of lovemaking, all of which he'd found tucked away in the family's vast library.

The medical book was written in excruciatingly turgid, almost indecipherable Latin. The manuals, written in Chinese, were even more impossible. They had, however, been elegantly illustrated, the detail as fine and exquisite as any of the hundreds of botanical texts that dominated his father's collection.

"I see that your intellectual interests have broadened recently," his father said, closing the door. *"So much for the new aquarium I bought you last week. I think it's time we had a talk."*

The Latin medical book and the illustrated manuals were still here in the library. He had planned to give them to his own son someday.

He looked at Victoria. "I don't quite understand what it is you expect me to do, Aunt Vicky."

She raised her chin in an ominous manner. "I will be the first to admit that I was somewhat taken aback when you brought Miss Hewitt into this house yesterday."

He stilled. "Let us be clear on one point. You are my aunt, and you have my affection and deepest respect. I will not, however, allow you to insult Miss Hewitt."

"Bah, there is no point insulting her now. The damage is done."

Anger and a chill of icy guilt sliced through him. "What the devil are you talking about?"

"Surely you are not that callous, Thaddeus. I have known you all of your life. I believed better of you."

"You are insulting me, not Miss Hewitt?"

"Do you think that I and everyone else in

this household, from Mrs. Gribbs and Mr. Gribbs, the cook and all the other members of the staff right down to little Mary, the new maid-of-all-work, don't know what happened out there in the conservatory last night?"

He felt as if he'd been struck by lightning. "Everyone was in bed when we came in last night."

"That doesn't mean we were all unaware of just when you returned to the house," Victoria snapped. *"Two in the morning."*

"Damn," he said, very quietly. He had not given the matter of Leona's reputation a second thought. He'd been too busy savoring the intense satisfaction he had felt.

"Some of your father's staff have known you from the cradle," Victoria reminded him in awful tones. "What must they be thinking this morning? Miss Hewitt wasn't even in this house one night before you took her out into the conservatory and seduced her."

"Damn," he said again. Nothing more useful came to mind. To think that only a moment ago he had been reflecting on the fine day and his uncharacteristically good spirits. So much for the power of positive thinking.

"Now that poor young woman is locked up there in her room," Victoria continued. "Too humiliated to come downstairs for breakfast. She probably believes that she has been ruined. I'll wager she's crying her eyes out."

"I suppose I should be grateful her dog didn't go for my throat," he said wearily.

He got to his feet, rounded the desk and started toward the door.

Victoria turned in her chair. "Where do you think you're going?"

"Upstairs to have a few words with Leona."

"Surely you do not intend to be private with her in her bedroom. Not with me and the servants in the house. Haven't you done enough?"

He stopped at the door, one hand on the knob. "I'll assume that is a rhetorical question."

Victoria made a tut-tutting sound. "One more thing before you go rushing upstairs."

Another ominous sensation splashed through him. "What?"

"I trust you have not forgotten the first Spring Ball?"

"Aunt Vicky, the damned Spring Ball is, at the moment, the very last thing on my mind. In fact, I do not give a damn about it."

"You, along with every other high-ranking member of the Society, will be expected to attend."

"What in blazes does that have to do with my intention to speak to Leona this morning?"

"That depends."

"On what?" he demanded, the last of his patience vanishing.

Victoria gave a ladylike sniff. "On whether or not you intend to escort Miss Hewitt to the affair."

"Damn it to hell, that does it. Aunt Vicky, in case you have forgotten, I am currently trying to recover a very dangerous relic from a man who has already poisoned two people in order to obtain it. In addition, I am attempting to discover the identity of a human monster who delights in slicing the throats of women. I do not have time to worry about escorting anyone to the Spring Ball."

Victoria's brows rose. "You had time to compromise a woman last night."

He did not trust himself to respond to that. Instead, he opened the door, strode out of the library and took the stairs two at a time.

When he reached the closed door of Leona's bedroom, he rapped sharply.

"Come in, Mary," Leona called.

In spite of his irritation, some of his tension eased. Her voice did not sound choked with tears.

Warily he opened the door. Leona was sitting at the small writing desk near the window. His breath tightened in his chest at the sight of her. She wore a dressing gown of spring green trimmed with yellow ribbons. The gown, with its long sleeves, prim neckline and floor-length hem, was modest in every respect. The style, imported from France, was meant to be worn casually indoors. It did not require tight lacing or a corset. Fashionable women like his mother wore their dressing gowns down to breakfast without a qualm.

But the dressing gown had created a great stir when it had first become popular. Critics railed against the comfortable style, declaring that its loose-fitting design would inevitably lead to even looser morals. For the first time he understood the shock and outrage among the priggish set. There was something undeniably sensual about the easy, flowing manner in which the gown draped a woman's body, or at least there was something very sensual about the way this particular gown draped this particular woman's body.

It occurred to him that he would not want any other man to see Leona in her dressing gown, regardless of that high neckline and those long sleeves.

"Just set the tray on my dressing table," Leona said. She did not look up from the leather-bound journal she was studying. "And please thank cook for me."

He folded his arms across his chest and propped one shoulder against the door-jamb.

"You can thank her, yourself," he said.

She started violently and turned in her chair, her eyes huge. "Thaddeus. What on earth are you doing here?"

"An excellent question. I was given to understand that you had ordered breakfast sent to your room because you could not face Aunt Vicky at breakfast, to say nothing of the staff."

"Good heavens, what nonsense."

"It was strongly implied that you were sobbing your heart out here in the privacy of your bedroom because you believed yourself to be ruined."

She frowned. "Who told you that?"

"My aunt."

Leona winced. "I see. I'm sure she meant well. How very awkward."

"For both of us."

She blinked. "What do you mean?"

"You are not the only one whose reputation is at stake here. Evidently my aunt and the servants have all leaped to the conclusion that I took ruthless advantage of you last night."

"I see." She closed the journal very carefully. "My apologies, sir. I had no notion that the simple act of requesting a breakfast tray would cause such a commotion. I shall get dressed immediately and come down to breakfast."

"Thank you. I'm not sure it will salvage my reputation, but at least I will not be obliged to face them all on my own."

She smiled. "I'm quite sure you could handle the situation, were it to prove necessary."

"Perhaps. But I can think of other things I would much rather do."

"Such as?"

"Have a couple of teeth pulled."

She laughed.

"One more thing," he said, straightening.

"Yes."

"Before we face the jury at breakfast I would like to speak to you in the library."

She brightened. "You have some news of the crystal?"

"No. I have a few questions for you."

She turned wary in a heartbeat. "What sort of questions?"

"Shortly before my aunt descended on me to defend your virtue, it dawned on me that you probably know more about the recent history of the aurora stone than most. Certainly more than Caleb Jones or I do. The last verified report we found was dated nearly forty years ago. You last saw the stone when you were sixteen. That would have been about ten or eleven years ago, correct?"

"Eleven." A closed, shuttered look cut off some of the light in her eyes. "I do not know what I can tell you that will help you find it."

"Neither do I. But if there is one thing I have learned in my career as an investigator, it is that sometimes even the smallest item of information can occasionally prove useful. You are the only person I know who can work the aurora stone. That gives you special insight. I want to go over every detail of your family history that relates to your career as a crystal reader."

A horrified stillness came over her. "Every detail? Is that really necessary?"

"I think so, yes. My method of investigation is somewhat primitive. I call it the turn-over-rocks-until-I-find-the-viper approach, but it is remarkably productive. Collecting as much information as possible is the basis of the method."

"I see."

"I'll wait for you downstairs."

Gently he closed the door and went along the hall to the staircase, wondering why his words had ignited a small flame of panic in Leona.

21

She put on her most severely tailored gown, the rust-brown one with the dark gold stripes, and pinned her hair up into a tight chignon. When she contemplated her reflection in the mirror she was not pleased. Pity she could not find an excuse to wear one of her heavily veiled hats as well, she thought. Knowing that Thaddeus could not see her face might have made things easier. Then again, perhaps it would not have helped.

Last night she had known this day might come, she reminded herself. But given her philosophy of positive thinking, she had told herself she would not dwell on the possibility.

She heard a soft whine from somewhere out in the hall. When she opened the door she found Fog waiting for her. He watched her intently with his wolf's eyes, as if he had sensed her distress and come to offer comfort.

She patted him lightly and rubbed the special spot behind his ears. "No need to worry about me. Mr. Ware will no doubt be somewhat shocked when I tell him who I really am, but that is neither here nor there. The important thing is the search for the crystal. We must get it back. If I possess some information that might assist in the recovery of the stone, then so be it. I will tell him everything I know."

She went down the hall, Fog pacing at her side. At the top of the staircase she saw Mary. The plump little maid was climbing the stairs with a great deal of enthusiasm, in spite of the heavy tray she carried. There was an air of barely suppressed excitement about her.

She noticed Leona and halted midstep, confused.

"Did ye change yer mind, then, ma'am?" she asked.

"Yes, I did." Leona summoned up a bright smile. "It is such a lovely morning, far too nice to spend alone in my room reading. I've decided I'd rather eat with the others."

Mary's face crumpled with undisguised disappointment.

"Yes, ma'am," she mumbled.

Dejectedly she went back down the stairs and disappeared in the direction of the kitchens.

I've just taken the wind out of her sails, Leona thought. So much for regaling the housekeeper, the cook and the rest of the staff with gossip about the poor houseguest who had been ruined by the master of the house last night. The lady was not a humiliated, shrinking violet hiding from the world in her bedroom. She was a woman of the world.

The small scene did wonders to elevate her spirits. Shoulders back, she went down the stairs and halted briefly in the open doorway of the library.

"I trust this won't take long, Mr. Ware," she said in her best stage voice, hoping it would carry as far as the kitchens. "I am very hungry for my breakfast."

Thaddeus put down a pen and got to his feet. Amusement etched his mouth.

"Not long at all, Miss Hewitt. I am as eager as you to get to the breakfast table. My appetite also seems to be in fine form this morning, probably because I slept so well last night."

He did not need to raise his voice in order to ensure that it carried. He merely added a little energy. His words rolled through the room and echoed along the hall. Fog tensed, suddenly very alert, and whined softly.

Leona glowered at Thaddeus and lowered

her own voice. "Stop showing off."

"Sorry." He crossed the library and closed the door behind her. "I was merely following your lead. I have noticed that, on occasion, you have a certain flair for the theatrical."

She knew she was turning pink, but by the time he had returned to the desk, she had composed herself on a chair, the folds of her skirts meticulously twitched into position. Fog stretched out beside her feet.

Thaddeus angled himself onto a corner of the desk, one foot braced on the floor. The amusement that had briefly lightened his hard features disappeared. A sober, intent expression replaced it.

"Tell me everything you can about the crystal," he said. "And about your family's connection to it."

"I never knew my father," she said. "He died when I was very young. I was raised by my grandmother and my mother. They supported themselves and me by working crystals. The women in my family have always had a talent for it. Mother and Grandmother managed a comfortable living. As you are no doubt aware, the rage for all things psychical has been quite strong for several years now."

"And unlike so many of the charlatans and frauds who pursue careers giving demonstrations, your mother and grandmother were the genuine articles. They really could work crystal."

"When I turned thirteen, my own abilities began to manifest themselves. It became apparent that I, too, had a talent for working crystals. Mother and Grandmother taught me the fine points of the business."

"Were your mother and grandmother members of the Arcane Society?" Thaddeus asked.

"No." She paused, choosing her words with some care. "They were aware of the Society, but neither of them ever applied for membership."

"Why not?"

"I suppose they simply never saw any point to it," she said smoothly. "The Society has always frowned upon their kind of talent."

"That attitude, I fear, is derived from an old legend within the Society."

"The legend of Sybil the Sorceress. Yes, I know."

"Actually, she is better known within the Society as Sybil the Virgin Sorceress."

She raised her brows. "Surely the status of her virtue is a minor point after all these years."

He smiled faintly. "It wasn't to Sylvester Jones, the founder of the Society. Evidently she refused his advances."

"Who can blame her? By all accounts he was not what any woman would deem a romantic man."

"Can't argue with you there," Thaddeus agreed dryly. "I do understand why your mother and grandmother were reluctant to get involved with the Society. Unfortunately, the organization has always been overly keen on tradition and legend."

"Yes, well, my mother and grandmother were not."

"How did they acquire the stone?"

"My mother found it when she was a young woman."

"She found it?" Thaddeus repeated a little too neutrally.

She gave him a steely smile. "That's right."

"Just lying about on the ground somewhere?"

"No, it was lying about in a dusty antiquities shop, I believe."

"Something tells me there is more to the story."

"If there is, my mother never told me. She said she went past a shop one day and felt a disturbing tingle of awareness. When she went inside she saw the stone. She recognized it instantly."

"I'll take your word for it. Please continue."

She gathered her thoughts again. "Things went quite well for the three of us for some time. Then Grandmother died. Two years later, the summer I turned sixteen, my mother was killed in a carriage accident."

"My condolences," he said gently.

She managed an austere little inclination of her head. "Thank you." Her hand stilled on Fog, who pressed closer to her. "She was being driven back to a railway station after visiting a wealthy, reclusive client. There was a storm. The vehicle went over a cliff into a river. My mother was trapped in the cab and was drowned."

"A terrible thing."

"She had the aurora stone with her at the time. The client had insisted that she use it, in particular, when she consulted for him."

Thaddeus's expression sharpened almost imperceptibly. "That was the day the stone disappeared?"

"Yes. I'm certain the thief assumed that anyone who was interested in the stone would conclude that it was lost in the river. But I did not believe that for a moment."

"You think that your mother's client arranged the accident to cover the theft of the crystal?"

"That was my conclusion at the time. I knew he was a member of the Arcane Society, you see. That was all the proof I needed. Only a member of the Society would be aware of the crystal and its power."

"What was the name of your mother's client?"

"Lord Rufford." She drew a deep breath. "I was convinced he had the stone in his possession. I determined to search his household. So I applied for a post as a maid."

For the first time Thaddeus looked nonplussed. "Good lord, woman, you took employment in the house of the man you thought had murdered your mother? Of all the idiotic —" He broke off, jaw hardening. "But I suppose it was no more of a risk than going into Delbridge's house dressed as one of his servants."

"Easier, actually. The turnover in servants being what it is, especially at the entry-level positions, I had no difficulty obtaining a position as a maid-of-all-work. As you know, it is the lowest position on any household staff."

"It cannot have been easy."

"It wasn't. But it gave me an excuse to be found anywhere in the house. I spent several days emptying chamber pots and scrubbing floors. But it proved fruitless. I picked up no trace of the stone."

"I take it you were never discovered?" Thaddeus asked.

"No. Rufford was a very old, very ill gentleman. He died shortly after I left his employ. In the end I was forced to conclude that someone else had arranged the carriage accident."

"Someone who knew that your mother had an appointment with Rufford and decided that that would be an ideal opportunity to get rid of her and steal the stone."

"Yes. I was unable to pursue my quest for the crystal for some time after that because I soon found myself penniless."

"Didn't you take on your mother's clients?"

"People, it turns out, are quite reluctant to consult a young woman of sixteen years on matters of a very personal nature such as their dreams."

"I see."

She straightened her shoulders and concentrated on her tale. "By the time I had buried my mother and completed my useless investigation of Lord Rufford, I discovered I had no clients left. In addition, the unscrupulous funeral director managed to erase most of what money my mother had left to me. The man cheated me, but there was no way I could prove it."

He went very still, watching her with an unreadable expression. "You must have been quite desperate."

"I was." She looked past him out the window. "The world makes it so difficult for a female to enter a respectable profession, and then everyone wonders why so many women end up on the street."

"I assure you, there is no need to lecture me on the subject. The women in my family hold forth on that subject on a regular basis."

"I was contemplating going into service for real when Uncle Edward showed up."

"Who is Uncle Edward?"

"My only remaining close relative. He was from my mother's side of the family. He was traveling in America at the time of her death. I did not know where he was, so I could not write or send him a telegram to inform him of what had happened. But he returned to England a couple of months later and came to see me immediately. He took in my financial circumstances at once and invited me to live with him."

"Did your uncle know about the aurora stone?"

"Of course. I thought I made it clear. The stone has been in my family for generations."

"Except when it isn't," Thaddeus said in

his maddeningly neutral way.

She shot him a withering glare. He did not appear to notice.

"Tell me about your uncle," he said.

She stifled a small sigh and continued her story. "To be honest, I did not know him well at that time. I had seen very little of him growing up. He rarely came to visit. I knew that my mother and grandmother were fond of him but they did not entirely approve of him."

"Why was that?"

"Among other things, he was an actor. He was always on the road, either here or in America. In addition, he had a certain reputation with women. Although, to be fair, from what I observed, he did not have to work very hard attracting female attention. He is a distinguished-looking and extremely charming man. Women are drawn to him like bees to honey."

"Did he treat you well?"

"Oh, yes." She smiled a little. "In his own way, he is quite fond of me."

"If that is the case, where is he now?"

She looked down at Fog. "He is traveling in America again."

"Where in America?"

She buried her fingers in Fog's fur. "I don't know."

"Your uncle took off for America and left you on your own?"

She frowned. "It is not as if I am still sixteen. I am quite able to take care of myself these days."

"When did he leave this last time?"

She hesitated. "About two years ago."

"Have you heard from him?"

"I received a telegram from a policeman in San Francisco informing me that Uncle Edward had died in a hotel fire. That was about eighteen months ago."

There was a long silence from Thaddeus. When she looked at him she discovered that he was watching her with a thoughtful look.

"You don't believe that he's dead," he said.

"Perhaps it is just that I do not want to believe it. Uncle Edward is my only remaining relative. It is difficult to imagine having no family left at all."

"I understand. Tell me about life with Uncle Edward."

"Is it really important to your investigation?"

"I don't know," he admitted. "But as I said, I like information; the more the better."

"It is a somewhat complicated story," she said.

"I'm listening."

"My uncle was aware that I had inherited my mother's talent for reading crystals. He suggested we go into the family business together, with him acting as my manager."

"How did he get around the fact that clients were reluctant to trust such a young person?"

"As I mentioned, Uncle Edward had some experience in the theater. He came up with the notion of dressing me as a stylish widow, complete with a heavy veil. Clients took me for a much older, more mature woman. They also liked the added air of mystery that the costume gave me."

Thaddeus looked amused. "Your uncle knew what he was about."

"Yes. It was so effective that I continued to wear widow's weeds even after I was in my twenties."

"Business went well?"

"Oh, yes, for several years we did quite nicely." She paused. "Until Uncle Edward came up with his investment scheme, that is."

Thaddeus narrowed his eyes very slightly. "Investment scheme?"

"You must believe me when I say that my uncle sincerely believed that there were fortunes to be made in the American West, especially in mining."

"Mining," Thaddeus repeated.

She could not tell what he was thinking so she hurried on. "Uncle Edward had ample opportunity to converse with my clients because he arranged all the appointments. He mentioned his conviction that a certain mining project in the Wild West promised great profits. The next thing we knew, several gentlemen insisted upon giving him money to invest in the venture."

Thaddeus's mouth twitched and then kicked up at the corner. "And two years ago good old Uncle Edward sailed for America with a few hundred thousand pounds of your clients' money and has not been heard from since."

She stiffened. "I'm sure he will come back with the profits one of these days."

His smile widened. "You're Edward Pipewell's niece."

She raised her chin proudly. "Yes, I am."

Thaddeus's eyes were gleaming with laughter now. "The woman who helped Dr. Pipewell fleece some of the wealthiest men in the Arcane Society."

"My uncle did not steal their money," she said, suddenly feeling quite fierce. "He put together an honest investment scheme. It is not his fault that things did not go well."

But she was wasting her breath. The laughter was spilling out of Thaddeus now. He was laughing so hard he could not possibly have heard what she was saying. He roared with laughter, howled with it, doubled over with it.

Fog watched him curiously, head tilted slightly to the side. Leona sat very still, uncertain what to do.

The door of the library opened.

"What on earth is going on in here?" Victoria demanded.

Thaddeus pulled himself together with a visible effort. He gave Victoria his wolfish smile.

"Nothing important, Aunt Vicky," he said. "Leona and I were just about to join you for breakfast."

"Humph." Victoria shot Leona a suspicious look before retreating back into the hall. The door closed with a distinctly disapproving little slam.

Leona looked at Thaddeus. "I will understand if you do not wish to continue an intimate liaison with Dr. Edward Pipewell's niece."

He rose from the desk, eyes still glinting with laughter. "Your connection to Pipewell is nothing to me. I didn't lose any money on your uncle's scheme."

He reached down, pulled her up out of the chair and tipped up her chin.

"Thaddeus?"

"I can think of nothing more that I would rather do than continue our intimate liaison, Miss Hewitt."

He kissed her with a thoroughness that ignited energy in the atmosphere around them. When he released her she had to grab hold of the edge of the desk to steady herself.

He smiled at her again, looking very satisfied. "I think it's time we went into breakfast, don't you?"

22

Leona knocked tentatively on the bedroom door.

"Is that you, Miss Hewitt?" Victoria called out in her brusque, no-nonsense tones. "You may enter."

Reluctantly, Leona opened the door. She was not looking forward to this meeting. The summons had been issued after Thaddeus had left the house for what he had described as a short meeting with Caleb Jones. Leona had gone into the garden with Fog and her mother's journal. She was sitting on a bench reading when Mary, the young maid-of-all-work, appeared.

"Lady Milden sent me to tell you that she wants to see you, ma'am." Mary kept a wary eye on Fog, who was sniffing some foliage at the base of the garden wall. "In her bedroom, she says."

It had been little short of a royal command.

Leona stood in the doorway and looked at Victoria, who was seated at a dainty little writing desk.

"You wished to speak with me?" Leona said politely.

"Yes. Stop dithering about out there in the hall. Come in and close the door."

Feeling rather like one of the servants, Leona obeyed.

"I wish to speak with you on a personal matter," Victoria announced.

Enough was enough, Leona thought. It had not been her idea, after all, to become a guest in this household.

"If this is about my association with Mr. Ware," she said coolly, "I have no intention of discussing it with you."

Victoria grimaced. "I have nothing to say on that subject. It is quite obvious that the two of you were meant to be lovers. This is another matter, entirely."

"I see," Leona said, utterly bewildered.

"I understand that you are something of an expert on dreams and insomnia."

Leona thought about the light that had burned so late under Victoria's door last night.

"I have a certain talent for dealing with the negative energy that can keep one from a restful slumber," she allowed cautiously.

"Very well, I wish to engage your services."

Leona swallowed. "Well —"

"Immediately."

"Uh —"

"Is there a problem, Miss Hewitt?"

"Uh, no, no, there's no problem," Leona said quickly. "It is just that I was under the impression that you do not approve of me."

"That is neither here nor there. For now, you may consider me a client."

Leona contemplated the situation from every possible angle and saw no escape, at least none that did not involve waving a flag of cowardice. *"You must control your audience. Never allow your audience to control you."*

"Very well," she said in her most professional tone. "What seems to be the problem?"

Victoria rose. Her posture was as rigid as ever, but the morning sun revealed the map of lines and creases on her face. When she moved to stand at the window, Leona sensed an aura of weariness about her.

"I have not had a good night's rest since my husband died, Miss Hewitt. Whenever I turn down the lamps I lie awake, sometimes for hours. When I do sleep I am troubled by dark dreams." She gripped a handful of curtains very tightly in one hand. "Sometimes I wake up in tears. Sometimes —"

"Yes?"

"Sometimes I think that I would rather not wake up at all," Victoria whispered.

The pain and sadness in the complaint swept aside Leona's irritation and wariness of the woman. In the blink of an eye Victoria was transformed into a client.

"I hear that from many of those who come to me," Leona said quietly.

"You no doubt think me weak."

"No," Leona said.

"I am an old woman, Miss Hewitt. But I have had a good life. I have been exceptionally fortunate in my health and also in having a family that has provided me with a comfortable home in which to pass my remaining days. Why does sleep elude me? Why, when I do manage to close my eyes, must I endure such disturbing dreams?"

Leona tightened her grip on her mother's journal. "All lives involve losses. The longer we live, the more losses we are obliged to endure. It is the way of the world."

Victoria turned her head and looked at her for a long, considering moment. "I can see that you have already endured loss although you are not yet thirty."

"Yes."

Victoria turned back to the view of the garden. "The sum can be quite staggering when one adds up the numbers after so many years. I have outlived my parents, a brother, my dear husband, one of my daughters and the infant who died with her in childbed, and any number of friends."

"My mother was convinced that it is the sheer accumulation of losses that destroys sleep in one's later years. The weight of all that negative energy takes its toll. One must fight it with positive thoughts."

"Positive thoughts?"

"Those of us who work crystal know the power of one's thoughts. There is energy in them. Negative energy creates more of the same. Positive energy can counteract the negative. Tell me, madam, what do you think about when you lie awake at night?"

Victoria stiffened. Then she turned very slowly. Leona knew that she was not seeing hallucinations as Thaddeus had the night he was poisoned. But there was about her a haunted quality that was disturbingly similar.

"I think about the past," Lady Milden whispered. "I think about all the mistakes I made. The things I should have done. I think about the losses."

"I'll go and get my crystals," Leona said.

23

An hour later she sat back in her chair and looked at Victoria, who was seated on the opposite side of the little writing desk. The glow in the blue crystal that rested on the table between them was fading rapidly now that neither of them was focusing on it.

"I warned you it can be an exhausting process," Leona said gently. "Are you all right?"

"Yes, just very tired." Victoria frowned at the crystal. "Was this the technique you used to save my nephew the other night when he was poisoned?"

"He told you about that?"

"He said you saved not only his sanity but very likely his life."

"I employed a different crystal, but, yes, the process is the same. Mr. Ware generates a great deal of power, so diffusing his negative energy was a bit of a challenge for both of us but we managed."

Victoria raised her brows. "I got the impression that it was actually a very near thing for both of you."

"Please remember, Lady Milden, I can help you deal with the insomnia and the bad dreams, but it is not within my power to affect the underlying causes of your melancholia."

Victoria straightened her shoulders. "If I can just get some sleep and if the troubling dreams cease I will be able to deal with my emotions."

Leona hesitated, uncertain of how far she should go. "Forgive me if I intrude too much into your personal life, but when I channeled your energy a few minutes ago I could not help but notice that you possess a great deal of paranormal power."

Victoria made a face. "I'm afraid it runs in the family. Both sides."

"In the course of my career I have channeled dream energy for many people, including a number who possess strong senses. People like you, Lady Milden."

"What of it?"

"I have observed that those with powerful talents often suffer greatly from depression and melancholia if they do not exercise their psychical natures."

"I see."

"They must find their passion if they wish to achieve some measure of contentment and satisfaction in life."

Victoria frowned, shocked. "What on earth are you talking about? I assure you, the very last thing I seek is an illicit relationship." She pursed her lips. "That is for women your age. In any event, I loved my husband very deeply; I have no wish to replace him in my heart."

Leona knew her face was turning quite pink, but she plowed on, determined to finish what she had started.

"I am not talking about sexual passion, Lady Milden. Nor do I mean the sort of love that one feels for the members of one's family. I refer to those things we do to satisfy something within ourselves. People who possess strong paranormal abilities usually discover that their passion is invariably connected to their talent."

"I really have no notion of what you are talking about."

"Mr. Ware has his career as an investigator. It allows him to employ his hypnotic talents in a positive fashion."

Victoria gave a soft snort. "And without the necessity of going on stage."

"Well, yes, that too. The point is, he has found an outlet for the psychical side of his nature that gives him satisfaction."

"They call him The Ghost, you know," Victoria said softly.

"Who calls him that?" Leona asked, startled.

"The people on the streets, his informants and those who seek his services but cannot afford to pay him. To be honest, I think he was in danger of becoming a real ghost until he invented his career as a private enquiry agent."

"Surely you do not mean that you feared he would do himself some harm?"

"No, he has far too much willpower," Victoria said firmly. "He would never hurt his family in that manner. But before he found his passion, as you call it, he had begun to withdraw more and more into himself. His parents had started to worry about his brooding moods. He seemed to be passing through life, as it were, rather than living it."

"I understand."

"His talent has made things very difficult for him in many ways," Victoria explained. "Other people who know of his abilities are often uneasy around him. One of the results is that he has never had many friends."

"I see."

Victoria watched her intently. "It is his talent that has kept him from finding a wife. Women quite naturally are unwilling to marry a man they fear can control them utterly with just the power of his voice."

"*Mmm,* yes, I can see the problem," Leona said briskly. The last thing she wanted to discuss was Thaddeus's problem finding a wife. She hurried to get the subject back on track. "He told me that the magnificent conservatory outside this house is the result of his parents' botanical talents. It is their passion."

Victoria hesitated and then nodded. "Yes, I suppose that is true. Odd, I never thought of Thaddeus's career and the conservatory in quite those terms."

"You know the members of your family quite well. Try to imagine any of them without their personal passions."

"Indeed, I cannot. If Thaddeus did not have his investigating business and if Charles and Lilly did not have their conservatory, well, I just cannot bear to contemplate what any of them would be like."

"Subject to bouts of melancholia, perhaps?" Leona suggested gently.

Victoria sighed. "You may be right. And to think that I always considered such things mere hobbies or pastimes."

"May I ask what form your talent takes?"

Victoria's expression tightened. "I'm afraid that my powers are of a useless nature."

"What do you mean?"

Victoria rose and went to lie down on the bed. She arranged the pillow beneath her head and closed her eyes. "I have always had a talent which, for lack of a better word, I call *un-matchmaking.*"

"I have never heard of such a talent."

"Unfortunately, it seems quite normal to me." Victoria put her arm over her eyes. "Show me any engaged couple or any husband and wife, and I can tell you immediately whether or not they are well suited."

"How extraordinary."

"And, as I said, quite useless."

"I don't understand. Why is that?"

Victoria removed her arm from her eyes and peered at her. "There is little point informing a married couple that they made a huge mistake. Divorce is out of the question for most, especially if there are children."

"But what of couples who are considering marriage? I should think they would want to know if they are well suited."

"Rubbish. I have discovered that very few people who are swept up in the first flush of mutual attraction wish to be told that they do not belong together."

Leona frowned. "Why is that, I wonder?"

Victoria put her arm back over her eyes. "Because they are generally dazzled or blinded, as the case may be, by more immediate concerns such as passion, beauty, financial or social status or simply the desire to escape loneliness."

Loneliness. That was the driving force that had motivated her interest in William Trover two years ago, Leona thought. She had been so alone in those days. At least until Fog had come along. Would she have been willing to listen to a matchmaker if one had tried to warn her that marriage to William would have been a mistake?

"I understand," she said quietly. "Those other factors can carry great weight."

"Even sharing a daring adventure together can inspire a great passion in some people," Victoria said dryly.

Leona wrinkled her nose. "I knew you would not be able to resist lecturing me about my association with Mr. Ware."

"Do not concern yourself. I told you I have no intention of wasting my time."

Leona smiled. "I am very grateful. Now, then, about your talent for un-matchmaking."

"What of it?"

"It strikes me that the main difficulty is that you exercise your talents on those who are already matched in one way or another."

Victoria made a face. "How else can one apply such a talent?"

"Well, for what it is worth, Uncle Edward always says that people do not appreciate advice unless they pay for it."

Victoria went very still. "Good lord. Are you suggesting that I go into the business of matchmaking?"

"No need to think of it as going into trade," Leona said quickly. "You could be a sort of consulting matchmaker. It would have to be very discreetly done, of course."

"To say the least."

"I suspect that if you let it be known in certain circles that you would be happy to consult for individuals seeking suitable marriage partners you would be overwhelmed with clients seeking your assistance."

"What an outlandish notion," Victoria said. "By the way, I spoke with Thaddeus this morning. He will escort you to the Arcane Society's first Spring Ball at the end of the week."

"*What?*"

"The new Master, Gabriel Jones, and his bride are hosting the affair. Evidently they feel that the members of the Society should socialize more. Mind you, I'm not sure that's an entirely sound notion, but Gabriel is now in charge of the Society and it is clear that he intends to make some changes."

"Lady Milden, I really don't think it would be at all wise for me to attend."

"Gabriel has concluded that the Society is far too hidebound and mired in tradition. He thinks there has been too much secrecy over the years. He wants the members to communicate more with each other. Some nonsense about preparing the organization to move into the modern era. Every ranking member of the Society, and that means every member of the Jones family, will be required to put in an appearance."

"I am not a member of the Jones family."

"No, but Thaddeus is."

"*What?*" She felt as if she were falling down the rabbit hole in the children's story. "Thaddeus is a Jones? That's impossible. His last name is Ware."

"He's a Jones on his mother's side. Prolific family."

"Good heavens." She was so stunned that she could not think of anything else to say. "Good heavens. A Jones."

"I have sent a message to my dressmaker," Victoria continued. "She will arrive here this afternoon at two o'clock to present us with some designs for your gown."

Leona struggled to recover her scattered wits. "Lady Milden, I don't want to sound rude, but attending an Arcane Society ball, especially with a member of the Jones family, is out of the question."

Victoria took her arm away from her eyes again. "Really, Miss Hewitt, if you are going to engage in an illicit liaison with my nephew, the least you can do is learn to conduct yourself with more composure. That expression of slack-jawed horror is not at all becoming."

"Lady Milden —"

"You'll have to excuse me. I am going to sleep now."

24

She was waiting for him when he walked into the library shortly before two o'clock. The moment Thaddeus saw her, he knew he was confronting a brewing storm.

Leona put down the old leather book that she seemed to carry with her everywhere and glared at him from the sofa.

"It's about time you got home, sir."

Amused, he reached down to pat Fog, who had ambled forward to greet him. "Such gentle words of feminine welcome are bound to warm the heart of any man upon his return to the bosom of his family, aren't they, Fog?"

Fog grinned and licked his hand.

Leona's scowl darkened. "This is no time for humor, sir."

"Very well, let's try another approach."

He crossed the room to the sofa, hauled her upright, straight off her feet, and kissed her soundly. He released her before she could even think of struggling. She dropped back down onto the sofa, momentarily stunned. He seized the opportunity to get to the safety of his desk.

"Now, then," he said, sitting down, "to what do I owe this charming greeting?"

"I spoke with your aunt this morning while you were out. She said that you were going to escort me to the Society's first Spring Ball."

He leaned back in his chair. "I seem to recall that she did say something to me along those lines." He raised his brows. "Is that a problem?"

"Of course it is a problem. I cannot possibly attend such a formal event with you."

Her unexpected vehemence twisted something deep inside him. Until now he had considered the Spring Ball as merely another move in the deadly game he was playing with the crystal thief. But suddenly it all became personal. Leona was his lover, damn it. Women were supposed to enjoy wearing spectacular gowns while they danced with their lovers.

Spectacular gowns. Of course. He should have understood immediately. Leona could not possibly afford a ball gown.

"I'm sure my aunt will see to an appropriate gown, if that is what you're worrying about," he said.

"As it happens, the dressmaker is due at any moment." She waved that aside. "The gown is the least of my concerns."

"Then what the devil are your concerns?"

"Lady Milden made it clear that the Spring Ball will be an important social event within the Society."

"Very important. You could call it a command performance."

"In which case," she concluded grimly, "we must assume that many of the investors in my uncle's investment scheme will be present."

"Ah, so that is the problem." He settled back in his chair, relaxing a little. It was not the fact that he would be her escort that alarmed her; it was her fear of being recognized as Pipewell's niece. That he could deal with.

"Rest assured, you have nothing to worry about," he said.

"Are you mad? Two years ago I worked crystals for all those investors. If I am recognized, someone will surely summon the police. Think of your own reputation, if you will not consider mine. Lady Milden says that you are a Jones."

"Mother's side."

"I'm sure your family would be appalled

if your name were to appear in the press in connection with mine."

He laughed. "It would take a good deal more than that to appall my family."

"Thaddeus, I am very serious about this."

"You told me that when you were with your uncle you were always careful to wear a heavy veil and conduct your appointments in darkened rooms."

"Uncle Edward always said that people prefer a bit of mystery."

"He's probably right, but I suspect that having you wear a widow's costume was his way of trying to protect you in case there was trouble."

She blinked, briefly sidetracked by that possibility. "I never thought of it that way."

"No doubt because your uncle never mentioned that there might be a very practical reason why you would need to remain anonymous."

She sighed. "I suppose he might have had some concerns along those lines."

"None of the investors saw your face, though, correct?"

"That is correct."

He widened his hands. "In that case, there is no reason to worry that anyone will recognize you at the ball. To be frank, I doubt that there would be a problem, even if your clients had seen you during those sessions."

"How can you say that?" she asked, bewildered.

He smiled. "People see what they expect to see. You would not be recognized for the simple reason that it would never dawn on anyone that Pipewell's niece would have the nerve to appear at the Spring Ball on the arm of the nephew of one of his most prominent victims."

"What?"

"You will recall Lord Trenoweth? The gentleman who first became suspicious of Pipewell and sounded the alarm that ignited the scandal?"

"Good heavens. Your *uncle?*"

"On my mother's side."

"Good grief." Staggered, she collapsed back into the corner of the sofa. "My uncle relieved Trenoweth of several thousand pounds."

"Taking the positive view, which, I have been assured, is always the best course of action, he was well able to sustain the loss. My uncle is a wealthy man. Pipewell hit his pride a lot harder than his bank account."

She lowered her face into her hands. "I don't know what to say."

"Say you'll allow me to escort you to the Spring Ball."

Slowly she raised her head, eyes narrowing. "Why are you so determined that I attend the ball?"

He leaned forward and folded his arms on the desk. "I will admit that when my aunt mentioned it this morning, it was not at the top of my list of priorities. But I have since changed my mind."

"Why?"

"Because it may help us recover the aurora stone."

For an instant she looked as if she had just been struck by lightning.

"Thaddeus." She leaped to her feet and swept across the room. Flattening her hands on the surface of his desk, she leaned forward, eyes brilliant with excitement. "Attending the Spring Ball is part of your plan to find the crystal? How?"

He lounged back in his chair again, enjoying the gentle wash of her highly stimulated aura. It aroused him in ways he could not even begin to describe.

"I have just come from speaking with Caleb, a man who can weave patterns from strands of chaos. Some say he does it to a fault. Be that as it may, it is his talent."

"Yes, yes, go on."

"He has done a great deal of research in recent days. As you know, the stone has traded owners many times during the past two hundred years, but there was always, according to Caleb, a pattern."

"What sort of pattern?"

"First, all those who have had possession of the stone have also had some connection to the Arcane Society."

"Of course. No one who is not aware of its history would be likely to know the legend."

"Right. In addition, those who have gone after the stone in the past have all been obsessive collectors."

"Or members of my family," she said very deliberately.

He inclined his head. "Or members of your family. The point is that they have all been individuals operating very much on their own. This time Caleb feels that the situation is quite different."

Comprehension sparked in her face. "Because so many people have died?"

"In part, yes. But also because, until now, Delbridge has never resorted to murder to acquire the antiquities that he covets."

"As far as you know."

"As far as we know," he agreed. "What we do know is that Delbridge is now willing to kill for the crystal even though there is no indication he can access its power."

"So the question becomes why does he

want this particular relic so badly, is that it?"

"Yes. Caleb is convinced that there is something more important at stake. He believes that the affair of the aurora stone may be connected to another attempt to steal the Society's darkest secret, a formula invented by Sylvester Jones."

"I see."

"Until recently the elixir was only a legend, but a few months ago Sylvester's tomb was excavated and the formula was discovered inside."

"Good heavens," she whispered, evidently quite awed. "I had no idea."

He felt the hair stir on the nape of his neck. Clamping his hands around the arms of the chair, he pushed himself to his feet and went to look out the window at the conservatory.

"Almost immediately after the formula was discovered, an attempt was made to steal it," he said. "Gabriel Jones and the lady who is now his bride foiled the scheme. At the time it was assumed that that was the end of the matter. And it was, at least as far as that incident was concerned. The madman who conceived the plot is dead."

"Is everyone quite certain of that?" Leona asked suspiciously.

"There is no doubt. Gabe and Venetia

both witnessed the death, but Caleb believes that Pandora's box has now been opened, so to speak. He fears that the near success of that first plot has inspired another."

"There is a certain logic to that line of thought, I suppose," she said. "But how could the aurora stone be connected to Sylvester's formula?"

He turned his head. She was watching him, transfixed.

"We don't know," he admitted. "The only thing of which Caleb is absolutely certain is that the members of this new conspiracy come from the highest ranks of the Arcane Society, men like Delbridge. It is no longer enough to stop him. We must discover the identities of the others."

Understanding lit her eyes. "And the highest-ranking members of the Society will all attend the first Spring Ball."

"That is the theory that Caleb and I are both going on at the moment, yes."

She frowned. "But how are we to identify them? If one of them had the crystal on his person, I would be able to detect it if I got close enough. But it seems unlikely that the thief would bring the aurora stone to a formal ball."

"I agree. It fits into the pocket of an overcoat, but it is too large to conceal in an evening coat. It would ruin the line."

She smiled faintly. "Spoken like a Jones."

"What?"

She glanced at the knot in his four-in-hand tie and then at his silver-and-onyx cuff links. "Uncle Edward once mentioned that the men of the Jones family were known for possessing a certain flair for style."

He shrugged. "It's in the blood. Our tailors love us. But to return to the topic under discussion. The goal will be to identify some of the others in the room besides Delbridge who are involved in this new conspiracy."

"How will you do that?"

"At some point during the evening, Gabriel Jones will rise and make a formal announcement to the effect that the aurora stone has just been returned to the Arcane Society. The stone is a great legend within the organization. The majority of those present will be thrilled to hear the news."

A slow smile curved her mouth. "But Delbridge and the others involved in its theft will no doubt panic."

"Panic creates its own unique kind of energy. It leaves a strong spore. There will be several trusted members of the Society present who are capable of sensing that kind of fear."

"What sort of talent confers that skill?"

"Several kinds, actually. Panic is one of the easiest emotions to detect because it is so powerful and so elemental. I can pick it up. You probably can, too, if you happen to be near someone who is in a state of panic. It is very difficult to conceal."

"What will you do if you succeed in identifying the other conspirators?" she asked.

"Some of the hunter talents will follow them and see where they go and what they do after the ball. Trust me, those involved in this affair will never know they are being trailed. With luck, one of the villains will lead us to the stone. Failing that, we will at least gain a great deal more information than we have now."

"In other words, the ball will be a trap for the conspirators."

"Yes," he said. "And you will be there to help us spring it. Now do you understand why it is important for you to attend the ball with me?"

Her shimmering excitement created so much energy in the atmosphere that Fog whined eagerly and thrust his nose into her hand.

Leona ruffled his fur, smiling her mysterious smile.

"I wouldn't miss it for the world," she said.

25

The commotion in the morning room reached all the way down the hall into the library. Madame LaFontaine, the dress-maker, was endowed with the grating, very carrying voice and the excruciatingly bad French accent of a woman who had probably emigrated from a neighborhood that was a lot closer to the docks than to Paris.

". . . *Non, non, non,* Miss Hewitt. Not the mushroom silk. *Absolument pas.* I forbid it. That is an excessively dull shade of gray, not at all suitable to your hair and eyes. Do you wish to fade into the woodwork?"

Thaddeus put down his pen and looked at Fog, who had taken refuge with him. The dog was at the window, gazing longingly out into the garden.

Thaddeus got to his feet. "I don't blame you for wanting to get out of the house. Come along with me."

Fog padded quickly after him, ears lowered against the booming voice.

"A hat with a veil? Have you gone mad, Miss Hewitt? One does not wear a veil in a ballroom, not with one of my gowns. Jeweled flowers only will I allow in the hair. Speaking of *les cheveux,* Maud, make a note. I will send Mr. Duquesne to dress Miss Hewitt's hair on the day of the ball. He, alone, can be trusted to create a style that is fashionable enough for one of my gowns."

Thaddeus smiled to himself. In spite of his reassurances, it sounded like Leona was doing her best to come up with a disguise for the Spring Ball. He had a feeling she was fighting a losing battle.

He opened the kitchen door and let Fog out into the garden. On his way back to the library he paused at the door of the morning room and watched the frenzied scene with some amusement. He had never seen Leona look so beleaguered, not even in the midst of fleeing from the scene of a murder.

Madame LaFontaine, a tiny, sharp-featured woman dressed in an elegantly draped dark blue gown, dominated the scene. Her diminutive size belied her formidable voice. She stood amid an array of fabric samples spread out on the carpet and strewn across the table, directing the actions of two harried assistants. In one hand she wielded a folded fan, waving it about as though conducting an orchestra.

"*Alors,* step away from the smoky satin, Miss Hewitt." Madame LaFontaine brought the fan down quite sharply across Leona's knuckles.

"*Ouch.*" Leona hastily dropped the swatch of gray satin.

"Madame LaFontaine is quite right," Victoria declared from the far end of the table. "You must stick to the jeweled tones."

"Quite right, Lady Milden." Madame LaFontaine bestowed an approving look on her and then whirled and pointed the fan at one of the assistants. "Bring me the amber silk. I believe it will complement Miss Hewitt's unusual eyes to perfection."

The swatch was produced and set out on the table. Victoria, looking more animated than Thaddeus had seen her in years, moved closer to consult with Madame LaFontaine. The pair pored over the amber-gold silk as though it were a treasure map.

"*Oui, parfait,*" Madam LaFontaine declared. "I will do it with the most elegant, the most delicate pouf of a bustle and, of course, a full train." She kissed her fingertips.

Leona looked toward the doorway at that moment and saw Thaddeus. He contemplated her desperate expression with a sense of satisfaction, gave her a small wave and went on down the hall. He was as eager to get out of the house as Fog.

He found a hansom on the street, stepped in and settled back to think about the intriguing new mystery that had occupied him for the past hour. It had come to light when he had explained to Leona that Caleb Jones believed they were dealing with a dangerous conspiracy to steal the founder's secret formula.

Leona had asked him a great many questions, but there was one very important one that she had not asked, one that any naturally curious person would have asked.

She had not inquired about the nature and properties of a formula so dangerous and so powerful that it could cause men to commit murder. He could only assume that was because she already knew the answer.

The truth about what the formula was intended to do was known to only a very few within the Society. The question of how Leona had come by that knowledge was tantalizing indeed.

26

"I have decided to become a consulting matchmaker," Victoria announced.

Thaddeus looked up from his salmon and potatoes. "What did you say?"

Victoria, seated halfway down the long table, fixed him with a challenging expression. "You heard me."

"I heard you," he agreed politely. "But I don't understand."

"I have concluded that the members of the Arcane Society require my special talents in order to form suitable marital alliances. Those possessed of strong abilities have a very difficult time with that sort of thing, you know. Take yourself, for instance."

Thaddeus looked at Leona, seeking enlightenment. "I think I am missing something in this conversation."

Leona smiled. "It is a brilliant idea. Your aunt has a talent for matchmaking."

"I see," he said.

"I am also well positioned to assist people in finding good matches," Victoria continued. "After all, I have been a member of the Arcane Society my entire life. Furthermore, I married into the Jones family. That means I have excellent connections throughout every level of the Society. I will be able to make inquiries about individuals to determine who should be introduced to whom."

"It is an interesting notion," Thaddeus said warily. "How do you plan to go about advertising your consulting services?"

"Word of mouth. Never fear, the news will get around very quickly."

"It certainly will," Thaddeus said, amused at the thought of what his mother would say when she learned of Victoria's plans.

"I will set up a registry of those seeking matches," Victoria said, excitement lighting her entire face. "I will conduct interviews and make notes. Miss Hewitt is convinced that I shall soon be overrun with clients."

He had not seen his aunt looking this enthusiastic about anything since his uncle's funeral. He had Leona to thank for the transformation. He smiled at her.

"I'm sure Miss Hewitt is right," he said. He turned back to Victoria. "Although I must admit that I never envisioned you setting yourself up in business, Aunt Vicky."

"Miss Hewitt has explained that people do not appreciate advice unless they pay for it."

He laughed. "Miss Hewitt would know."

27

Leona awoke with a start and lay still for a moment, willing the last fragments of the unpleasant dream to fade. Then she sat up slowly, trying to decide what had jarred her out of her restless sleep.

A soft growl sounded again from the shadows. She realized it was not the first time Fog had uttered the warning.

"What is it?" She pushed the covers aside and got to her feet. "What's wrong?"

Fog was at the window, forepaws braced on the sill, his head silhouetted in the moonlight. She went to join him. When she touched him she could feel the rigidly tense muscles beneath his fur.

Together they looked down into the garden. For a moment she could see nothing out of the ordinary. Then she noticed the flickering light. Someone was moving through the shrubbery. He held a dimly lit lantern in one hand. Her fingers stilled on Fog.

"An intruder," she said. "I must sound the alarm."

But just as she was about to turn away to rush toward the door, another figure emerged from the kitchens and walked swiftly to meet the figure with the lantern.

"It's Thaddeus," she said to Fog. "What on earth is going on?"

Down below the pair spoke briefly. The man with the lantern left the same way he had come, disappearing into the night. Thaddeus returned to the house.

She hurried to the bedroom door and opened it gently. Fog trotted eagerly after her and tried to stick his nose through the tiny opening. Footsteps, barely audible, echoed from the ground floor. Thaddeus had gone into the front hall.

She opened the door wider. Fog practically leaped out into the hall and dashed toward the stairs. She grabbed her robe off the hook and followed.

By the time she reached the top of the stairs, she could see Fog at the bottom, prancing excitedly around Thaddeus. Both were illuminated in the low light of a downstairs sconce. Thaddeus was dressed in the black linen shirt, black trousers, boots and long black coat that he had worn the night she encountered him in Delbridge's museum.

Alarm flashed through her. Clutching the lapels of her robe, she grabbed the banister in her right hand and rushed down. Thaddeus waited for her in the shadows at the foot of the staircase.

"I should have known I could not leave without arousing the dog and you, as well," he said.

"Where are you going at this hour?" She halted on the last step. "Who was that man in the garden? The one with the lantern?"

"You saw Pine?" He smiled and brushed her cheek with the back of his fingers. "You must not have been sleeping any more soundly than I was."

"Thaddeus, please, what is going on here?"

He dropped his hand. "I do not have time to explain. I promise I will tell you everything in the morning."

She sensed his determination and his urgency and knew that nothing she could say would stop him.

"I could come with you," she said quickly.

That startled him for an instant. Then he smiled wryly. "Yes, you could. But you will not."

"Take Fog, in that case."

"His job is to guard you. Do not worry about me, my sweet. I will be fine. I have had some experience in this sort of thing."

"Does this have something to do with your profession as an investigator?"

"Yes."

He leaned forward and kissed her somewhat ruthlessly, as if she belonged to him and he intended that she never forget that fact.

A moment later he was gone out into the night, closing the door behind him.

28

His real name was Foxcroft, but everyone had called him Red for so long, he doubted that anyone but his mother remembered. He was wiry, red-haired and cunning, having survived the city's roughest streets since birth. His instincts were well honed. From the start of his association with the man who awaited him in the alley, he had known that his employer was dangerous.

It had not been difficult to come to that conclusion. Any gentleman who was not afraid to conduct meetings in dark alleys in this part of town was either extremely dangerous or a complete fool. After their first encounter, some two years ago, Red had quickly determined that his employer was certainly no fool. That left only the other alternative.

Red paused within the weak circle of light cast by the street lamp and peered into the alley. He thought he sensed a presence there, but he could not be certain.

"Are ye here, sir?" he asked cautiously.

"Yes, Red, I'm here. I got your message. You have news?"

The voice always made him think of the distant thunder of a gathering storm, low and ominous. Red had never seen the gentleman's face and could not have described him. He did not know his name. But at night on the streets the man was known as The Ghost.

It gave Red cold chills sometimes to think that he might actually be working for a dead man, but there was no denying that, at least in this case, the dead paid a good deal better than the living, and Red had six mouths to feed at home.

"Aye, sir," he said. He moved out of the safety of the lamplight and closer to the black mouth of the alley. "They're saying in the tavern that there's another girl dead tonight and one gone missing last night."

There was a short silence from The Ghost. It lasted just long enough for Red to begin to wonder if the specter had melted away into the shadows.

"What are the names of the girls and where do they live?" The Ghost asked.

"The dead one is Bella Newport. They say her body is still where the Midnight Monster left it, in a basement below her room in Dalton Street. The man who found her was afraid to summon the police for fear they'd think he was the one who killed her. Her throat was cut, like the others."

"What of the other girl? The one who is missing?"

"Annie Spence. She works the street in front of the Falcon. The owner of the tavern says she was out in front beneath the street lamp all evening. Never brought any of her customers upstairs, though. He reckoned her business was just slow, like his. He closed early and went out to see if she was feeling like a bit of sport. But she was gone. He's very worried about her. Says it's not like her to go off with a customer."

"Did anyone notice either girl talking to a man earlier in the evening?"

"Can't say about Bella Newport. But the tavern owner told me that Annie had bragged about a gentleman who had been watching her off and on for the past few days. She thought he looked very elegant, but she said he seemed a bit shy when it came to approaching a girl."

"Thank you, Red."

A carriage appeared momentarily out of the light mist, then rolled past. Red kept his attention on the night-filled alley. He thought he caught the faintest shifting of shadows, but he couldn't be sure. The rattling of wheels and the clop of the horse's hooves masked any sound of footsteps, assuming there had been footsteps.

By the time the vehicle had once again vanished into the mist, Red knew that he was alone. He went forward slowly. Sure enough, the usual envelope was there on the paving stones. There would be money inside, enough perhaps to buy his wife a new bonnet. Bessie would be thrilled. She did not approve of his new career as an assistant to a ghost, but she was happy with the income.

He stuffed the plump envelope inside his coat and hurried away toward home. Once he was sipping hot tea and sitting in front of a warm fire he would be able to convince himself that he was not really working for a dead man.

There was no constable standing guard in front of the darkened, rundown building, no crowd gathered in the street. It appeared that Bella Newport's murder had not yet been reported to the police, although, with the rumors already flowing through the underworld, it would not be long. Thaddeus knew that he would not have much time.

He listened carefully, all his senses wide

open, making certain that he was alone in the street. He neither saw nor heard anything to indicate that there was anyone else about. No currents of energy stirred, at least none that he could detect.

Satisfied, he left the shadows of a stone doorway, gripped the iron railing and dropped down into the below-street-level front area of the old building. There was enough light from the street lamp above to reveal the debris and decaying leaves that had accumulated in the small space.

He heard a rustling, skittering sound. An instant later two rats, evidently annoyed at having been interrupted in their foraging, flashed up the steps and disappeared beneath the low edge of the railing.

The narrow windows designed to allow light and air into the below-stairs kitchens during the day were black and impenetrable at this hour. He tried the door handle with one gloved hand. It turned easily.

The stench of death struck him the instant he opened the door. He raised one arm to cover his nose and mouth with the sleeve of his coat.

He stood on the threshold for a moment, giving himself some time to become more accustomed to the dreadful atmosphere. After a few seconds he realized that none of the light from the street lamp penetrated the room through the windows.

He closed the door, struck a light and saw immediately why no illumination from outside passed through the glass. The windows were shrouded with the stained canvas that had once covered the kitchen floor. In addition, small squares had been cut out of the fabric and nailed over the glass panes set high in the door.

The murderer had made preparations before the kill. He had stalked his victim.

The body lay on the kitchen table, bound and gagged. Her blonde hair and faded gown were saturated in the blood that had spilled from the ghastly wound in her throat.

Thaddeus forced himself to move closer to what was left of Bella Newport. This was the first time he'd had an opportunity to examine one of the Midnight Monster's victims.

He was prepared for the fact that the woman had been murdered with a knife. Word had circulated that the other two victims had died in the same fashion. Knives were, after all, the weapon of choice for most in the criminal underworld. Unlike guns they were silent, efficient and easily obtained.

What he had not anticipated was the little pot of rouge on the table beside the body.

29

"You think Annie Spence was killed by the same man who murdered that poor woman we found in Delbridge's mansion?" Leona could scarcely believe what she had just heard. Then again, she reflected, she was still reeling from the shock of discovering that Thaddeus was investigating the murders perpetrated by the Midnight Monster.

Victoria stared at Thaddeus, openmouthed. "Are you saying that the Midnight Monster was invited to Delbridge's party? That he was a guest?"

"I do not know if he received an invitation." Thaddeus rubbed the back of his neck. "But I am quite certain that he was there that night. I'm also sure that he is the hunter I've been chasing these past few weeks."

It was shortly after five in the morning. They were gathered in the library. Leona and Victoria were in their dressing gowns. One of the cooks who had risen to start the preparations for breakfast had sent in a tray of tea and toast. Leona could not help but notice that the staff appeared unfazed by what would have been perceived as decidedly odd behavior in other households.

Thaddeus was the only one who was not seated. He stood at the window, still dressed in his black shirt, trousers and boots. A restless energy shimmered invisibly in the air around him. Fog had sensed it the moment he had walked through the door a short time ago. The dog now hovered near Thaddeus, pacing when Thaddeus paced.

"Remember that rouge pot beside the body in the gallery, Leona?" Thaddeus asked. "You kicked it with the toe of your shoe."

She frowned. "I remember kicking some object when I tried to break free of your grasp —" She stopped suddenly, aware that Victoria was looking at her with a fascinated expression. Hastily she cleared her throat. "I meant to say, I recall my toe striking some small object. You picked it up, but I never saw what it was."

"A rouge pot." He went back to the desk and held up a little white porcelain pot decorated with tiny pink roses. "The one I found next to Bella Newport's body tonight looked very similar to it."

They all contemplated the rouge pot. Victoria turned back to Thaddeus.

"What is so unusual about a rouge pot?" she asked. "You said that poor girl was a prostitute. Everyone knows that women of that sort use cosmetics."

Thaddeus frowned. "Women of that sort? Are you telling me that only prostitutes use them?"

Victoria looked at Leona.

Leona cleared her throat. "Actresses also employ cosmetics."

"And Frenchwomen, of course," Victoria added with a judicious air. "An English lady, however, uses only the most delicate of beauty aids. One may bathe one's face in a gentle bath of purest rainwater infused with a few slices of cucumber or lemon, but that is all."

"Well, one might occasionally apply a wholesome lotion made of cream and egg whites to the skin," Leona offered.

"But never anything as vulgar as rouge," Victoria concluded firmly.

Thaddeus planted his hands on his hips. "I don't believe this. Are you two going to sit there and tell me the rosy blush one sees on the lips and cheeks of every lady in a ballroom is due to daily baths of rainwater and cucumbers?"

"The ladies' magazines do provide some

hints for achieving that youthful glow," Victoria conceded. "The merest trace of artifice, you understand."

"What hints?" Thaddeus demanded.

Leona leaned forward to pour more tea into her cup. "One is advised to bite one's lips and pinch one's cheeks quite vigorously before one enters a room."

Thaddeus looked grim and irritated. "This is all rubbish, and well you know it. The makers of cosmetics and beauty aids do very nicely in England. Do not try to tell me that they are making their fortunes selling their products solely to actresses, prostitutes and the occasional French tourist."

Leona sipped her tea, silently deferring to Victoria.

"Very well, Thaddeus," Victoria said, tight-lipped. "I will allow that, in truth, there are a great many rouge pots sitting on the dressing tables of England. But you must not breathe a word about that outside this room. Do you understand?"

Leona hid a smile. "The reputations of the women of England are in your hands, sir."

Thaddeus shoved his fingers through his hair. "I can't believe all this nonsense about whether or not a woman uses cosmetics."

Victoria gave him a repressive glare. "What respectable women may or may not do in the privacy of their bedrooms is not the point. What I am trying to make clear is that the use of cosmetics is considered quite vulgar."

Leona pondered that observation and then looked at Victoria. "If a killer wanted to make a point about his victim being a prostitute, he might leave a rouge pot behind at the scene."

Victoria nodded. "Yes, it would be a symbolic way of accusing her of being a streetwalker."

The lines at the corners of Thaddeus's eyes tightened a little. "In Bella Newport's case, he did more than just leave the pot behind. He applied a great deal of the paint to her face."

Victoria stared at him aghast. "The murderer put rouge on her cheeks? Are you sure it wasn't the victim, herself, who did it before her death?"

"I could see where the Monster was forced to wipe away some of the blood before he applied the rouge," Thaddeus said quietly.

"Good lord." Victoria shuddered.

Leona frowned. "What of the woman in Delbridge's museum?"

"I cannot say in her case," Thaddeus admitted. "The light was very poor, if you will recall, and I did not have an opportunity to examine the body." He studied the little pot he held. "But given that this rouge was at the scene, I think we can now be reasonably certain that whoever murdered that woman is the Midnight Monster."

"A guest in Lord Delbridge's house." Victoria shook her head, amazed. "But why would he do such a thing? There is no logic to such an action."

"There is no logic to slaughtering prostitutes," Thaddeus pointed out. "I suspect that he enjoys the business. Perhaps the rouge pots at the scene are his way of leaving a signature."

"The man must be insane," Leona whispered.

"Mad, perhaps," Thaddeus agreed, "but not dim-witted. He is clever, and he manages to keep to the shadows."

"If Caleb Jones is right, and the Monster is a hunter, it is no wonder he has been able to avoid detection," Victoria observed.

Thaddeus continued to study the little pot. "A hunter who, for one night, it seems, selected different prey. The question is, why would he change his pattern?"

Leona raised her brows. "You refer to the dead woman in Delbridge's gallery?"

"Yes." Thaddeus leaned back against the side of the desk. "Whatever else she was, the woman we found was not a common streetwalker. She was a fashionable and no doubt expensive member of her profession. What is even more interesting is that my friend at Scotland Yard tells me that her murder has not yet been reported to the police."

"Delbridge is concealing the crime," Leona said.

"Murder will out," Victoria quoted softly.

"Not, it appears, in this case," Leona said.

"Not yet, at any rate," Thaddeus corrected. He looked at Victoria. "We need more information, and we need it quickly. I could use an assistant, Aunt Vicky."

Victoria's eyes widened. "You want my help in your investigation?"

"If you are willing," Thaddeus said. "I'm quite certain there will be no danger involved."

An unfamiliar animation lit Victoria's normally stern face. "I would be delighted to help bring this dreadful killer to justice. But what can I do?"

"You clearly know a great deal about cosmetics. I want you to go on a shopping expedition this morning to see if you can locate the establishment that sold this rouge pot. It is obviously quite expensive. That should shorten the list of shops that might sell such items."

"Yes, it will," Victoria said, still looking somewhat dazed. "Indeed, I can think of only a handful of places that sell such fine cosmetics."

"What about me?" Leona said to Thaddeus. "I'm certainly not going to sit around here waiting for my fitting while you and your aunt investigate."

He smiled. "You and I are going to pay a couple of visits to certain individuals today. The first one, I think, has met the killer and will be able to give me a detailed description of him."

"Really? That would be wonderful. Who is it?"

"Someone you know rather well."

She stared in disbelief. "I am acquainted with a person who has met the Midnight Monster?"

"I'm afraid so," Thaddeus said.

30

"Now, see here, Mrs. Ravenglass, I've told you before, you can't bring that dog into my shop." Dr. Wagner Goodhew leaped to his feet behind his desk, nervously watching Fog. "It isn't sanitary."

"Perhaps not," Leona said. She smiled behind the black veil of her hat. "But I have discovered that, thanks to the poor quality of the clients you have been sending to me lately, I require some physical protection."

Fog, unaware that he had been insulted, settled down on the floor, paws outstretched, and studied Goodhew with an unwavering gaze.

Thaddeus entered the premises behind Leona and Fog. He now stood nearby, wrapped in his invisible cloak of stillness and shadows, and contemplated the doctor with an expression that, in Leona's opinion, bore a remarkable resemblance to Fog's. Both looked as though they would enjoy nothing more than going for Goodhew's throat.

Goodhew noticed Thaddeus for the first time.

"My apologies, sir," he said quickly. "I didn't see you standing there. I expect you've come to inquire about the special sale on Goodhew's Vital Elixir for Men. I'll be right with you."

"No hurry," Thaddeus said. He infused his voice with just a touch of energy, enough to fill the room with a sensation of impending doom. *"I'm with the lady."*

Goodhew went quite pale. He pulled himself together with a visible effort and swung back toward Leona. "What's this about the quality of the clients?"

"We have an agreement, Dr. Goodhew," she said crisply. "Your side of the bargain includes ascertaining that the people you send to me are legitimate clients in need of my crystal-working services. In return you receive a rather hefty referral fee from me. But the gentleman you sent to me the day before yesterday, Mr. Morton, seemed to believe that I am in a somewhat different line of work."

Goodhew bridled. His gaze shifted uneasily from Fog to Thaddeus. "I have no idea what you're talking about."

She took two steps closer to the desk. "Just

how did Morton gain the impression that I might be agreeable to providing certain *therapies* designed to relieve congestion of the masculine nervous system?"

The instant she moved, Fog surged to his feet, growling softly. Goodhew started visibly and jumped back. He came up hard against the wall.

"I have no idea what you're talking about," he said forcefully. "If Morton made certain assumptions, that is not my fault."

"On the contrary," Leona said, "he specifically stated that you had diagnosed his dreams as the products of a congestion of certain masculine fluids which, in turn, created stress on his nerves and caused disturbing dreams."

"I'm sure he simply misunderstood."

"He said you promised him an hour of private therapy in an *intimate* setting."

"Well? Isn't that how you perform your crystal work, madam? Privately and in an intimate setting?"

"You know very well that you deliberately gave Morton the wrong idea of what to expect from a consultation. What's more, you charged him extra for my *special services.*"

"Now, see here, business has been slow of late, you know that, Mrs. Ravenglass."

"What does that have to do with marketing me as a prostitute?"

Goodhew spread his hands. "I was trying to be creative."

"*Creative?* You were assuming the role of a brothel keeper."

"Morton had no luck with my Vital Elixir for Men, and, to be frank, he was not at all keen on trying your crystal therapy. Didn't have any faith in psychical nonsense, he said. I would have lost him as a client altogether if I hadn't come up with an innovative concept. I gave him no specific reason to expect other than some crystal work for his dreams."

"Mr. Morton most certainly expected something more."

"That is not my fault."

"In that case, why did you charge him extra?"

Goodhew drew himself up and squared his shoulders. "I did it for both our sakes. I thought it time to increase our prices. I fully intended to give you half of the additional fees I collected."

"Rubbish. You never even intended for me to find out that you were charging the higher fees. How many other clients have you diagnosed with masculine congestion?"

"Calm yourself, Mrs. Ravenglass." Goodhew flapped his hands. "I only recently hit upon the notion of sending such clients to you, and I assure you that I only refer those gentlemen who do not first have success with my elixir."

She took another step closer to the desk. "How many others, Goodhew?"

He cleared his throat, loosened his tie and glanced uneasily at Thaddeus. "Hardly any."

"How many?"

Goodhew seemed to cave in on himself. "Two. Morton was the first. The second gentleman's appointment is for today."

Thaddeus stirred and walked toward the desk in a deceptively leisurely manner. "Show us your appointment book, Goodhew."

Goodhew scowled. "Why?"

"Because I want to find out how many more clients with erotic dreams induced by masculine congestion I can expect to see in my consulting rooms," Leona said coldly.

"I told you, there is only one other appointment of that nature." Goodhew edged warily back to his desk, reached down and flipped open a leather-bound journal. "See for yourself. I told you, it has been a very slow week."

Thaddeus spun the appointment book around with a quick twist of his wrist. Together he and Leona looked down at the page that covered the week. There were three appointments for ladies but only two for men, Morton's and one other.

Thaddeus pinned Goodhew with a cold-eyed look. "Are these the only two men you have referred to Mrs. Ravenglass in the past week?"

"Yes, yes, just the two," Goodhew muttered.

Thaddeus pointed toward the square marked WEDNESDAY. "When did Smith make his appointment?"

"The day before yesterday."

"Morning or afternoon?" Thaddeus asked.

Goodhew hesitated. "Midmorning, I believe. See here, what does it signify?"

Thaddeus ignored the question. "Describe the client."

Goodhew raised both of his thin shoulders in an elaborate shrug. "Late twenties. Light-colored hair. Very elegant. The sort of gentleman women would find quite handsome, I believe." He glowered at Leona. "There was nothing objectionable about him, I assure you."

"Tell me about his clothing," Thaddeus said.

"Expensive," Goodhew snapped.

"Was his coat light or dark?"

"I don't recall."

"Was he wearing any jewelry? Rings? A stickpin?"

Goodhew assumed a mulish expression. "See here, you can't expect me to remember so many details about a client who was only in this office for a few minutes."

"Yes, Goodhew," Thaddeus said, each word he uttered now riding a current of mesmerizing power. *"You will remember every detail about the client who called himself Mr. Smith."*

Leona shivered as if she had brushed up against a ghost. Thaddeus was not aiming his talents at her, but she nevertheless sensed the energy swirling in the atmosphere. So did Fog. He whined softly and never took his eyes off Goodhew.

Behind his desk, Goodhew turned into a human statue. He stared into the middle distance. All traces of emotion vanished from his expression.

"I remember," he said tonelessly.

Relentless, Thaddeus took him through a detailed description of Mr. Smith. By the time he finished, Leona knew there could no longer be any doubt. From the pale blond hair to the walking stick, he matched the description of the man Mrs. Cleeves had glimpsed briefly in Vine Street. Goodhew, having viewed Smith from a closer vantage point, was able to offer more details.

". . . a large onyx ring set in silver on his right hand," he droned.

". . . walking stick has a silver handle carved in the shape of a hawk's head . . ."

". . . very pale gray-blue eyes . . ."

When the interrogation was finished Thaddeus looked at Leona. His own eyes still burned hot and fathomless. Leona got the feeling that if she looked too long into the fire she would not be able to resist walking into the flames.

"He went to your consulting rooms in Marigold Lane and kept watch until you left the premises," Thaddeus said. "Then he followed you home and waited for an opportunity to search the house."

She shuddered. "The man enjoys killing. Fog was no doubt the only thing that stopped him from coming in while Mrs. Cleeves and I were inside. If it had not been for him —"

She broke off, unwilling to finish the sentence.

They both looked at Fog who regarded them, in turn, with an expression of polite inquiry.

Leona ruffled his fur and then turned back to Thaddeus. "Do you think Mr. Smith really is the Midnight Monster?"

"There is no doubt in my mind." Thaddeus turned toward the door. "Come. We must be off to our next appointment. It is critical that we learn the name of the dead woman we found in Delbridge's museum."

Leona glanced at the motionless man behind the desk. "What about Dr. Goodhew?"

"What of him?" Thaddeus opened the front door of the shop. "He can stand there until hell freezes over as far as I'm concerned."

"You can't leave him like that, Thaddeus. How long will the spell last?"

The heat in his eyes, which had begun to cool, blazed hot once again.

"It's not a spell, damn it," he said.

The harsh response caught her off guard.

"I'm sorry," she said, hurrying toward the door with Fog. "I didn't mean to offend you."

He looked at her as if he could see straight through the heavy netting of her veil.

"I'm not a sorcerer," Thaddeus said evenly.

"Of course not," she agreed. "There is no such thing as sorcery. I used the term *spell* in a metaphoric sense."

"I would prefer that you not use it in any sense," he ground out. "Not in reference to me. I'm a hypnotist, a very powerful hypnotist to be sure, but my talents are psychical in nature, not supernatural."

"Yes, I know, but —"

He angled his chin at the frozen man. "There is nothing magical about hypnosis. I used my talents to temporarily neutralize his senses. A number of practitioners can do it to varying degrees. While in that state the subject is susceptible to suggestion, but there is no sorcery involved. It is purely a matter of manipulating certain currents."

She suddenly understood.

"Rest assured that you are not the only one who has suffered from accusations of dabbling in the occult," she said quietly. "When I was in business in Little Tickton I was lectured more than once by a member of the clergy on the evils of my ways and strongly advised to give up my profession. In previous generations, the women in my family were often forced to practice their skills in secret or risk being arrested and burned at the stake. More than one had to flee for her life from some overzealous fanatic who thought he had been appointed by God to rid the world of witches and sorceresses. Even today, even within the Society, there are those who consider crystal workers little better than carnival entertainers."

He stood there, tense and still for another few seconds, and then the tension seemed to ebb from him. His eyes cooled.

"Yes," he said. "You understand. You have always understood, right from the beginning. Come, let us be on our way."

She cleared her throat. "You really must not leave Dr. Goodhew in that condition, Thaddeus. What if he doesn't return to his senses? What if someone walks in and believes him to be the victim of a stroke or a paralytic fit?" A horrifying thought struck her. "Good heavens, what if people think he's *dead.* Except that he's still *alive?* There are tales about that sort of thing, ghastly stories about people being accidentally buried alive because everyone thought they were dead."

He startled her again with his quick, wolfish grin. "Has anyone ever told you that you have an excellent imagination?"

She winced. "The result of channeling other people's dreams for so long, I suppose. Thaddeus, I have no great fondness for Dr. Goodhew, but I really do not think we should leave him in a trance. He is helpless."

"Calm yourself, madam. If I do not give specific instructions regarding the termination of the trance, the mesmeric effects fade away within a matter of hours. The thing about hypnosis, even psychically enhanced hypnosis, is that eventually the compulsion always wears off. It can be quite annoying in cases like this."

"Release him," she ordered, losing patience. "He is too vulnerable in that state. What if a thief came into his shop?"

Thaddeus's mouth twitched. "Very well. I can't imagine that there are a great many thieves running around London who are in need of a year's supply of Goodhew's Vital Elixir for Men. Nevertheless, if it will put your mind at ease, I will release him."

"Thank you."

Thaddeus's voice rolled softly through the room, filling it with the endless power of a great sea. *"Goodhew, you will awaken when the clock strikes a quarter past the hour. Do you understand?"*

"Yes," Goodhew said.

Thaddeus took Leona's arm and escorted her out onto the front steps.

She glanced back over her shoulder. "Will he remember what he told us while in the trance?"

"No, not unless I return and instruct him to remember." Thaddeus smiled again, this time with amused satisfaction. "But rest assured he will most certainly recall that you were very annoyed about the type of clients he had begun to refer to you. And I do not think he will forget Fog anytime soon."

She sighed. "It appears that, what with one thing and another, I shall be requiring a new referral agent when this affair is concluded. I am going to be very short of clients for a while."

31

At three o'clock that afternoon they arrived for their appointment in Bluegate Square. Fog no longer accompanied them, having been left to his own devices in the Ware gardens.

They were ushered into a large library decorated in the latest fashion. Dark red velvet drapes were tied back from tall windows with gold cords. The floor was covered in a red, blue and gold carpet decorated with an elaborate floral design. The wallpaper was a finely striped design picked out in the same colors.

Adam Harrow lounged with languid elegance on the corner of a vast, highly polished desk.

Mr. Pierce sat behind the desk. He was not tall, but there was a square, solid look about him that would not have seemed out of place on the docks. His black hair was shot with the first hints of silver. He regarded Leona and Thaddeus with brilliant blue eyes.

Sprawled on the carpet in front of the fire was a massive hound. Leona had explained to Thaddeus that the beast was the primary reason why Fog could not accompany them. Caesar did not tolerate the presence of other dogs on his territory.

He got to his feet with an air of aging royalty and walked stiffly forward to greet the newcomers.

"Hello, Caesar." Leona rubbed his ears respectfully with one gloved hand.

Caesar turned to Thaddeus, who repeated the greeting. Satisfied, the big dog returned to his place in front of the fire and settled back down.

Mr. Pierce was on his feet behind the desk.

"Miss Hewitt," he said in his brandy-and-cigar voice. "A pleasure as always."

Leona smiled warmly. "Thank you so much for seeing us today, Mr. Pierce."

"Of course. Please sit down." He inclined his head toward Thaddeus. "Ware."

"Pierce." Thaddeus returned the brusque, masculine nod and then did the same with Adam Harrow. "Mr. Harrow."

Adam's mouth curved in a bored, humorless smile. "Why is it that every time I turn around lately, I find you underfoot, Ware?"

"Coincidence is an odd force," Thaddeus said.

Adam looked pained. "I do not believe in coincidence any more than do the members of your Arcane Society."

Thaddeus smiled slightly. "In that case, I can only hope that you will not feel it necessary to take more drastic steps to get rid of me."

Pierce's brows rose in amusement. "I have a hunch that making you disappear would require considerable effort, sir."

But probably not an entirely unfamiliar sort of effort, Thaddeus thought. "I will do my best to avoid putting you to the trouble," he said.

Pierce chuckled. "I think we understand each other very well, indeed, sir. Please take a seat."

The door of the library opened soundlessly. A young footman appeared with a tea tray. He set it down on a low table and looked at Pierce.

"Thank you, Robert," Pierce said. "That will be all."

Thaddeus studied the delicate line of Robert's jaw and the curve of his calf outlined by the snug-fitting livery. The footman was another female in men's clothing, like the butler who had escorted them into the library. Pierce's entire household appeared to be composed of women living as men.

Pierce looked at Leona. "Will you do the honors?"

"Of course." Leona leaned forward and picked up the teapot.

Adam slipped off the corner of the desk and began to hand around the teacups as Leona filled them. When she gave a cup to Pierce, Thaddeus noticed the subtle air of intimacy that imbued the small, prosaic gesture. When he had seen the pair together for the first time he had been almost sure that they were lovers. Today he was certain of his conclusion.

"Now, then," Pierce said, "I have the guest list for Delbridge's party, as you requested. Forgive my curiosity, but before I give the names to you I must ask why you require them."

Leona set down the teapot. "We are hoping that the name of the woman whose body we found that night will be on that list."

"Yes, Adam told me about her." Pierce frowned. "If you do not even know her name, why are you pursuing an inquiry into her death?"

Thaddeus settled back into his chair. "I have reason to believe that whoever killed her is the same person who recently murdered at least two prostitutes."

Adam stared at him, astonished. "Do you refer to that fiend the press is calling the Midnight Monster?"

"Yes," Thaddeus said. "I have been engaged by the Arcane Society to find the murderer."

Pierce looked intrigued. "And why does the Society care about these murders?"

"We have reason to believe that the killer possesses certain dangerous abilities that will make it difficult for the police to catch him."

"I see." Pierce was not particularly impressed. "And the Society feels an obligation to hunt down this killer, is that it? How very noble."

"It is not an entirely altruistic endeavor," Thaddeus said dryly. "The Society is concerned, of course, that his talents may allow the killer to operate unhindered by the authorities indefinitely. But it also fears that, if and when the police do apprehend him, the paranormal aspects of his nature may be revealed to the press. The newspapers and penny dreadfuls would create a great sensation, one that could have lasting effects on public opinion."

"Ah, yes, I understand now." Pierce nodded once, satisfied. "You fear the results of such a revelation."

"By and large, the public views the whole business of the paranormal with either skepticism or deep curiosity," Thaddeus said. "At worst, it considers those who claim to possess strong talents as frauds. At best, they are seen as providers of controversial medical cures or merely as entertainers."

Adam settled one hip on the corner of the desk again. "But if it got out that the Midnight Monster possessed some very dangerous paranormal talents, the public's attitude could become extremely hostile. People might well turn on all those who claim to possess psychical abilities, including those who happen to be endowed with genuine powers."

"The Arcane Society would naturally prefer that did not happen," Thaddeus said mildly.

Pierce and Adam exchanged looks of intimate understanding.

"It is quite true that the public can make life very difficult for those who do not conform to what is considered to be the respectable norm," Pierce said quietly.

"Will you help us?" Leona asked.

"I will give you the list." Pierce opened a drawer in the desk and withdrew a sheet of paper.

Thaddeus rose from his chair and picked up the paper. He glanced at the names. "I will not ask how you came by this list."

Pierce shrugged. "I don't mind telling you. There was no great trick to it. On the occasions when Delbridge entertains, he employs a secretary who happens to be a friend of my own secretary."

Leona smiled. "It is a small world."

Adam grinned. "It certainly is when one is dealing with the world of private secretaries employed by the elite. Their circles are even smaller and tighter than those of their employers."

Thaddeus studied the list. "The majority of these names are those of Delbridge's male guests. The Midnight Monster may well be among them. But at the moment, I wish to concentrate on the women. I see that there are a dozen of them."

"All expensive ladies of the night," Pierce said.

"One of them will no longer be among the living," Thaddeus observed. "Although the murder has not been reported, I would expect that some of the other women on this list might have noticed her absence. The world of exclusive courtesans is also quite small."

Pierce leaned back in his chair. "I do not

know whether it is of any importance, but there is one woman who may well have been there that night who is not on that list."

Thaddeus looked up at that. "Who?"

"Delbridge's mistress. I have seen the two of them together at the theater. We have not been introduced, but she is extraordinarily beautiful. No one knows much about her. There are rumors, however."

"What sort of rumors?" Leona asked.

"It is said that she was once an actress. In addition, I have heard gossip that she is not particularly faithful to Delbridge."

Leona glanced at Thaddeus. "The dead woman in the gallery apparently had an assignation planned that night."

"I have heard that Delbridge's mistress has engaged in a number of brief affairs while she has been under his protection. All were with gentlemen who collected antiquities."

Thaddeus looked at him. "And Delbridge has a penchant for stealing those relics that he cannot acquire by other means. I wonder if he was in the habit of using his mistress to gain access to the collections of some of his rivals."

"It would not be the first time a man has used a beautiful woman to achieve his objectives," Pierce said.

"Delbridge might not have bothered to

send a formal invitation to his mistress because he planned to escort her, himself," Leona offered.

"Or perhaps her name was left off the invitation list because Delbridge knew in advance that she would not survive the night," Thaddeus said quietly. "In case of an investigation he did not want any formal record of her presence in the mansion that evening."

They left the house a short time later. A hired carriage waited for them in the street. Thaddeus handed Leona up into the cab. The skirts of her deep violet gown whispered past his arm. He caught a tantalizing glimpse of one delicately curved, stocking-clad leg. It vanished quickly beneath a flurry of petticoat ruffles. Memories of the interlude in the conservatory seared his senses. Everything inside him clenched tight.

He followed Leona into the cab, closed the door and sat down across from her. He watched her adjust the elaborate folds and flounces of her skirts.

"I can understand why a lady might find it comfortable and convenient at times to wear men's clothes," he said. "But speaking from a man's point of view, I must tell you that there is a great deal to be said for the sight of a woman in a gown."

Leona smiled coolly. "Speaking from a woman's point of view, I can assure you that there is a great deal to be said for having the choice."

The carriage rumbled forward. Thaddeus looked back at Pierce's handsome townhouse. "I have the impression that the women in Pierce's life have all chosen to give up the option of wearing gowns and petticoats in favor of living their lives in men's clothes."

"You noticed that the servants were all female?" Leona asked, startled.

"Yes."

"How could you tell?"

He shrugged. "Once you start to question the obvious, you begin to look beneath the surface."

Leona followed his gaze to the front door of the townhouse. "The fascinating thing is that very few people do look beneath the surface. Mr. Pierce and Adam and their close associates at the Janus Club go about as men on a regular basis, and no one ever seems to notice."

"It is not the fact that they are all women disguised as men that intrigues me," Thaddeus said.

"What does intrigue you?"

He smiled and stretched out one leg, letting it brush against her violet skirts as though by accident.

"It is the thought of the reaction of all the gentlemen presently nursing their brandies and cigars in their St. James Street clubs if they were to learn that one of the wealthiest, most mysterious criminal lords in London is a female."

32

A feverish thrill of excitement swept through Delbridge when he walked into the hushed chamber. He had waited for this moment for months.

The ancient stone room was windowless. Power as heavy and as ominous as the fog outside pooled within the four walls.

The aura of menacing energy was not a product of his imagination. His own senses were wide open, registering the strong paranormal currents that swirled in the chamber. They emanated from the five men seated at the large, horseshoe-shaped table. Each possessed a high degree of talent.

He did not yet know the identities of any of the men. The five members of the Third Circle of the shadowy conspiracy known to him only as the Order of the Emerald Tablet wore cowled robes embroidered with cryptic alchemical designs. The hoods of the robes were pulled up so that each man's face was cast in deep shadow. Beneath the hoods, each man wore a half mask. Four of the masks were silver. The fifth, that of the leader, was gold.

"Good afternoon, Lord Delbridge," the leader said. His eyes glittered through the openings of the mask. "The members of the Third Circle of the Order of the Emerald Tablet look forward to receiving your offering."

Delbridge's blood beat heavily in his veins. They both knew that the crystal wasn't an offering; it was his initiation fee. He had accomplished the task these men had set him. He had proven his worthiness to sit among them.

"I have brought the aurora stone to you, as you asked," Delbridge said.

He sensed the sudden greed and — there was no other word for it — lust that flared in the chamber. He had known from the start of this affair that the five wanted the crystal very badly. With luck he would finally discover just why the stone was so important to them.

"You may present your gift to the Third Circle," the leader intoned.

With a small flourish, Delbridge removed the velvet pouch from his coat pocket. There was an audible murmur of excitement from the members.

Savoring the moment, he walked into the curve of the table and set the pouch in front of the leader.

"With my compliments," he said.

The gold mask glinted again when the leader picked up the pouch. Delbridge and the others watched him untie the cord and withdraw the stone. He placed the crystal on the table. It sat there, dull and unprepossessing in the dim light.

There was a short, uncertain silence.

"Doesn't look like much," one of the men commented.

A little jolt of anxiety touched Delbridge's nerves. It was the right crystal. It had to be. He had risked everything, most importantly his position in Society, to obtain it for them. If it ever got out that he had joined forces with a mad scientist and a cold-blooded killer in order to gain entrance to a secret club he would be ruined. Given his wealth and his connections he might avoid prison, but the scandal would haunt him to the end of his days.

The leader picked up the stone and held it in the palm of his hand. Beneath the edge of his mask, his thin lips curved with satisfaction. "I can feel its power."

"Many crystals have power," grumbled

one of the Order members. "How do we know it's the stone we require?"

The leader rose. "By putting it to the test, of course."

When he crossed the stone floor, steel clanked lightly on steel, as though he wore old-fashioned armor beneath the thick robes. A shiver ruffled the hair on the nape of Delbridge's neck. He wondered if the leader carried a sword. That possibility made him swallow hard. Intuition warned him that this group would not take failure well.

They could not murder him outright if the crystal did not do whatever it was they expected it to do, he assured himself. He was Lord Delbridge. His family connections were impeccable. He moved in some of the best circles of society.

Yes, and he had recently set the Midnight Monster on two other gentlemen who had possessed excellent connections. He had gotten away with murder. Who was to say these men could not perform a similar feat?

Calm yourself. You have given them what they demanded, the real aurora stone. You will soon be one of them.

The leader halted in front of a low, vaulted door in the ancient stone wall, reached inside his long robes and produced a key. That explained the clanking noise, Delbridge thought. The leader wore a steel chatelaine with a number of keys on it beneath his gown, not a sword. That realization came as a distinct relief.

"Yes, the test," one of the men hissed, jumping to his feet. "If it unlocks the strongbox we will know immediately if Lord Delbridge has brought us the right stone."

The others followed quickly. For a moment Delbridge thought that he had been forgotten, but the leader turned once more to look at him, pinning him with his cold gaze.

"Come with us, sir. You will witness the results of your efforts together with the rest of us."

Do not show any fear, Delbridge warned himself.

"As you wish," he said, managing to maintain what he hoped was a coolly polite air.

They filed through the narrow doorway and into another, smaller chamber. The leader turned up a lamp. Delbridge looked around with a mix of curiosity and dread. This room, too, appeared to date from ancient times. It also lacked windows. Delbridge glanced at the heavy, ironbound door with its massive lock and concluded that the little chamber had probably once functioned as a secure storeroom.

A large steel strongbox sat on a thick carpet in the center of the room. It looked old. Late seventeenth century, Delbridge decided, the era of Sylvester Jones, founder of the Arcane Society. Had the Third Circle managed to obtain an artifact connected to Sylvester? Excitement sparked through him, driving out some of the apprehension. The founder's secrets were the stuff of myth and legend within the Society.

Lamplight flickered on the gold foil that covered the curved top of the strongbox. Words and symbols were inscribed on the gold. Delbridge recognized some of the symbols as alchemical and some of the words as a mix of Latin and Greek but could not decipher their meanings. A private code, he thought. The old alchemists were notoriously secretive.

There was no lock on the strongbox and no visible line to mark the lid. In the center there was a deep indentation lined with some dark, glassy substance.

The leader looked at Delbridge. "I can see from the expression on your face that you have some notion of the value of this ancient strongbox."

"Did it belong to Sylvester Jones?" Delbridge asked, awed in spite of himself. "A while back there were rumors about a burglary at Arcane House."

"This was not stolen from Arcane House," the leader said.

Delbridge's sense of intense anticipation dimmed. "I see."

The leader gave him a mysterious smile. "It did not belong to the founder," he said softly. "It was, instead, the property of someone who was privy to his greatest secrets. We believe those secrets are locked inside."

Delbridge frowned. "One of Sylvester's rivals?"

"His greatest rival, Sybil the Virgin Sorceress."

Thunderstruck, Delbridge stared at the strongbox. "I thought Sybil was just another Arcane Society legend. Are you saying that she actually existed?"

"Oh, yes." The leader indicated the ancient book he held. "She existed. This is one of her notebooks. I searched for it for years before I finally located it in the library of an aging member of the Arcane Society. Upon his death, I was able to acquire it."

The death of the former owner had probably not been of natural causes, Delbridge thought.

"The entire notebook is written in the Sorceress's private code, of course," the leader continued. "I have devoted the past decade of my life to deciphering it. I succeeded, and the contents led me to the location of the strongbox."

"What is inside?" Delbridge asked, hardly daring to hope. "A copy of the founder's formula, by any chance?"

"Yes," one of the other cowled figures said impatiently. "According to the notebook, Sybil did, indeed, steal the formula and conceal it in that strongbox."

"I don't understand," Delbridge said, searching the masked faces around him. "Haven't you looked?"

"Unfortunately, that has not been possible until now." The leader's hand tightened on the journal. "The strongbox is sealed with a most unusual locking device. According to the warning written on the gold foil, any attempt to force the chest open will result in the destruction of the secrets inside."

Delbridge frowned. "How will you get into it?"

The leader held up the velvet pouch. "Sybil's warning makes it clear that the aurora stone is the key."

Another thrill shot through Delbridge. At last he comprehended the enormity of the gift he had provided to the Third Circle. No wonder he had been promised a seat at the table in the other room if he brought them the stone. He had given these men the key to something they valued above all else, something they had not been able to obtain for themselves. He felt his own aura shift and pulse more strongly. Power fed on power.

The leader handed the notebook to one of the other robed figures. Then he held up the aurora stone. For a moment they all stared at the dull, colorless crystal.

With great precision, the leader lowered the stone into the black glass depression set in the top of the strongbox. There was an audible click. It fit perfectly, as if it had been made to sit there.

Delbridge held his breath. He sensed the others, including the leader, doing the same.

Nothing happened.

There was a short, tense silence. Perspiration broke out on Delbridge's brow.

"It isn't working," someone muttered.

Everyone looked at Delbridge. Raw fear briefly paralyzed him. But with an effort of will, he managed to pull himself together.

"This is the stone you demanded," he said as coolly as possible. "I can feel its power, even if you cannot. It's not my fault it isn't opening the strongbox."

The leader wrapped one hand around the

aurora stone. He concentrated intently for a moment. "I think you are correct. I can feel the resonating power of the stone. It is stronger now that it is in contact with the strongbox. But the energy is murky and unfocused. It appears that the last words of Sybil's warning are true, after all. I had hoped they were intended merely to discourage any attempt to open the box."

"What does the warning say?" Delbridge demanded.

"'Only she who can command the aurora stone may open this strongbox,'" the leader quoted.

"That is the answer, then," one of the others whispered excitedly. "The energy in the crystal must be properly channeled and directed in order to unlock the strongbox."

The leader straightened and contemplated Delbridge with a basilisk gaze. "You have brought us the aurora stone, but it is useless to us unless we can find someone with a talent for working the crystal."

For the first time in several minutes, Delbridge relaxed. He gave the leader a cold smile. "You should have mentioned that earlier when you set me the task of delivering the crystal. I'll be happy to bring you a woman who can work the aurora stone. Will that satisfy you?"

“Bring us a female who can unlock this strongbox and the sixth seat at the table of the Third Circle is yours,” the leader vowed.

33

"Her name was Molly Stubton," Thaddeus said. "No one has seen her since the night of Delbridge's party. I got a description from one of her rivals today. I'm certain she was the dead woman Leona and I found in the gallery."

It was late in the afternoon. They had gathered once again in the library to share the information they had collected. Thaddeus was impatient for the arrival of night. He had plans for the evening.

"I realize that Miss Stubton did not move in society," Victoria said. "Nevertheless, I find it astonishing that her murder has gone unnoticed in the press."

"That is because no body has been found, according to my associate at Scotland Yard," Thaddeus said. "But among her acquaintances in the world of high-class prostitutes, there are rumors circulating."

Leona looked at him. "What do her friends

and rivals believe happened to her?"

"The current theory is that Delbridge murdered her in a jealous rage and got rid of the body that night." Thaddeus went to stand at the window. "There is some support for that possibility."

"What support?" Leona asked.

"It was widely known within her own social circles that Molly Stubton had other lovers. But given the manner of her death and the presence of the rouge pot, I think it more likely that the Midnight Monster killed her."

Victoria frowned. "I agree. I have met Delbridge on a number of occasions. He strikes me as a rather fastidious man. I cannot imagine him wanting to commit such a gruesome murder. The killer no doubt would have been splashed with the victim's blood."

Thaddeus propped himself against the side of his desk and folded his arms. "I agree with you. And, as it happens, there is some other evidence that supports our theory. Although Miss Stubton's associates all agreed that she took other wealthy lovers, some of them believe that she did so to please Delbridge."

Leona's hand stilled on Fog's head. "Why would a gentleman want his mistress to form a liaison with another man?"

Victoria sniffed disdainfully. "When you have lived as long as I have, Miss Hewitt, you will understand that when it comes to that sort of thing there is no limit to the range of perversions that exists."

Leona blinked and then turned pink. "Good heavens. You mean Delbridge might have actually enjoyed the notion of his mistress and another man —" She broke off, waving one hand vaguely to finish the sentence.

"That his lordship might have enjoyed watching her in bed with other men?" Victoria concluded coolly. "Yes, that is exactly what I meant."

Leona swallowed. "How odd."

"Odd, indeed," Thaddeus said grimly. "However, in this case I think we can absolve Delbridge of the charge of voyeurism. He is an obsessive collector. The other gentlemen with whom Miss Stubton conducted affairs were also collectors." He paused for emphasis. "Her last two paramours were Bloomfield and Ivington."

Leona's eyes widened with excitement. "The two men who were murdered with the poisonous vapor."

"Right," Thaddeus said. "Delbridge used his mistress to gain access to the collections of those two men. It was after Bloomfield's death that the rumors about the theft of the aurora stone started to circulate. He must have been the last one to possess it before Delbridge stole it. Caleb has done some research. It seems that Bloomfield very likely acquired the stone some eleven years ago."

Leona went very still. "Then Bloomfield was the one who murdered my mother."

Thaddeus watched Fog lean more heavily against her. "It appears so," he said gently.

"After all these years," she whispered. "I was never able to find her killer. And now he is dead, thanks to another killer."

To Thaddeus's astonishment, Victoria leaned closer to Leona and patted her hand.

"Justice, however bizarre, has been done, my dear," she said quietly.

"Yes," Leona said. She blinked very rapidly. "Yes, I suppose that is true."

Thaddeus unfolded his arms, reached into his pocket and took out his handkerchief. Without a word he handed it to her.

"Thank you," she said. She dabbed at her eyes with the square of pristine linen.

"Bloomfield was every bit as obsessive as Delbridge," Thaddeus continued. "He was also known for being extremely reclusive and secretive. He kept his possession of the stone a great secret. But I have a hunch that at least one other collector was aware that he had it."

Victoria frowned. "Do you refer to Ivington?"

"Yes. If you will recall, Ivington was poisoned first. I suspect he was killed after he revealed that Bloomfield was in possession of the stone. Delbridge wanted to cover his tracks."

Leona crumpled the handkerchief in one hand. "Do you think Molly Stubton was the one who gave both men the poison?"

"No," Thaddeus said. "In the course of my investigation before I encountered you, I interviewed the servants in both households. They were all quite certain that there was no one else with their employers on the nights of their deaths. Both men were sound asleep, alone in their beds, when they awoke and went mad."

Victoria nodded at once, understanding. "The murders were carried out by someone who could sneak in and out of the victims' bedrooms undetected. A hunter talent."

"The same hunter talent who is killing the prostitutes," Thaddeus said.

"But last night there was another murder and a rumor that another prostitute has gone missing," Leona pointed out. "Why would the hunter resume killing prostitutes if he is now in the employ of Lord Delbridge?"

Thaddeus looked at her. "Anyone who murders women in such a savage, senseless manner is clearly mad. Delbridge got himself a hired killer, all right, but he has employed a crazed fiend who is unable to resist returning occasionally to his favorite prey."

Leona shuddered. "I see what you mean."

Victoria made a face. "If I were Delbridge, I would be very worried about such an unstable employee. This hunter may have his uses, but judging by the rouge pots, he cannot help leaving clues behind at the scene of his crimes."

"Speaking of the rouge pots," Thaddeus said, "did you have any luck locating the shop that sells them?"

Victoria assumed a smug expression. "I certainly did. They are French, as I suspected. The two pots were sold in a small, very exclusive establishment in Wilton Lane. Quite expensive, by the way."

Leona turned toward her, excitement flaring. "Did you get a description of the person who bought them?"

"It was a man," Victoria said. "But I regret to say that I do not think it is the one you are looking for. The shopkeeper told me he had gray whiskers and longish gray hair."

"A disguise, perhaps," Leona said quickly.

Victoria raised her brows. "Yes, I suppose that might be the case."

"Did the shopkeeper offer any other details?" Thaddeus asked.

"The man carried a very fine walking stick," Victoria said. "The shopkeeper admired the silver handle. It was fashioned in the shape of a hawk's head."

Satisfaction and anticipation flashed through Thaddeus. "The Midnight Monster, shopping for his next victim."

34

The townhouse that Molly Stubton had rented echoed with the silent, hollow sensations that characterized an uninhabited residence. Thaddeus was well aware that there were some endowed with a specific talent for detecting the psychical residue left behind by those who had inhabited a room. People with that ability could distinguish the type and strength of the various emotions embedded in the walls. But even those with other sensitivities could sense the unique resonance of emptiness.

He stood quietly for a moment in the back hall, listening with all of his senses. There was no trace of fresh energy in the atmosphere. Molly had no doubt employed a housekeeper, at least, and possibly a maid or a cook. But those who had once worked here had evidently concluded that their employer was not going to return. They had packed their things and left.

Perhaps they had heard rumors of just how Molly Stubton had died, he reflected. Servants talked, just as their employers did. Although Delbridge's mansion was miles away, the staffs of the two households would have been aware of the liaison. Gossip flowed freely in all levels of society, and, as Victoria had reminded him, murder will out.

Satisfied that he had the premises to himself, he began a methodical search. A short time earlier he had engaged in a brisk argument with Leona concerning his intentions here tonight.

"You'll be taking a great risk," she said.

"Not as great as the one you took the night you entered Delbridge's mansion," he countered.

"I do wish you would cease throwing that in my face every time we quarrel."

"I can't seem to help myself. Finding you there was a very unnerving experience."

"That incident only goes to show that I am very good at that sort of thing. I'll come with you."

"No, you will not," he said. "Two people would mean twice the risk."

"What will you look for in Molly Stubton's house?"

"I'll know it when I see it."

That last remark had only served to

heighten her anxiety, but it was the truth. He did not know what he hoped to find here or if there would, indeed, be anything to discover. But he had learned over the course of his career as an investigator that he usually recognized a clue when he saw it. It did not always follow, unfortunately, that he knew how to make sense of said clue, but that was another matter. When one applied the turning-over-rocks approach to solving a crime, one had to turn over a lot of rocks.

The curtains were all drawn tightly closed. He struck a light and made quick work of the kitchen and the housekeeper's tiny room. Both were bare of anything remotely resembling a clue. The same was true of the small parlor.

He went out into the front hall and took the stairs two at a time to the upper floor. There were two bedrooms. One appeared to have been used as a dressing room. Two large wardrobes were stuffed with a number of expensive gowns, shoes, hats and petticoats. The jewelry box, which sat in a position of honor on top of a high chest of drawers, was empty. He wondered if the staff had helped themselves to the contents on their way out the door or if Delbridge had sent someone to collect the jewels he had bestowed on his mistress.

He checked the wardrobes for concealed drawers and pulled up the carpet to see if there was a floor safe. Satisfied that he had done what he could, he made his way through the connecting door into the bedroom.

Ten minutes later he found the unfinished letter under the mattress. He struck a fresh light and started to read.

My Dear J.
I have thrilling news . . .

There was no sound but something shifted in the brooding atmosphere of the house. A whisper of disturbed air wafted through the bedroom door.

He put out the light and opened his senses to the fullest, probing for the telltale pulse of energy that would tell him he was no longer alone in the house.

The hot flash of murky, chaotic, paranormal currents slammed across his senses. The soundless manner in which the intruder had managed to get into the house was evidence enough that he was a hunter.

The Midnight Monster had arrived.

. . . The power of the aurora stone is a double-edged sword. It must be used with the greatest discretion and only in the most

extreme cases. The crystal worker who would command the psychical currents of the stone risks being overwhelmed by them. Only the strongest should attempt to manipulate this energy.

The greatest hazard of all is that any crystal worker who is powerful enough to control the stone will also be strong enough to transform it from a healing device into a weapon.

In the hands of one who possesses such power the stone can be used to cast the victim into a waking nightmare . . .

A shock of dread as unnerving as a jolt of electricity snapped across Leona's senses. The realization that Thaddeus was in deadly danger trapped the breath in her lungs. Her mother's journal fell from her hand and tumbled onto the floor beside the bed.

Fog rose from the rug and padded across the room to the bed. He whined softly.

"I'm all right," she said.

The immediate sensation of alarm eased somewhat. At least she could breathe again. Nevertheless her hand trembled when she reached out for Fog. Instead of giving him the reassuring pat she had intended, she clutched him with both hands and buried her face in his fur.

The ominous feeling hovered, an invisible vapor in the small room.

"It's just my nerves," she told Fog, trying to reassure herself. "Things have been somewhat stressful of late."

Fog licked her hand and pushed his head against her, offering silent comfort.

"Who am I fooling?" She shoved aside the covers and swung her feet to the floor. "I'm terrified. He's in danger, and there is nothing I can do. I should never have let him go to that house alone tonight."

As if she could have stopped him.

Dread cascaded through her again.

Thaddeus had given her Molly Stubton's address.

"Number 21 Broadribb Lane. A quiet, respectable neighborhood. Do not worry about me, I'll be fine."

She was on her feet without thinking about it, hurrying across the room to the wardrobe. She yanked open a drawer and took out the shirt and trousers that she had worn the night she had gone to Delbridge's mansion.

35

The midnight monster was, as Thaddeus had guessed, not entirely sane. The madness was there in his erratic, unstable aura, which was flaring high and hot now because the Monster was hunting.

It was extremely difficult to hypnotize those who were truly mad because such individuals generated such wildly fluctuating, unpredictable currents of power. The very nature of their disordered minds made it difficult for them to sustain any sort of trance, even one that was psychically induced.

The question tonight was just how crazed the Midnight Monster really was.

Thaddeus dropped the letter he had found into his pocket and circled the bed, putting it between himself and the open door. Not that a mattress and quilt would be much protection against a man who could see clearly in the dark and who was as fast and lethal as any beast of prey.

He eased the pistol out of his pocket and pointed it toward the gray rectangle that marked the open door.

The shadows shifted in the hall, but no one appeared in the opening. So much for finishing this with one quick, lucky shot.

The man out in the hall laughed. The sound was a little too loud, a little too excited, almost a giggle. The air seemed to crackle, as though some strange form of electricity had ignited it.

"You're armed, I'm sure, Ware," the Monster said. "But you are a member of the Arcane Society so you must know that a pistol is of little use against a man with my talents." There was another unwholesome giggle. "I'm a hunter, you see. Tell me, what kind of talent are you? I know you're no hunter. I met another hunter once. We recognized each other's true natures immediately. He is dead now, by the way. I was the stronger."

The Monster wanted to boast; more than that, he *needed* his prey to comprehend his powers and fear him. It was important to him that his intended victim experience as much terror as possible. Who better to understand and respect just how dangerous he truly was than a member of the Arcane Society?

The Monster's compulsion to chat was a very good thing, Thaddeus thought. Indeed, it might be his only hope. With luck the bizarre conversation would point to the nature of the compulsive obsession that drove the beast to kill. A good mesmerist could work with that sort of knowledge.

"You're the one the newspapers call the Midnight Monster, aren't you," Thaddeus said. He did not take his attention off the doorway.

"An amusing title, is it not? A correspondent for *The Flying Intelligencer* bestowed it on me. You must admit it has a certain ring to it. You should see the looks on the girls' faces when they finally realize who I am. They've all read about me in the penny dreadfuls. They are so beautiful in their fear."

The Monster's voice altered slightly on the last sentence, becoming almost a caress. For a moment, the erratic currents of power emanating from him steadied. The thought of the women's terror was linked to the compulsion that drove him. He fed on fear.

"If they are beautiful why do you put rouge on them after they are dead?" Thaddeus asked.

"Because they are cheap whores and such women paint their faces. Everyone knows that. Only prostitutes use cosmetics."

The waves of furious energy leaped higher,

but they steadied briefly again. The rouge was linked to the compulsion and whenever the Monster came close to thinking about his kills, he was able to focus. It was a strange irony that the only time the Monster's energy was close to stable was when he was sunk deepest into the pool of his insanity.

Just a few seconds of such mad clarity might be enough, however. Thaddeus kept the pistol pointed at the doorway. If conversation failed, he would only get one shot, and that one shot had to count. Merely wounding the bastard would not be enough to stop him, not in his crazed mental state.

"You haven't told me the nature of your talent," the Monster said, his voice suddenly conversational in tone, as though they were sitting side by side in their club.

"You haven't told me your real name," Thaddeus said gently. He paused. "Or do your associates just call you Monster?"

"Very good, Ware. I'm impressed that you can summon up a sense of humor at this moment. My name is Lancing. But I do not expect you to recognize it. We are not acquainted."

"I'm surprised to learn that. You move in Delbridge's circles, and he belongs to all the right clubs. Surely we've brushed up against one another on some occasion?"

"I don't move in your circles." Rage caused Lancing's aura to flare wildly. "Nor in Delbridge's either."

"He invited you to his party the other night."

"Bah. He tolerates me on the fringes of his exclusive set," Lancing said, bitterness like acid in his voice. "It sticks in his craw, but it is the price he pays for my services." He paused. "You were the one who found her that night, weren't you?"

"Molly Stubton? Yes. I recognized your signature at the kill. The rouge pot."

Energy flared. "Why the devil do you keep harping on the rouge?"

"It interests me. What happened to the body? I've been curious. Such a murder should have made a great sensation in the press, just as your other kills did."

"After the rain stopped I dumped her body into an unmarked grave in the woods. No one will ever find her. No one will even look for her."

"But you left the rouge pot by her body there in the gallery."

"She was just a cheap harlot like the others."

"Not so cheap from what I heard. She was Delbridge's mistress."

"I don't care how many jewels and gowns

he gave her. She was a whore, no better than any other whore. So I killed her like the whore she was."

"Delbridge did not object?"

Lancing giggled. "He *instructed* me to get rid of her. She had served her purpose."

"Seems a little odd that he would want you to kill her in his house on a night when the mansion was filled with guests."

"He ordered me to bring her back here after the party and take care of the business then. But I realized that she had become suspicious of me so I had no choice but to make the kill there in the gallery."

"That must have annoyed Delbridge."

Lancing laughed. "He was enraged, but he knew better than to lose his temper with me. It was a pleasure to watch him fume. It made him realize that he is not my master, after all."

"Do you worry that some day he will decide that you, too, are no longer useful?"

"Unlike Molly, I cannot be replaced. Delbridge knows that."

"In other words, you are merely a tool for him to use."

"That is not true," Lancing roared. "I am far more powerful than Delbridge. I am a superior form of man."

"Yet you do Delbridge's bidding. Sounds

like you're just a tool to me."

"I am my own master, you son of a bitch." Lancing's voice rose shrilly. "It suits me to let Delbridge think I take his orders, but in the end I will have it all, everything, do you understand? Including the seat at the table of the Third Circle that he covets so highly."

"What is the Third Circle?"

"He doesn't know that I am aware of what he is about," Lancing continued, as though he had not heard the question. Energy pulsed fiercely now, growing darker and steadier. "He thinks that because my mother was a drunken whore I am less than nothing."

"Your mother was a prostitute?" Thaddeus kept his tone coolly thoughtful, as though the subject were only of academic interest. "That would certainly explain Delbridge's reluctance to allow you into his inner circles."

"My mother was a respectable woman who was driven into the streets by a man just like Delbridge, a man of status and power," Lancing shrieked. "The bastard got her pregnant and then abandoned her. She had no choice but to become a whore in order to survive."

"And you hated her for what she became, for what it cost you."

"I am the son of a *gentleman,* damn you."

"But you will never be able to claim your birthright because your father never married your mother. Instead, she became a drunken whore and she dragged you into the gutter with her. Every time you kill a prostitute, you punish your mother for what she did to you."

"You don't know what you're talking about. I kill because it enhances my power and because it proves that I am a highly evolved man who is naturally superior to you and Delbridge and every other so-called gentleman in England."

"You're a wild beast pretending to be human."

"Stop it," Lancing shrieked.

Energy pulsed hotly in the darkness.

"A truly superior man, a hunter who believed that he should have the rights and privileges of a gentleman, would choose prey that was his equal," Thaddeus said softly. "He wouldn't kill helpless prostitutes like his mother."

"Shut your damned mouth."

"Where's the challenge in your sort of hunting? It doesn't require any special ability to slit the throat of an unarmed woman. That kind of killing only proves that you are a far lower form of life than your victims."

"Stop saying those things."

"Delbridge knows what you really are. When he is through with you, he'll send you back to the gutter. That is obviously your natural habitat."

Lancing howled. There was no other word for the strange, inhuman sound that came from his throat. Simultaneously his aura flared.

Although Thaddeus was braced for it, had the pistol pointed toward the doorway, he was not fast enough. The Monster leaped through the opening with the speed of a leopard taking down prey.

Thaddeus glimpsed a dark figure silhouetted briefly against the dull gray light in the hall and pulled the trigger.

But even as the gun roared, shattering the stillness, he knew he had missed Lancing. An instant later, the silhouette was gone. The killer was in the room with him, invisible in the darkness, stalking him.

Lancing giggled again. The sound came from the shadows beside the wardrobe. "This is too easy. Why don't you make a run for it? That will add a bit of sport to the business."

Lancing was invisible in the darkness, but his aura was strong and steady now. His bloodlust was unleashed. It completely dominated all other traces of energy. Bloodlust was violent and fierce, but it was also very strong and steady.

Thaddeus spoke, each word freighted with hypnotic power.

"You cannot move, Lancing. You are a rabbit cowering before a wolf, a fawn frozen in fear. Your arms and legs will no longer obey your mind."

There was no movement in the vicinity of the wardrobe. Thaddeus kept talking while he struck a light.

"You cannot kill tonight. You are helpless."

The light flared, revealing Lancing, who stood, frozen, in the shadows of the wardrobe. Thaddeus brought the barrel of the pistol up, aiming for Lancing's heart. But before he could squeeze off the shot, Lancing's features twisted with fear. Simultaneously his aura spiked and pulsed in a wildly erratic pattern, shattering the trance.

Abruptly free of the mesmeric command, Lancing leaped for the door with his hunter's speed. But he was no longer driven by his bloodlust. The chaos of panic had overwhelmed him.

"Stop," Thaddeus commanded. But panic was a form of madness, unstable and uncontrollable, especially in one who was already insane.

Lancing fled through the door and vanished into the hall, moving once more with a hunter's paranormal speed.

Thaddeus followed, but he knew there was no way he could catch him.

He expected to hear the sound of Lancing's footsteps on the staircase. Instead a door was flung open somewhere in the hall behind him. He whirled and turned up a nearby sconce just in time to see Lancing disappear through the doorway.

He ran after him, pistol at the ready. A cornered hunter in the grip of terror would be every bit as dangerous as one in the throes of a killing bloodlust.

When he reached the open door he found himself looking into a narrow stairwell that led up toward the top of the house. Lancing, in his disoriented state, or perhaps driven by some primal instinct to seek higher ground, had fled up toward the roof, not down to the street.

Footsteps pounded on the stairs above. Thaddeus entered the dark stairwell cautiously, one hand planted on the wall to help him feel his way. He kept his senses wide open, tracking Lancing's crazed energy.

At the top of the stairs another door was flung open. Night air poured into the stairwell. Lancing went out onto the roof.

Thaddeus followed. The currents of the

panicked hunter's fear were easing somewhat. Rage and bloodlust once again became the dominant forces.

Thaddeus stepped out onto the roof and struck another light. He saw Lancing hovering a short distance away, face contorted in a terrible mask. The Monster stiffened, preparing to spring.

"You cannot move, Lancing. You will stand still while I secure your hands behind your back. You will then go to Scotland Yard and confess that you are the Midnight Monster."

For a few seconds the hypnotic instructions worked. Lancing stood, frozen, while Thaddeus walked swiftly forward. He had to get close enough to make certain of his shot this time.

But Lancing's instinct for survival, fueled by his natural talent and his own mental instability, once again swamped the mesmeric currents of the trance.

He screamed, jumped up onto the stone parapet and launched himself out into the night.

Perhaps he had intended to try to leap onto an adjoining rooftop. But if that was the case, he had made a disastrous error. He went over the edge that faced the street.

The long, howling scream ended in shocking silence a heartbeat later.

36

The silence did not last long. A horse whinnied in terror. A dog started to bark. Someone shouted furiously.

Thaddeus looked over the edge of the parapet. Down below, the street lamps illuminated a chaotic scene. A carriage had just set down a passenger. Lancing's body had landed almost directly in front of the vehicle, frightening the horse. The beast was greatly agitated, shifting nervously in its traces. The coachman struggled to control his nag while yelling at the passenger.

"'Ere now, what about my fare? And the tip you promised if I got ye here in a timely manner?"

The passenger ignored him to run toward the body. There was something very familiar about the way the figure moved, Thaddeus thought. At that moment, the man's cap fell off. Long dark hair spilled free.

"What the devil?" the coachman yelped.

A large dog leaped out of the carriage, barking furiously. The dog, too, looked very familiar.

"And don't forget the extra charge for the bloody dog," the coachman shouted.

Thaddeus felt the tight, hot energy generated by the confrontation with Lancing suddenly change focus. A rush of anger spilled through him. How dare Leona follow him into what could have been mortal danger? Had she arrived five minutes earlier, *just five minutes,* she might have been dead by now.

"Bloody hell."

He turned away from the parapet, crossed the roof at a dead run and plunged recklessly down the dark stairs. When he arrived in the front hall, he yanked open the door and went out into the street.

Fog noticed him first. Ferocious barking gave way to an excited greeting.

Leona was just straightening from the body. When she caught sight of him she flew toward him as if chased by demons.

"I thought it was you," she shouted. "God help me, I thought it was you."

She sounded as angry as he was. Before he could start yelling at her, she was in his arms, clinging to him with what had to be every ounce of her strength. She pressed her face into his shoulder.

"I thought it was you, Thaddeus," she whispered again. "I was so terrified."

He groaned and locked his arms around her, burying his face in her hair and inhaling her scent. "What the hell are you doing here? Do you have any notion of what could have happened if you had walked in that front door a few minutes ago? He would have murdered you in the blink of an eye. Or used you as a hostage."

"Thaddeus."

His name came out a half-choked sob. She tried to raise her head. He pushed her face back into his coat.

"What about my fare?" the coachman grumbled.

Pinning Leona against his chest with one arm, Thaddeus reached into his pocket, took out some coins and tossed them to the driver.

"Thaddeus," Leona mumbled, her face still muffled by thick wool. "I can't breathe."

"Thought I'd seen everything," the coachman said, pocketing his money. "But a whore dressed in men's clothes is something new under the sun."

Thaddeus infused his voice with the full strength of his hypnotic powers. *"Be still or I'll wring your bloody neck for you."*

The coachman froze. His horse shifted uneasily, responding as all animals did, to the heavy currents of energy in the atmosphere. Fog, too, reacted. He lifted his muzzle to the sky and began to howl. The unearthly cry echoed through the streets.

It was too much for the horse. The creature flattened its ears, screamed in panic and plunged violently in its traces. The coachman, in the grip of the trance, did nothing to control him.

"You may move," Thaddeus shouted, lifting the compulsion. *"Control your damned horse."*

The coachman came out of the trance in an instant and immediately set about working the reins. But it was too late. The beast took off in a mad rush. The carriage rolled forward and careened out of sight, the coachman still shouting at the hapless horse.

An upstairs window was flung open. A head crowned with a nightcap looked down at the scene.

"Sound the alarm," the woman shouted. "There's a wolf in the street."

Farther along the way, another window opened.

"Harold, come and see," another woman called out. "There's a wolf down there. *And a body.* The wolf has killed a man. Dear God, someone summon a constable."

"Damnation." Thaddeus seized Leona's arm and hauled her away toward the far end of the street. "What a charming fiasco. We must get out of here immediately before someone else notices that you are a woman. I cannot hypnotize everyone in the neighborhood."

Fog bounded enthusiastically after them, eager for the new game.

"For heaven's sake," Leona said, breathless. "You are worrying about nothing. No one around here could possibly recognize me."

"As I recall, you said something similar the night we were obliged to make a hurried escape from Delbridge's mansion. But his pet killer not only found you, he entered your house and stole the damn crystal."

"Really, sir, are you going to hold that one small incident over my head forever?"

"I think so, yes."

37

It took some time to find another carriage and drive to the address of Thaddeus's Scotland Yard acquaintance. Leona waited in the shadows of the cab with Fog while Thaddeus rapped on the door of the detective's modest house. When a sleepy-looking man in a dressing gown appeared, candle in hand, the two conducted a low-voiced conversation for several minutes.

Eventually the detective retreated swiftly into his front hall and closed the door. Thaddeus loped down the steps and got back into the cab. Leona sensed immediately that notifying the man from Scotland Yard of Lancing's death had done nothing to diminish the prowling tension in him.

"Detective Spellar will deal with the body and conclude the investigation," Thaddeus said in a controlled yet furious tone. "He is the one who first suspected that the Midnight Monster was a hunter. With luck he will find some evidence to confirm Lancing's guilt when he searches his lodgings. A killer that deranged no doubt kept some record of his crimes. He was very proud of his work."

It did not require a crystal to know that Thaddeus's mood was not what anyone would call pleasant. Fog reacted by keeping his attention respectfully on him, a soldier awaiting orders from a commanding officer. Leona drummed her fingers on the seat. The initial shock and horror of seeing Lancing's body had turned into nerve-shuddering relief. Now, however, that unsettling emotion was mixed with a growing exasperation bordering on anger.

By the time they walked back into the darkened mansion, she'd had quite enough.

"Go to bed," Thaddeus said. "We will talk in the morning."

That did it. The fact that she had been about to do exactly as he had commanded only served to infuriate her all the more.

"How dare you?" she said tightly.

He stalked into the library, ignoring her. He slung his coat over the back of the sofa, turned up a lamp and went straight to the brandy table. She rushed after him, closed the door behind her and leaned back against it, her hands gripping the knob.

"You have no right to give me orders, Thaddeus," she whispered, low and fierce.

"I have every right." He yanked the stopper out of the brandy bottle and splashed the contents into a glass. "As long as you are a guest in this house you will do as I say."

"I would remind you that you demanded that I come here to stay. I can see now that acquiescing to your orders on that occasion gave you a serious misunderstanding of the nature of our association."

"Our association?" He gave her a look of savage amusement and then tossed back half the brandy in the glass. "Is that what you call it? You make it sound like a business arrangement."

"Well, it is, in a way."

She knew at once that she had made a serious mistake. The currents of intense energy flaring invisibly around Thaddeus leaped like wildfire to a new and dangerous level.

He set the brandy glass down much too gently and crossed the room in three long strides. He halted in front of her, trapped her against the door and captured her face in his hands. When he spoke his voice came from the heart of a storm. The mesmeric cadences rolled through her senses.

"Damn it to hell and back, whatever else this

is, this is no business arrangement between us, madam."

It took every ounce of her own energy to stop him from overwhelming her will. Heat flooded through her. She wondered if she had a fever.

"Why are you so angry?" she demanded.

"Because you nearly got yourself killed to-night."

"So did you."

He paid no attention to that piece of logic.

"You will never again put yourself at such risk. Do you understand me, Leona?"

"You were in danger," she shot back. "I had no choice. And stop trying to give me hypnotic commands. I'm immune to your power, remember?"

His hands tightened on her face. His eyes were seas filled with dangerous but unbear-ably exciting currents.

"Unfortunately," he said softly, "I am not immune to yours."

He took her mouth captive, and she dis-covered that his kiss held more mesmeric power than his voice. She did not even want to try to resist. As if he had given her an hypnotic command, the volatile mix of fear, frustration, hurt and anger twisting through her suddenly flashed into a raging passion.

She wrapped her arms around him, fighting him for the embrace. In between damp, heated, hungry kisses, he yanked off her men's clothing. Coat, shirt, shoes and trousers landed in a heap at her feet. In her hurry to dress, she had put on no undergarments so she was soon nude.

He traced the shape of her body with his hands, his palms gliding possessively, hungrily, down her back, along the curve of her waist and over the swell of her hips. He found the melting core between her legs and stroked her until she was wet, until she almost screamed aloud in frustration.

He picked her up and carried her across the carpet. Excitement heating her blood, she closed her eyes against the spinning room. When he lowered her, she expected to feel the cushions of the sofa or perhaps the carpet beneath her back. Instead, she felt hard, polished wood beneath her bare backside.

She opened her eyes, startled, and discovered that she was perched on the edge of the broad desk. Before she could ask any questions, Thaddeus had the front of his trousers open and was moving between her thighs.

He gripped the nape of her neck with one hand and put his mouth very close to hers. She sensed that he was willing her to acknowledge the force of what was happening between them.

"Whatever the hell this is, it is not a business arrangement," he said again.

His mouth closed over hers. Simultaneously he drove himself slowly, relentlessly into her, letting her know in the most elemental way that he was staking a claim. The pressure was unbelievably exciting and exhilarating.

He moved inside her with long, hard thrusts. Instinctively she wrapped her legs around him, staking her own, feminine claim. He groaned in response. Beneath her palms his linen shirt was damp. He released her neck, gripped her hips with both hands and went deeper still. So deep she thought she would shatter, so deep she thought that for a moment they were one being.

She fell back onto the desk and stretched her arms out on either side. There were a number of soft thuds as several small objects went flying onto the carpet. She gripped the edges of the desk so tightly she thought that it would be amazing if she did not leave small gouges in the wood. She hung on for dear life.

A moment later her climax slammed through her. That's all it took to pull Thaddeus over the edge with her. When his own release surged through him, Leona sensed that, for a few timeless seconds, their auras were fused together.

The sensation was so exquisitely intimate, so incredibly strong, that she could not stand it. She convulsed one last time and then went limp, faintly aware of the tears leaking out of the corners of her tightly closed eyes.

38

Thaddeus came back to his senses, aware of a nearly boneless sensation. It dawned on him that what he really wanted to do was collapse. He was still leaning over Leona, his hands braced on either side of her warm, soft body. Her legs, only a moment ago a snug vise around his waist, had fallen away and now dangled over the side of the desk.

He took in the sight of her sprawled beneath him, her eyes closed, her mouth soft and full, and felt a sense of euphoric satisfaction unlike anything he had ever known. Gently, reluctantly, he pulled free of her tight, swollen core. Leaning against the desk, he wiped himself with a handkerchief and put his pants to rights. Then, he managed to fall into the nearest chair.

He leaned back, rested his arms at his sides, stretched out his legs and simply enjoyed the site of Leona displayed like a luscious banquet before him. The red crystal at her throat still glowed faintly.

When she stirred and opened her eyes a moment later, he was shocked to see the glitter of tears. Guilt ripped through him. He got to his feet and used the edge of his finger to wipe away the traces of moisture.

"Did I hurt you?" he asked.

"No." She gave him an odd smile and sat up cautiously, turning her back toward him, as though struck by a sudden pang of shyness. "The experience was somewhat intense, that's all."

"Somewhat? Try unbelievably, indescribably intense. Try exhausting. I'll be lucky if I can climb the stairs to my bedroom."

"I may have a similar problem."

She slid off the table and hurried across the room to pick up her clothes. Idly he watched her pull on the masculine shirt and trousers, enjoying the sight of her getting dressed in the wake of passion, savoring the intimacy of it.

"Do you suppose all of our quarrels will end like this?" he asked, smiling a little at the possibility.

She paused in the act of buttoning the shirt and gave him a quelling look. "One would hope that we will not have such arguments often."

He thought about the reason for the quarrel, and his amusement faded.

"You're right," he said, narrowing his eyes a little. "I do not want a repeat performance of what happened tonight."

Her brows scrunched together in warning. "Thaddeus . . ."

"I don't think my heart could sustain the shock," he concluded dryly.

She looked as if she was about to argue further but instead wrinkled her nose. "Mine, either."

He smiled at her. She smiled back.

Quarrel or no quarrel, he thought, the gossamer strands of their invisible bonds linked them. There is no escape for either of us. But he did not speak the words aloud. It was too soon, the moment too fragile.

She finished dressing and then stood there, looking at him, somber and concerned. Now what? he wondered.

"That beast, Lancing," she said. "Did he really jump to his death tonight?"

So that was it. She was unnerved by the possibility that he had killed a man. He should have expected that reaction. He exhaled slowly, reliving the confrontation on the rooftop.

"Yes," he said. What the hell, it was the truth, as far as it went.

Relief lightened her expression. "I see."

He rose and went to the table where he had left the half-finished brandy. He took a swallow, waited until the heat hit him and then lowered the glass.

"But I deliberately drove him to it," he said.

"I don't understand."

"I could not hold him in a trance for more than a few seconds at a time." He met her eyes across the room. "He was . . . unhinged. Much of his energy was chaotic. He kept slipping in and out of my control. But he comprehended what was happening, and it threw him into a panic. He ran up the stairs to the roof."

"And you went after him?"

"Yes." He did not take his eyes off her. "I think he meant to jump to a neighboring roof, but in his confusion and fear he chose the wrong side of the building. His leap took him out over the street."

"I see."

"I'm the one who put him into that state of extreme disorientation. I killed him, Leona, as surely as if I had pushed him over the edge. When I followed him up the stairs, I meant to destroy him because I was certain that he could not be safely confined in prison. He was deranged, but his talents were very powerful. Very dangerous. I intended to shoot him, but —"

She nodded once in that same solemn manner and walked to where he stood. He realized he was holding his breath.

She stopped in front of him and touched the side of his face. "He was a rabid dog. You did what had to be done."

"But now you look at me with different eyes because I plotted a man's death."

She shook her head slowly, her fingertips gentle on his cheek. "Not different eyes, worried eyes."

That caught him by surprise. "What are you worried about?"

"Unlike Lancing, you are a civilized man with a sense of decency and a conscience. Civilized men do not kill with impunity, no matter how righteous the cause. The act always exacts a toll. If it did not, you would be no better than an animal, yourself. There will be dreams, Thaddeus. Perhaps not tonight. Perhaps not tomorrow night. But sooner or later, there will be dreams."

He did not stir, afraid that she would lower her hand if he moved.

"Yes," he said. "I expect there will be dreams."

"Promise me that you will come to me when they strike. I cannot prevent them entirely, but I can keep them from becoming . . . overpowering."

She was not repelled by what he had done. She was offering to help him deal with the inevitable results of his actions. He exhaled slowly, aware of an enormous sense of relief.

He caught her fingers in one hand, brought them to his mouth, and kissed them. "I will come to you if I need your assistance with the dreams."

She nodded, satisfied, and stepped back. "At least we now have some answers and the Midnight Monster is dead."

"Which reminds me." He turned away, picked up the coat he had tossed over the sofa, and removed the sheet of paper from a pocket. "I found this letter under Molly Stubton's mattress. She never finished it. For some reason she felt it necessary to conceal it."

He read it aloud.

"My Dear J.

"I have thrilling news. My plans are unfolding, just as I had hoped. Last night I informed D. that I expected to be paid a great deal more than he is presently giving me for the risks I am taking. He argued at first — called me vile names and pointed out that if it had not been for him I would

not be mingling with my 'betters' in the social world. It was all very tiresome. But when I reminded him that if not for me, he would never have discovered the name of the collector who possessed that chunk of rock he coveted so highly, he finally saw the light of sweet reason.

"I asked him why the crystal was so important. I thought it might be useful to know. But all he would tell me is that it is the entry fee required to join a very exclusive club.

"Although I expect to do well with the income from D., I know better than most that I cannot trust him. Therefore, I have decided to find another paramour. A woman alone in the world cannot afford to be without the protection of a wealthy gentleman. I have my eye on a certain Mr. S., a man of great wealth and very little intelligence. A nice combination."

The letter ended abruptly. When he looked up Leona was watching him with an intent expression.

"It would appear that your friend Caleb Jones was right to suspect a larger scheme," she said thoughtfully. "Delbridge did not steal my crystal merely to add it to his own collection. He wanted it because it was the price required to join a secret club of some sort."

Thaddeus slowly refolded the letter. "A club in which he deemed membership so important, he was willing to commit murder."

"She mentions that she is looking for a new paramour. It must have been the gentleman who came into the gallery to meet her that night."

"Perhaps," Thaddeus said. "One thing is certain, I need to get back inside Delbridge's mansion as soon as possible."

Eagerness lit her eyes. "Do you think we will find the crystal there again?"

"I doubt it. If, by some chance, Delbridge is still in possession of the crystal, he will have taken care to hide it in a less obvious place this time."

"Then why go back to the mansion?"

"Because I want to look for something that may prove even more important than the damn crystal."

She appeared startled at the notion that there might be anything more important than the aurora stone.

"What?" she asked, frowning a little.

"Information on the secret club he seeks to join. Perhaps, if I am fortunate I'll discover the names of some of the other members."

"Oh, I see. Well, I suppose that would

be useful information for you and Caleb Jones."

He walked to the desk, opened a drawer and took out the schedule of Delbridge's customary activities that he and Caleb had prepared at the start of the affair.

"If Delbridge follows his usual routine, he will be at his club tomorrow night until quite late. Only two servants live in the house with him: his housekeeper and her husband, the butler. The others come in on a daily basis but they are never there at night."

"How odd. Most servants live in their employer's household."

"Delbridge has secrets to protect, a lot of them," he reminded her. "And servants talk, just like everyone else. In any event, tomorrow night is the regular evening off for the pair that reside in the mansion. They always go to their daughter's house on those evenings. They'll spend the night there."

"What if Delbridge changes his customary habits when he learns that his pet Monster is dead?"

"I don't think that is likely. If anything, the news of Lancing's death will go far to ensure that he sticks to his regular schedule. He will be extremely nervous lest anyone connect him with Lancing's crimes."

"I take your point," Leona said. "By now

a number of Delbridge's associates must be aware that he was acquainted with Lancing and even invited him into his home."

"Delbridge will feel compelled to disassociate himself from the Monster and to assure people that he is just as shocked as the rest of Society to learn that Lancing is connected to a series of awful crimes. The best way to do that is by not doing anything out of the ordinary. And if he is worried about the long arm of the law, there is an additional benefit to be gained by going to his club."

"What is that?"

"Few places on earth are as far beyond the reach of a police detective as the inside of a gentlemen's club."

Leona squared her shoulders. Her face was set in an all-too-familiar expression of determination. His gut tightened. He knew what was coming.

"I'll go with you tomorrow night," she said.

"No."

"You'll need me."

"No."

"Yes, you will, and for the same reasons you needed me last time. Please be reasonable, Thaddeus. There is a slim chance that the crystal is somewhere inside that mansion. If that is so, I am the only one who can detect it. And if you accidentally trigger another one of those hideous poison traps, what will you do without me? Whether you like it or not, we are partners in this affair. It has been that way from the beginning. We need each other."

She was right, he thought. He certainly needed her — in ways he had never dreamed that he would ever need a woman.

"I will think about it," he allowed quietly.

She smiled, not in victory, he realized, but rather in relief. She really had been terrified for his safety tonight.

"Good night, Thaddeus," she said softly. "And thank you for being reasonable."

Reason had little to do with this, he thought. When it came to this woman, he was in the grip of a compulsion as binding as an hypnotic trance.

He crossed the room to open the door for her.

"One thing before you go," he said when she made to move past him. "How did you know that I was in danger tonight?"

She hesitated, looking first startled and then mildly troubled. Finally she shook her head. "I have no idea. I just suddenly knew it."

"That is because the bonds that connect us are growing stronger," he said quietly.

Anxiety shadowed her eyes. Before she could argue with him, he kissed her lightly on the mouth.

"Good night, Leona."

39

The following morning Detective Spellar arrived just as Leona, Thaddeus and Victoria were sitting down to breakfast. He was shown immediately into the room.

He greeted Victoria with a respectful but familiar air.

"Lady Milden," he said.

She gave him a regal nod. "Good morning, Detective. You're here early today."

Leona blinked at the calm, polite reception. It was more than a little extraordinary for a household such as this one to entertain a police detective at breakfast.

Thaddeus introduced Spellar to Leona.

She smiled. "Detective."

Spellar inclined his head politely. "A pleasure, Miss Hewitt."

"Help yourself," Thaddeus said. He waved a hand at the heavily laden sideboard. "And tell us your news."

"Thank you, sir, don't mind if I do."

Spellar regarded the array of silver serving dishes with enthusiasm. "Been up most of the night, and I don't mind admitting I'm half-starved."

Leona studied him with deep curiosity. She had never met a detective before. Uncle Edward had not been keen on associating with policemen.

Last night she'd had only a shadowy glimpse of Spellar when he'd answered the door and spoken with Thaddeus. This morning she saw that he was of medium height, with a sturdy, rounded figure that suggested he enjoyed his food on a grand scale. His thinning hair was going gray. A full mustache dominated broad, cheerful features and served to distract the viewer from the razor-sharp intelligence that gleamed in his blue-green eyes. His coat and trousers were immaculately tailored to flatter his portly frame.

Thaddeus noticed her scrutiny. He looked amused. "I believe I may have mentioned that Detective Spellar is a member of the Arcane Society. He possesses a talent that is especially useful in his profession. He can read a crime scene as though it were a book."

"Mind you," Spellar said from the sideboard, "some books are harder to read than others."

"Were Lancing's lodgings difficult to interpret?" Thaddeus asked.

"No." Spellar heaped eggs and sausages onto a plate in an efficient manner. "Rest assured, the man who jumped to his death off that rooftop last night was the Midnight Monster."

"What did you find?" Leona asked.

"Souvenirs of his kills, if you can believe it. And a written record, as well." Spellar sat down and picked up a fork. "The son of a bitch —" He broke off, reddening furiously. "My apologies, ladies."

Victoria waved an impatient hand. "Never mind, Detective. Please continue. We are all very anxious to hear the outcome of your investigation."

Spellar cleared his throat. "As I was saying, the Monster kept tokens of each of his kills and a detailed account of how he stalked each victim." His mouth twisted in disgust. "There was a button from one of the women's dresses. A scarf from another poor girl, a ribbon from the third and a locket from the fourth. All neatly displayed in a little chest next to their names."

Leona put down her fork, unable to finish her eggs. "You said there were four victims in all, Detective?"

"Sara Jane Hansen, Margaret O'Reilly, Bella Newport and Molly Stubton."

"What of the three who disappeared?" Leona asked urgently.

"We still haven't found any bodies," Spellar said. "All I can tell you at this point is that there were no souvenirs or accounts for those three. It's quite possible those disappearances were unrelated to this case. They don't fit the Monster's pattern."

Thaddeus contemplated that for a moment and then shook his head. "The tavern owner said that the third woman, Annie Spence, described the man who was stalking her as elegantly dressed with pale blond hair."

"Sounds like Lancing," Spellar agreed. "Perhaps he disposed of her body and those of the other two in a different manner."

"As he did with Molly Stubton's body," Leona said.

Thaddeus's eyes tightened a little at the corners. "Lancing made it clear to me that killing Molly Stubton was a task assigned to him by his employer. He enjoyed the business and tried to make her fit into his pattern. But because he was following Delbridge's orders, he could not follow his usual routine. He buried her in the woods because he was ordered to do so."

Victoria frowned. "Perhaps Delbridge also ordered him to get rid of the three girls who vanished in a similar manner."

"Why would he do that?" Leona asked. "It is clear that Molly Stubton had become a problem for Delbridge. He wanted her out of the way. But why would he concern himself with a poor prostitute like Annie Spence? She was the sort of woman the Monster stalked and killed for his own pleasure."

Spellar's broad shoulders rose and fell. "As I said, the three disappearances may not be related to this case. We may never know what happened to Annie and the other two. They would certainly not be the first poor girls to vanish without a trace from the streets of London. But at least we have gotten rid of the Monster. Over the course of my career I have learned to celebrate what small victories come my way."

"What of Lord Delbridge?" Victoria asked. "Did you find any proof that connects the Monster to him?"

Spellar heaved a heavy sigh. "Not yet. They were acquainted, obviously. But Delbridge managed to keep Lancing at arm's length socially. As far as I have been able to determine, the party the other night was the first time Lancing was ever invited to the mansion."

"He was brought in to get rid of Molly Stubton," Thaddeus said. "Lancing probably demanded an invitation to the party as his fee for the murder. He envied Delbridge's place in Society. Felt he had every right to a similar position."

"Speaking of Lord Delbridge," Spellar said, patting his mouth with his napkin. "I went past the mansion before coming here. I knew his lordship would never agree to an interview with me, but I thought it wouldn't hurt to watch the place for a time, just to see if there was any interesting activity. I was curious to see what he would do when he learned that the Monster was dead."

Leona glanced at Thaddeus. His expression remained impassive, but she got the message. He did not want her to so much as even hint at their plans to search the Delbridge mansion. She understood. Detective Spellar was the person who had quietly asked the Arcane Society to investigate the Midnight Monster, but he could not afford to be seen condoning an illegal search of a gentleman's home. Such an action would have been professional suicide. Better for all concerned if he remained blissfully uninformed.

"Did you note anything of interest at Delbridge's address?" Thaddeus asked as though only mildly curious.

"Wasn't anything to note." Spellar's mustache twitched. He reached for a slice of toast. "Place was empty and locked up tight. No servants about. No sign of Delbridge."

Thaddeus stilled. "Delbridge has left London?"

Leona straightened abruptly. The villain had decamped with her crystal. She might never find it now.

Evidently sensing her outrage and alarm, Thaddeus sent her a subtle, silencing look. Resentfully, she bit back the questions she wanted to aim like arrows at Detective Spellar and tried to appear only politely interested.

"Delbridge must have got wind that his hired killer had plunged to his death in what would have struck him as very suspicious circumstances," Spellar said, buttering his toast. "The Monster, a suicide in the street in front of the house previously occupied by Delbridge's own mysteriously vanished mistress. Quite alarming."

Victoria frowned. "But how did he learn of Lancing's death so soon after the event?"

"Can't say." Spellar bit into his toast. "Perhaps he and Lancing had an appointment and Lancing failed to show. Or perhaps he heard the rumors of the death at his club, rushed home, packed and fled."

"But why would he leave?" Leona asked. "By all accounts, he was careful to keep some social distance between himself and Lancing. Why would he panic and run upon learning that Lancing was dead? It would make more sense for him to remain in town and pretend to be as astonished by the news of the identity of the Midnight Monster as everyone else."

Spellar's bushy brows bobbed up and down a few times. "This is mere speculation, you understand, but it occurs to me that perhaps the peculiar circumstances of Lancing's death gave Delbridge cause to fear that he might be the next one to die in a similar fashion."

Thaddeus's expression did not alter by so much as an eyelash, but Leona nearly choked on her tea.

He knows, she thought. With his psychical intuition Detective Spellar had guessed that Lancing's death was neither an accident nor a simple suicide. He knew what had really happened up on that roof last night; he knew and he was going to bury the secret in a grave of silence.

It occurred to Leona that over the course of a long career, a policeman probably kept a great many secrets. A policeman who was also a member of the Arcane Society no doubt kept even more than the usual number.

40

The Delbridge house loomed in the fog-shrouded moonlight, a haunted mansion straight out of a gothic novel. On the evening of the party, the lower floors had been ablaze with lights, but tonight every window was darkened.

Leona stood with Thaddeus just inside the gate at the back of the sprawling gardens. Tension and excitement and a sense of dread shivered through her. She was doing her best to conceal her emotions from Thaddeus, however. She knew it would take very little for him to change his mind and refuse to allow her to accompany him inside the mansion.

"Detective Spellar was right," she said. "The house appears deserted."

"The fact that the servants have departed along with their master indicates that Delbridge intends to be gone for some time," Thaddeus said. "He has a hunting lodge in

Scotland. Perhaps he retreated to it."

"Scotland." She was aghast. "How will I ever find the crystal there?"

"The Arcane Society has a very long reach," Thaddeus said. He sounded as though he was suppressing a laugh.

She raised her chin. "I would remind you that the crystal belongs to me, not the Society."

"And I would remind you that we agreed to postpone a discussion of ownership until after we recovered the damned stone. Are you ready?"

"Yes."

Thaddeus was in his familiar black attire tonight. She, too, was dressed for midnight work. In addition to the servant's coat and trousers that Adam had provided her for the first expedition into the Delbridge mansion, Thaddeus had given her one of his dark linen shirts.

The shirt, naturally, was much too big for her. She had managed to stuff some of the excess fabric into her trousers, but there was no denying that the remainder created a decidedly bulky effect beneath her close-fitting coat. She felt rather like a stuffed toy animal and suspected she looked that way, too.

"We will go in through a library window," Thaddeus said.

"What if he has set one of his nasty little poison traps there?" she asked.

"I think it unlikely. He obviously left in a great hurry. There was little time to set elaborate snares. Why bother? He will have taken the crystal with him."

"Yes, I know," she said glumly. "All the way to Scotland."

"Where's that famous and ever so irritating streak of unbridled positive thinking?"

She decided to ignore that.

They threaded a path through the unkempt, overgrown garden. In spite of Thaddeus's conviction that Delbridge had not set any traps, they both took care to cover their noses and mouths with heavy cloth when he applied his pick to the window lock.

In less than a moment they were inside the library. The draperies were pulled tightly closed, veiling the space in utter darkness. A disturbing energy stirred in the atmosphere. Thaddeus turned up the lantern he had brought along. The yellow glow revealed an array of strange relics scattered around the room. Leona knew that the trickling currents of paranormal power emanated from the antiquities.

"These he likely considers his less valuable artifacts," Thaddeus said. "Unworthy of display in the museum upstairs."

She shivered, well aware that the unpleasant tingling of her senses was nothing compared to what awaited upstairs in the gallery that housed the main portion of Delbridge's collection.

"He must have spent years of his life acquiring these objects," she said.

"Delbridge is nothing if not obsessed with paranormal antiquities." Thaddeus went to the desk, opened a drawer and took out some papers. "Any indication of the crystal?"

She turned on her heel, opening her senses fully. The unnerving aura produced by the objects around her intensified, but there was no trace of the aurora stone's distinctive currents.

"No," she said.

"Not much in the way of helpful information here, either." Thaddeus opened another drawer. "Some bills from his tailor and glove maker that have gone unpaid for several months and a handful of invitations."

"Don't look so disappointed. It was too much to expect that Delbridge would have jotted down the address of that club he hopes to join."

"You're right. But I was thinking positive." He tossed the letters back into the drawer. "Let's try upstairs."

They made their way up the staircase. The

house seemed to echo with a strange sort of silence. It was as if the mansion was inhabited by ghosts, Leona thought.

A short time later they stood in the doorway of Delbridge's bedroom.

"Hmm," Leona said.

Thaddeus gave her a quick, searching look. "What is it?"

"There's no sign that he packed in a frantic hurry. Indeed, everything appears neat and orderly as if he had just walked out a few minutes ago."

Thaddeus held the lantern aloft and surveyed the room. "He would likely have instructed his housekeeper to pack for him. She would have taken care to keep things tidy."

"Perhaps." She hesitated. "Still, one would have expected some indication of anxiety or haste. Delbridge would have been quite desperate to get out of town. Look, his shaving things are still on the dressing table."

Thaddeus crossed the room and opened the wardrobe door. They both looked at the array of clothes inside.

"He never left London," Thaddeus said.

Anticipation sparked through Leona. "Maybe my crystal is still here, too."

"Can you sense it?"

"No, not in this room. Let's try the museum."

They went back down the dark hall to the old stone staircase that linked the new section of the house to the older portion where the museum was housed. Leona braced herself for the nerve-stirring aura produced by the collection of antiquities in the gallery. Nevertheless, the whispers of unpleasant energy sluiced through her senses with the same jarring impact she had experienced the first time. She knew that Thaddeus, too, was reacting to the sensation.

At the top of the staircase they walked across the worn stone floor and entered the long gallery. The lantern light splashed cold hellfire on the artifacts and cases of relics.

They passed the door to the old stone stairwell they had used to escape the night of Delbridge's party. Leona looked at the cabinet in which the crystal had been stored. There was no trace of crystal energy seeping from it.

"It isn't anywhere in this gallery," she said, crushed.

"No, but something else is." Thaddeus held the lantern higher.

Leona followed his gaze down the long gallery and saw the massive stone altar they had used for concealment on their previous visit. There was something different about it tonight. It took her a few heartbeats to realize that the ungainly dark shape sprawled on top of the altar was a body.

"Dear heaven," she whispered, stopping quite suddenly. "Not another one."

Thaddeus went to the altar and stood looking down at the motionless figure. In the fiery light Leona could see a small river of drying blood that started at the point where the ancient dagger was sunk into the man's chest, saturated the expensive coat and once-white shirt, streamed across the stone surface and pooled on the floor.

"Delbridge is certainly not in Scotland," Thaddeus said. "I suspect that the crystal isn't there, either."

41

Some time later Thaddeus lowered himself into one of the two wingback chairs in front of the hearth. He turned the brandy glass between his palms, absently noting the way the firelight transmuting the contents into liquid gold, the color of Leona's eyes.

"We can only presume that Delbridge was murdered because of the crystal," he said. "The possibility that he was stabbed by a conventional housebreaker stretches coincidence too far."

"I agree," Leona said from the other chair. "My crystal has disappeared yet again. *Damnation.* After all these years." She slapped the arm of the chair with her free hand. "To think that only a few days ago I actually held it in my hands."

Fog was stretched out in front of the hearth, his nose on his paws. He did not open his eyes but one of his ears twitched, registering Leona's frustration and tension.

Ever the barometer of his mistress's moods, Thaddeus thought.

As for the connection between himself and Leona, he needed no more evidence that it existed than the sensation of completeness that he felt in her presence. He had been looking for her all of his life without knowing it. She filled in all the empty places, making him whole. He took an elemental satisfaction in just being alive and in the same room with her.

He relaxed deeper into the chair, allowing himself to savor the sight and sensation of Leona sitting here so close to him. She had removed her coat and was now dressed in only her close-fitting trousers and the oversized shirt he had loaned her.

When they had walked back into the house a short time earlier, she had yanked the billowing shirttails free of the trousers. The garment now flowed loosely around her, emphasizing the delicate bones at her throat and at her wrists, where she had turned back the cuffs. How could a woman appear so enticingly sensual dressed in men's clothing? he wondered. He thought about his first impression of her the night she had rounded the corner in the long gallery and flown straight into his arms. *A lady of secrets and mysteries.*

At the moment she was also a woman seething with outrage.

"We'll find the crystal," he said calmly.

She did not seem to hear him. Instead she gazed into the fire he had built, eyes fierce and shadowed.

"It's enough to make one wonder if she really was a sorceress," Leona whispered. "Maybe she cursed the stone."

Thaddeus said nothing, just let the words hang in the air for a moment, waiting for her to realize what she had said.

Leona froze. Then, with an obvious effort of will, she managed to raise the glass in her hand and toss back a large quantity of brandy.

He winced and waited for the inevitable.

Leona inhaled sharply when the brandy hit. Her eyes watered. She gasped and started to cough. Frantically she reached into her pocket and came up empty.

Thaddeus withdrew a square of linen from his own pocket and handed it to her.

"Next time you put on men's clothes you might want to remember that a gentleman never leaves the house without a clean handkerchief," he said.

She ignored him, dabbing at her eyes while she caught her breath. Eventually she regained her composure.

"I'm more accustomed to sherry," she said weakly.

"Obviously. Now, then, I believe we have played this particular game long enough."

"Game?" Her voice was still breathy from the fire of the brandy. "What game?"

He rotated the glass in his hand again. "I think it's time you told me why you are so convinced that you have a claim on the aurora stone."

She stilled as if he had put her into a trance. Fog raised his head and fixed her with an intent expression.

"Old family heirloom," Leona said smoothly.

"Which your family seems to be in the habit of losing on a regular basis."

"Primarily because people connected to the Arcane Society keep stealing it," she shot back.

He shrugged and drank some more of his brandy.

She exhaled deeply, stretched out her legs toward the hearth and slumped into her chair.

"You know, don't you?" she said.

"That you are a descendant of Sybil the Virgin Sorceress? It was a guess until now, but, I think, a fairly reasonable and logical one under the circumstances."

She made a face. "We all hated the title the Society gave her, you know."

"Sybil the Virgin Sorceress?" He shrugged. "Seems rather catchy to me. Just the sort of thing you expect from a legend."

"She did not practice sorcery, no more than you or I do. She was a brilliant, psychically gifted alchemist, just like your infamous Sylvester Jones. Today, she would have been called a scientist."

"Sybil the Virgin Scientist doesn't have quite the same ring."

"She wasn't a virgin, either," Leona said dryly. "At least not for the whole of her life. I'm proof of that. So are my mother and my grandmother and the whole long line of my female ancestors before them. We are all descended from Sybil."

"All right, I'll grant you that the term *virgin sorceress* may have been something of a theatrical embellishment."

She gave a disdainful little sniff. "Typical Arcane Society legend."

"We're good at that sort of thing," he agreed.

Leona frowned. "I understand the sorceress part, but why on earth did she get labeled a virgin?"

"Blame that on Sylvester. He was furious because she refused to surrender said virginity to him. According to his journal she told him that she had consecrated herself to alchemy."

"He didn't love her," Leona said tightly. "He just wanted to use her as part of an experiment to see if his own psychical talents could be passed down to his off-spring."

"I know. He found a couple of other talented women instead, one of whom was my own ancestress. But it always infuriated Sylvester that Sybil had refused him."

Leona leaned her head against the back of the chair. "How long have you known?"

"Your skill with crystals, of course, was the main clue."

"I'm hardly the only crystal worker in the world."

"No, but according to the legend, the aurora stone was different from other crystals. Sylvester was of the opinion that the talent required to channel energy through it was extremely rare. Sybil was the only person he ever found who could work it. Stands to reason that someone who had inherited her unique abilities would also be able to employ it."

Leona's mouth tightened. She did not take her attention off the fire.

"Mmm," she said.

He waited a moment longer. When it became obvious she was not going to say anything more, he looked at Fog.

"The legend also states that Sybil had a loyal wolf for a companion. Sylvester suspected that she and the beast shared a psychical bond. He found that fascinating because until then he had believed that only humans possessed the potential for paranormal talents."

"It sounds like all you had to go on were a few coincidences with a legend."

"There is also the brief description of Sybil that Sylvester wrote in his journal. It bears an uncanny resemblance to you."

She turned her head to look at him. "Uncanny?"

"*'The sorceress is exceedingly dangerous, with hair as dark as night and* eyes *of a strange shade of amber,'*" he quoted. "*'She possesses the power to control one's very dreams.'*"

Leona looked suddenly interested. "You think I am exceedingly dangerous?"

"In the most delightful way."

"Did Sylvester describe Sybil in more detail?" she asked.

"As I recall, the terms *treacherous vixen, shrew, she-cat* and *virago* were thrown about somewhat liberally in his journal."

"Hardly a flattering description."

"Depends on one's point of view, I suppose. I found it . . . intriguing."

"That was it? You leaped to the conclusion that I am Sybil's descendant based on that rather unflattering description and a few thin coincidences?"

"There was one final clue that was not so frail," he admitted.

"What was it?"

He rose, picked up the brandy bottle and splashed more of the contents into his glass. "You failed to ask the right question when I told you that Caleb Jones believes there is a plot afoot to steal the Arcane Society's most closely held secret."

She watched him, wary and bemused. "As I recall, I asked any number of questions when you told me about the conspiracy."

"Ah, but you did not ask me the most obvious question. You did not ask me to explain the nature of a secret that could cause men to kill."

She blinked once and then sighed in disgust. "Damn."

"You didn't need to ask, did you?" He saluted her lightly with the glass and sat down again. "You already knew all about the formula."

"The legend of the founder's formula is

part of my family's heritage," she admitted. "It was passed down from mother to daughter. Sybil said Sylvester's obsession with perfecting the elixir that he believed would expand and enhance his paranormal powers was madness. He thought it would even extend his life. She was convinced that, in truth, it killed him."

"Nevertheless, she stole the formula?"

Leona glowered. "She was his assistant for a time. She made a copy and took it with her when she left. She didn't steal it."

"Why did she take it if she thought it wouldn't work?"

"For a time she had dreams of perfecting it, thereby proving herself superior to Sylvester. They were fierce rivals until the end. But Sybil finally came to believe that the elixir would always be too dangerous to use. Still, she could not bring herself to destroy her copy of the formula. Or so she implies in her letters."

"Fascinating."

Leona spread her hands wide. "Very well. You know who I am. I suppose it does not matter how you came to that conclusion. Sybil's journal of experiments was lost early on. No one in my family knows what happened to it or the strongbox where she supposedly kept it and her other secrets. But I have two of the notebooks she used more or less as diaries and some letters she wrote. In those she made her feelings about Sylvester excruciatingly clear."

"What else did she have to say about him?" he asked.

"Among other things, she referred to him as an arrogant mountebank and a great liar."

"Why did she call him a liar?"

"He tried to woo her by promising her that they would work side by side, sharing their secrets and developing their powers. She fell in love with him and believed that he loved her, too. But when she realized that all he really wanted was to use her in his breeding experiment, she was outraged. She understood then that there would only be one great passion in Sylvester's life and that passion was his search for a formula. So she left."

"Taking the aurora stone and a copy of the formula with her."

"She had a right to both," Leona said forcefully.

He smiled.

"What do you find so amusing about all this?" Leona demanded.

"What I find vastly entertaining is the notion that I will be escorting the descendant of Sybil the Virgin Sorceress to the Arcane Society's first Spring Ball. Nothing the Society or my family loves more than a good legend."

42

"She's the direct descendant of Sybil?" Gabriel Jones smiled widely. "Wait until Venetia hears about this."

The new Master of the Arcane Society sat behind his desk in his library, every inch the modern English gentleman. One would never know, Thaddeus thought, that Gabriel was one of the most dangerous men in London, thanks to his talents.

Like many of those in the Jones line, he was a parahunter with reflexes, senses and instincts as keen as those of any large beast of prey. Even when he was calm and at ease, the telltale traces of the prowling paranormal energy in his aura were distinguishable if one was sensitive to such things.

"Wait until I hear about what?" Venetia said from the doorway of the library. She smiled when she noticed Thaddeus. "Thaddeus. How nice to see you. I didn't know you were here."

"Good day to you, Venetia." Thaddeus got to his feet. "You're looking lovely as always. Have you just come from taking a portrait?"

"Yes, as a matter of fact."

In addition to her new role as the wife of the head of the Society, Venetia was also a fashionable photographer whose skills were much in demand. Very few of her wealthy, elite clients, however, were aware that her talents went beyond the ability to take stunning pictures.

With her talent, Venetia could view auras quite clearly. It was true, of course, that many, even those who laughed at the entire notion of the paranormal, were somewhat sensitive to auras. Most attributed the occasional tingle of uneasiness or fascination or other inexplicable reaction they experienced around certain individuals to their own intuition.

The truth was that they were actually sensing some faint whisper of the aura of the person in question. Those who were endowed with strong paranormal abilities were naturally more acutely sensitive to the traces of energy that emanated from others. But only a few people possessed the rare type of second sight required to see the full and unique spectrum of another individual's entire aura, the way Venetia could.

"You will never guess who Thaddeus will be escorting to the Spring Ball," Gabriel said. He went forward to greet her. "A crystal worker who just happens to be a direct descendant of Sybil the Virgin Sorceress."

Venetia looked at him, astonished. "I thought the tale of Sybil and the aurora stone was just another Arcane Society legend."

"You know what they say, there's a grain of truth in every good legend."

He kissed her, a brief, affectionate, husbandly welcome, but Thaddeus sensed the currents of heat, intimacy and love in the embrace. The Master of the Arcane Society was a happily married man.

"There are also, it turns out, two versions of any good legend," Thaddeus said, watching Venetia sit down in the chair across from him. "Leona feels very strongly that the aurora stone belongs to her. She says it was Sybil's to begin with, and I suspect she is right."

"The problem," Gabriel said, "is that, like the formula, the stone is said to be dangerous."

"In what way?" Venetia asked.

"It's not clear." Gabriel sat down behind his desk. "According to Sylvester's journal it has the ability to destroy a man's powers."

Venetia's mouth twitched at the corners. "Oh, my. You mean it can render a man impotent? No wonder you Jones men are so anxious to get it back under lock and key."

Thaddeus laughed. "We think, or at least we hope, that the powers in question refer to psychical abilities, not the other sort."

"Nevertheless, a man can't be too careful," Gabriel said. He grew more serious. "Sylvester believed that Sybil somehow tuned the crystal so that only she could control its energy. Evidently some of her descendants inherited the ability."

"Leona can work it," Thaddeus said quietly.

Venetia frowned. "But if no one else can work the crystal, why are so many people willing to kill for it?"

"We don't know," Gabriel admitted. "But Caleb suspects that, in one way or another, this is all connected to another attempt to steal the founder's formula."

Venetia sighed. "That is one Arcane Society legend that should have remained a legend, if you ask me. If you and Caleb had not discovered it when you excavated Sylvester's tomb, we wouldn't be having all these problems."

"I can't argue with that," Gabriel said. "But the damage has been done. What's more, something tells me that damned formula is going to be a problem for the Society from now on."

"And so will men like Lancing," Thaddeus said. "For obvious reasons the police will always have difficulty stopping such criminals."

"I agree." Gabriel folded his hands on top of the desk. "As it happens, I have given such matters a great deal of thought lately. I believe the Society has a responsibility not only to protect its most dangerous secrets but also to try to control powerful rogues such as Lancing."

"What have you got in mind?" Thaddeus asked.

"I think the time has come to establish an office dedicated to security matters within the Society. It will be under the control of the Council and the Master."

"Who will you put in charge of this new office?" Venetia asked.

Thaddeus smiled slowly. "Someone who is preternaturally good at seeing patterns where others see only chaos, perhaps? A first-rate conspiracy theorist?"

"How did you guess?" Gabriel laughed. "I intend to speak to Caleb immediately."

43

The shoemaker was a skeletally thin, rumpled man with a nervous air and a pair of gold-rimmed spectacles. He employed two burly assistants.

"I do apologize for the confusion concerning the time of my appointment here today," he said. "But Madame LaFontaine sent a message informing me that I was to arrive promptly at eleven to fit Miss Hewitt with her dancing slippers."

"We were not expecting you until three o'clock," Victoria said, "but as we have just finished with the milliner we may as well deal with the slippers. It will be one less thing to bother with this afternoon."

"Yes, of course." The shoemaker turned to Leona and gave her an anxious, ingratiating smile. "This won't take long. Madame LaFontaine was adamant that the slippers complement the color of your gown. I have brought several pairs with me so that you will have a wide selection."

Leona looked at the large wooden box the two assistants had set down on the carpet. More decisions, she thought glumly. Under normal circumstances she would have savored the process of selecting dancing slippers to go with the gorgeous gown Madame LaFontaine had designed. Indeed, the whole business of preparing for the Spring Ball should have been utterly intoxicating. She had never been invited to such a grand affair in her entire life. Not only would it be a glorious, glittering occasion, she would be on the arm of the man with whom she had fallen head-over-heels in love.

But the circumstances were anything but normal. The only reason she would be attending the Spring Ball was so that she could help Thaddeus identify the people involved in a dangerous conspiracy. In addition, if it got out that she was Edward Pipewell's niece, the woman who had, however unwittingly, helped fleece a dozen of the most important men in the Arcane Society, she would be lucky to get through the night without being arrested. Those two facts had removed a lot of her enthusiasm for the business of choosing such things as dancing slippers.

Victoria, however, was remarkably animated. Evidently she'd had another good night's sleep. She eyed the box with a look of great expectation.

"Let us see what you have brought," she said to the shoemaker.

"But of course, madam." He gestured toward his two assistants. "The samples, if you please."

One of the men went to open the large crate. The hair stirred on the nape of Leona's neck. Why did the shoemaker need two such large assistants? she wondered.

She glanced at Victoria, whose attention was focused on the long, coffin-sized box. The assistant had the lid open now. He reached inside. Leona did not see any shoes.

"If you don't mind, I'll just close this door so that we won't be interrupted," the shoemaker said softly.

Leona swung around, an inexplicable alarm shafting through her.

"No," she said. "Don't —"

But it was too late. One of the big assistants seized her, pinning her arms and clamping a beefy hand across her lips. She heard Victoria's horrified gasp and then an ominous silence. The strong odor of chemical fumes filled the air.

She struggled fiercely, digging her nails into her captor's arms and kicking wildly.

"Hurry," the shoemaker snapped. "We have only moments."

"She's a right little she-devil," the man holding Leona muttered. "I should just throttle the bitch."

"She must not be harmed," the shoemaker yelped, furious now. "Do you hear me? I need her alive."

"I hear ye," the man muttered. "Be quick about it, Paddon."

The second man was in front of her now. He held a damp rag in one hand. She could smell the noxious chemicals in which it had been soaked.

He forced the fabric across her nose. She tried to kick him in the vicinity of his cock, but her skirts impeded the effort. Should have worn my men's clothes, she thought.

The vapors flooded her senses. The world tilted. Darkness poured into the sunny morning room, sweeping her away into an endless night.

The last thing she heard was Fog. Out in the gardens he started to howl. He sounded like a lost soul in hell.

44

"I do wish that wretched dog would cease that interminable howling," Victoria muttered. She reclined on the sofa, a damp cloth across her forehead, a bracing cup of tea at her side. "The servants told me he started at about the time the kidnappers attacked us. He hasn't stopped. It is beginning to affect my nerves."

Thaddeus looked at Fog, who was still out in the garden. The dog was visible through the glass panes of the French doors. He raised his head and loosed another blood-curdling howl.

Thaddeus sympathized. He wanted to shout his rage to the skies, too, but he managed to suppress the impulse. He could not afford the luxury of venting his emotions in such a pointless manner. Time was of the essence, he knew that as surely as he knew who had taken Leona. The kidnapper needed her but probably not for long.

He decided not to further alarm Victoria by informing her that it was undoubtedly the necessity of keeping Leona alive and sane that had saved both of them. The bastard had used chloroform, not the nightmare vapor.

Fifteen minutes earlier he had returned home to discover the disaster. The staff had not realized that anything was amiss until shortly before he had walked through the front door. The scene had been one of panic and chaos.

"Found Lady Milden on the carpet," Gribbs, the butler, had explained sadly. "The shoemaker and his assistants had been gone for some time, along with Miss Hewitt, of course."

The kidnappers had stuffed Leona into the wooden crate and taken her out through the tradesmen's entrance. No one had thought it amiss that the shoemaker and his assistants had departed so soon after their arrival. The shoemaker had explained in the most apologetic manner that there had been a dreadful mix-up in the appointment times and that Lady Milden had instructed him to return at a more convenient hour.

The crate was loaded into a waiting carriage, and the entire lot had disappeared into the fog.

But with a touch of hypnosis Thaddeus had elicited detailed descriptions of the shoemaker and his assistants from Gribbs. He had not recognized the shoemaker, but there was no doubt in his mind as to the identities of the two burly men who had helped him kidnap Leona.

"They were the two guards Delbridge employed the night of the party at the mansion," he said to Victoria. "The bastard probably didn't know any other men in that line of work so he contacted them."

She frowned. "I don't understand."

"Neither do I, but it is a place to start."

"Dear heaven, she is in mortal danger, isn't she?"

"Yes."

He crossed the library and opened the French doors.

Fog stopped crying vengeance to the heavens and looked at him, ears pricked, cold death in his eyes.

"Come with me," Thaddeus said quietly. "We are going to find her."

45

Leona awoke to nausea and the murmured ravings of a madwoman. For one horrified moment she thought she was the one carrying on the crazed, fearful conversation.

"The demon is from hell. Ye'd never know it to look at him but comes straight from hell, he does. Is that where you come from?"

Leona opened her eyes cautiously. The world was no longer spinning as it had been when she had slipped away into unconsciousness, but it was still a very dark place. The shoemaker's box. Perhaps she was trapped inside.

A wave of terror shot through her. She sat up quickly, too quickly. Her stomach rebelled. For a few seconds she thought she was going to be quite ill. She squeezed her eyes shut and tried to breathe deeply. Gradually the roiling sensation calmed.

"He's a demon but ye'd best not tell him that. Thinks he's special, he does. Calls himself a scientist."

Leona risked opening her eyes again and discovered that she was sitting on the edge of a cot positioned against the wall of a small stone chamber. Bands of lantern light filtered through the iron bars set in the door of the cell, but there were no windows. That explained the deep shadows.

"It was the demon's servants that brought ye down here to hell."

Leona considered closely for a few seconds and decided she was not hearing voices in her head. There was someone else in the cell. She looked around and saw the woman huddled in the corner.

The other prisoner wore a faded brown dress. She peered at Leona through a tangle of matted blonde hair. There was a desperate, hollow-eyed look about her.

"Says he's a scientist, but he's really a demon," she explained to Leona.

"If you're talking about the man who pretends to be a shoemaker, I agree with you," Leona said softly.

"No, no, no, not a shoemaker." The woman twitched violently in her agitation. "A scientist."

"I understand," Leona said gently. "The scientist is really a demon."

"Yes, that's right." The woman seemed

relieved now that her main point had been grasped. "A terrible demon. He's got magic potions that make the nightmares real."

Leona shivered. "I know."

A tiny thrill of awareness fluttered through her, stirring the hair on the nape of her neck. Thaddeus and Fog were searching for her. She knew it as surely as she knew the sun would rise in the morning. She needed to buy time for them to find her.

"Says he's a scientist, but he's a monster, just like the other one," the woman explained in a terrified whisper.

Leona frowned. "Who are you talking about? Who is the other one?"

"I thought he was a gentleman, ye see. So handsome, he was." The woman's voice changed to a wistful sigh. "So fine and elegant. He has the prettiest hair. Like gold. He looks like one of those angels in the old paintings."

Leona gripped the edges of the cot. "Did you say he has gold hair?"

"Smiled so nicely ye'd never know he was a monster." The woman's voice roughened in despair. "Knew he'd had his eye on me. Thought he'd pay well. But he lied. Brought me down here to hell, he did."

"Dear heaven," Leona whispered. "You're Annie Spence."

Annie jerked wildly and pressed deeper into the grimy corner. "How do ye know my name? Are you a demon, too?"

"No, I'm not a demon. Annie, listen to me, the golden-haired monster who brought you here is dead."

"No, no, ye can't kill monsters and demons."

"His name was Lancing, and I swear to you that he is dead." She tried to think of some way to get through Annie's fantasies. "The Monster died when he encountered The Ghost."

"I've heard about The Ghost." Hope sparked briefly in Annie's voice. "They whisper about him on the street."

"Lancing tried to run from The Ghost. He fell to his death."

"No, that can't be true." Annie sank back into despair. "The Monster's one of the demons. Not even The Ghost can kill a demon."

"I saw the body myself, Annie. What's more, The Ghost will soon come here to rescue us."

"Nobody can rescue us," Annie explained sadly. "Not even The Ghost. It's too late. We're already in hell."

"Look at me, Annie."

Annie cringed, but she met Leona's eyes.

"Too late."

"No, it's not too late," Leona insisted fiercely. "The Ghost will come straight down here into hell itself, and take us out."

Annie looked doubtful.

A door opened somewhere outside the cell. Annie buried her face in her hands and started to sob quietly.

A familiar figure appeared on the other side of the iron bars. Lamplight gleamed on the shoemaker's bald head and sparkled on the frames of his spectacles.

"I see you're awake, Miss Hewitt." He beamed. "Excellent. Your audience is gathering even as we speak. They're counting on you to give a thrilling performance. Indeed you may consider it the performance of your life."

Leona did not move from her position on the cot. "Who are you?"

"Allow me to introduce myself. I am Dr. Basil Hulsey. Like you, Miss Hewitt, I am an expert in the energy of dreams. Unlike you, however, I specialize in creating nightmares."

46

Shuttle had grown up hard on the streets, and he'd seen a lot of things in his time, things that could make a grown man shiver in his shoes. But few were as frightening as the shadowy figure standing in front of him now. He'd heard rumors of The Ghost, but he'd always laughed at the tales. Tonight he was not laughing.

"It was just another bit of employment for me and Paddon," he said urgently, desperate to be believed. "We didn't hurt the ladies, I swear. Just put 'em out for a bit with one of the doctor's potions."

"You kidnapped one of the women," The Ghost said.

Shuttle trembled. There was something strange about the voice. It turned everything in the vicinity, including The Ghost himself, to shadows. The phantom stood no more than a couple of steps away, but Shuttle could not make out his face. Part of the trouble was that it was almost midnight. Nevertheless, there was a street-lamp nearby. He should have been able to see The Ghost more clearly.

"It wasn't a kidnapping," he said, eager to explain. "We just tucked her into the box and loaded her into the carriage. A kidnapping is when you hold a person until someone pays ransom, ye see. This weren't like that. Not at all. Just a job of work, see. Paddon and me got paid for a day's labor, and that was the end of it."

"Where did you take the woman you kidnapped?"

The voice rolled over him like a great wave. He was helpless in its grip.

He told The Ghost where he and Paddon had taken the woman.

47

"It's a pity you and I did not meet under other circumstances, Miss Hewitt," Hulsey said through the iron bars. "We would have made an excellent team in the laboratory."

"Do you think so?" Leona could not think of anything else to do except keep Hulsey talking.

"Yes, indeed," Hulsey said, waxing enthusiastic. "Your knowledge of the power of crystals to influence the dream state would have been most welcome. I am hoping that after you have satisfied the members of the Third Circle, they will give you to me. It would be so interesting to see if you could use the aurora stone to free yourself from one of my chemically induced nightmares."

Annie whimpered quietly in the corner.

Leona got to her feet and went to the door of the cell. She studied Hulsey. The man looked like an oversized insect.

"I'm amazed that a researcher who prides

himself on being a scientist would give any credence to the powers of a woman who claims to make her living working crystals," she said. "Never say that you actually believe in the paranormal, Doctor."

Hulsey chuckled and clasped his hands very tightly in front of his thin chest. "Ah, but I do, Miss Hewitt. You see, I also possess psychical abilities. In fact, I have been a member of the Arcane Society for many years."

An icy chill went down her spine. "What is the nature of your talent?"

Hulsey preened. "I am no ordinary chemist, Miss Hewitt. I possess a genius for the science that is positively preternatural. I have devoted my talent to the study of the dream state."

"Why?"

"Because it fascinates me. You see, the dream state is the one condition in which the barriers that separate the normal and the paranormal are blurred. Everyone dreams, Miss Hewitt. It is proof that everyone possesses a paranormal side to his or her nature, whether or not the individual is aware of it."

She forced a careless little shrug. "I happen to agree with you. What of it?"

"I congratulate you on your insight. But

evidently you have not taken your understanding of the nature of dreams to the logical conclusion."

"Which is?"

Behind the lenses of his spectacles, Hulsey's eyes glittered. "Don't you see? If one can manipulate a man's dreams, one can control that man utterly."

The ancient abbey ruins loomed in the moonlight. Thaddeus stood in the shadows at the edge of the woods, Caleb on one side, Fog on the other. They studied the pile of stone.

"She is in there," Thaddeus said.

"Unless the bastards moved her to another location after Shuttle and his associate delivered her here," Caleb said.

"She's in there," Thaddeus repeated. "Look at Fog. He can sense her, too."

They studied Fog, who stood tense and alert, nose pointed at the abbey.

"Hard to believe his canine senses have caught her scent at this distance and through all that stone," Caleb said, sounding very thoughtful.

"I think he shares some sort of link with her. So do I."

Caleb did not argue. "Can you keep him under control when we go in after her? If he gets loose and starts howling, the bastards will realize what we are about."

Thaddeus tugged gently on the leash attached to Fog's collar. The dog did not react in any way. All of his attention remained fixed on the abbey.

"To tell you the truth, I don't know if I'll be able to restrain him once he gets closer to Leona," Thaddeus said. "All I know is that we need him. He's our best hope of finding her quickly in that pile of stone."

48

"Why did you bring Annie here?" Leona asked.

"Annie?" Hulsey looked baffled. "Is that her name?"

In her corner, Annie cried out as though she had been struck.

"You don't even know her name?" Leona asked.

"She isn't important. Just a research subject. The last two died in the course of the experiments. I told Delbridge that I needed another. He sent the Monster out to collect one for me."

"You're the one responsible for those girls disappearing from the streets. You conducted experiments on them."

Hulsey chuckled. "I could hardly conduct experiments on myself now, could I?"

"How dare you," Leona said fiercely.

"Really, Miss Hewitt, there's no need for such strong emotions. I'm a scientist, and

I require test subjects. Annie is not important. Neither were the other two. They were merely common prostitutes."

"What have you done to her?"

"I have been trying to create an antidote for my nightmare vapor. It would be useful to have in the event of accidents. As it stands now, the nightmares are irreversible. Annie inhaled the vapor yesterday. I gave her the antidote last night."

Leona tightened her hands into small fists. "It does not appear to have been effective."

"Actually, Annie has survived longer than the other two girls, but I must admit, this experiment has not been a success." Hulsey exhaled a little sigh of regret. "Annie is quite insane now. She will not recover. I shall have to get rid of her and find another girl for the next phase of my experiments."

Leona wanted to wrap her fingers around his scrawny throat and squeeze the life out of him. She forced herself to find another topic instead.

"Lancing is dead," she announced.

"Yes, I heard." Hulsey's sharp face twisted in disgust. "Fell trying to jump from one rooftop to another, they said. Good riddance. The man had some extremely primeval talents that I admit were of limited use, but he was mentally unstable. I told

Delbridge he was dangerous, but his lordship was quite taken with the notion of having his own parahunter for a hired killer."

"Delbridge died only a few hours after Lancing. He was stabbed with one of his own artifacts, an ancient dagger. Was that your work?"

"Of course not." Hulsey was affronted. "I'm a scientist. I have no interest in physical violence. If I'd wanted his lordship dead, I would have used my nightmare-inducing vapor."

"Who killed Delbridge?"

"The leader of the Third Circle."

"Why didn't he kill you as well?"

Hulsey chuckled, genuinely amused. "Now, why would he want to kill me? I am the only one who knows enough about the science of chemistry to be able to comprehend the founder's formula when it is recovered. I am the only one who is brilliant enough to prepare it and conduct the tests necessary to ensure that it is safe to use. No, no, my dear, I assure you the members of the Third Circle need me."

"This is about the founder's formula, then? In that case, why is everyone after the aurora stone?"

"The aurora stone is necessary to unlock the formula, as you will soon discover. The members of the Third Circle need you to work the crystal for them to open a certain strongbox. They expect to find the formula inside the box."

A conspiracy, Leona thought, just as Caleb Jones had deduced but perhaps far more complex than he assumed. It sounded as if the conspirators were organized in ascending circles of power. If there was a third circle, it stood to reason that there was probably also a first and second, perhaps more.

"Speaking of the stone," Hulsey continued, "I wish to inquire what, precisely, happened that night in Delbridge's gallery? Someone triggered the trap, but we never found a body. It was Ware, wasn't it?"

She shivered. "You know about Mr. Ware?"

"Yes, of course. Delbridge made inquiries and determined that Ware is a member of the Arcane Society." Hulsey frowned. "He is a psychical hypnotist, is he not?"

There was no reason to give him any more information than necessary, Leona thought. She said nothing.

Hulsey nodded to himself. "That is what I thought. He must have been in a very bad state after he inhaled the vapor. I am very curious to know how you used the crystal to save him."

"What makes you think I saved him?"

"It is the only explanation. No one has ever come out of one of my nightmares." Hulsey's head bobbed again. "Yes, indeed, I really must be allowed to have you after the members have finished with you tonight. I will make it clear that if they want my expertise with the formula they must give you to me." Hulsey took out his pocket watch and flipped open the cover. "Won't be long now. The last member of the group arrived a short time ago. They'll be sending someone along shortly to escort you to the chamber."

Hulsey turned and hastened away. Leona heard a door open and close. Silence descended on the outer room.

Annie whimpered again. "We're both in hell. Don't ye understand?"

Leona turned around. "We're in hell, Annie, but we're going to get out."

"No." Annie shook her head in despair. "We're trapped here until the end of time."

Leona walked across the small space. She undid the top three buttons of her bodice and pulled out the red crystal pendant.

"Look at my necklace, Annie. Concentrate on it as hard as you can and tell me about your dreams."

Annie was bewildered, but she was too

exhausted to disobey. She looked at the crystal.

"I'm in hell," she whispered. "There are demons all around, but the most dreadful one of all is the scientist . . ."

Leona felt the familiar stirring of troubled dream energy. She focused on the small storm brewing inside the stone, channeling her own psychical currents.

The crystal started to glow.

The door in the outer chamber opened again. Leona watched through the bars of her cell as two men wearing black cowled robes tromped into the room. The light glinted on the silver half-masks that covered their faces. She swallowed the sick dread that threatened to choke her and summoned up all of the acting skills that Uncle Edward had taught her.

"Nobody mentioned that the invitation was to a costume ball," she said.

"Watch your tongue if you want to stay alive for the rest of the night," one of the men said. "The Order does not tolerate insolence."

She thought about what Hulsey had said earlier. Evidently the members of the organization required her crystal-working skills. As long as the villains needed her services, there was hope. Uncle Edward's words rang in her ears. *"Always think positive, Leona. It is not as if there is anything to be gained by dwelling on the negative."*

"Evidently the Order doesn't tolerate a sense of humor, either," she said, surveying the two men through the bars. "Tell me, does one go to a tailor to acquire robes and a mask like those or does one buy them ready-made in Oxford Street?"

"Shut your mouth, you foolish woman," one of the men hissed. "You have no conception of the kind of power you are playing with tonight."

"But you will learn soon enough," the other vowed.

Rough words but spoken with upper-class accents. These two were not from the streets; their kind inhabited exclusive gentlemen's clubs.

One of the pair reached inside his robe. Keys jangled. A moment later the cell door swung open, hinges grinding. The first man reached inside, grabbed her arm and hauled her out of the tiny chamber. The one with the keys hurriedly closed and locked the door.

Neither of them paid any attention to Annie, who was huddled in her corner, conversing softly with herself.

"Brought us down here to hell, y'see," she whispered. "Demons everywhere."

The two robed figures forced Leona through the door in the outer room and along a shadowy stone hall. Candles smoked and flickered in wall sconces.

"You know, you really should think about installing gas," Leona said. "Candles are so old-fashioned. They give the impression that the Order is not terribly modern in its thinking."

One of the men tightened his grip on her arm so violently she knew she would have bruises in the morning. Always assuming she survived until morning. *No, don't think like that.* She forced herself to concentrate, the way she did when she channeled dream energy. *Where are you, Thaddeus? I know you're looking for me. Can you sense me? I am here. I do wish you would hurry. The situation appears to be getting somewhat dire.*

The two men brought her to a halt in front of an iron-and-wood door. The cowled figure on the left opened it. The other man pushed Leona into a candlelit chamber.

"The crystal worker," one of the men announced.

Three men in robes and masks occupied a horseshoe-shaped table. There was no sign of Hulsey.

"Bring the woman to me," commanded the man at the head of the table.

One of the men who had brought her into the room reached for her arm again. She sidestepped him neatly and walked to stand in front of the figure who had spoken. When she got closer she saw that his mask was gold.

"My name is Miss Hewitt," she said coldly. "And I really must tell you that mature adults consider dressing up in long robes and wearing silly masks a game that is best reserved for children. Such activities do not imply any degree of maturity."

There was a murmur of anger from around the table, but the leader seemed unperturbed.

"I applaud your spirit, Miss Hewitt," he said, amused. "As it happens, you're going to need it. Do you know why you are here?"

No need to mention that Hulsey had said they needed her quite urgently, she decided. As cards went, it was not the highest one in the deck, but neither was it the lowest.

"I assume you want me to work some crystal," she said. "Really, you needn't have gone to such overly dramatic lengths to obtain my services. I take appointments. I'm sure I could have fit you in early next week."

"Tonight works much better for us," Gold Mask said. "We have been informed that you can control a certain crystal known as the aurora stone. I hope, for your sake, that is true."

Her pulse, already racing, began to pound more heavily.

"I have never encountered a crystal that I could not work."

"This one is quite unique. It is the key to an old strongbox. If you are successful in opening the box, we of the Third Circle will be very pleased. Indeed, in future we might have more employment for you."

"I'm always in the market for new clients."

"If you fail, however, you will be quite useless to us," Gold Mask concluded softly. "Indeed, you will become a liability."

She chose to ignore that. *Think positive.*

"I will be happy to see what I can do for you," she said briskly. "I assume you are acquainted with my usual fees?"

There was a short, startled silence. No one had planned to pay her a fee for this night's work. That probably did not bode well.

"Never mind, I'll send you my bill later," she continued smoothly. "Now, then, why don't you show me this aurora stone and let me see what I can do with it?"

Gold Mask rose. "This way, Miss Hewitt."

He walked toward a door. The others got up, formed a tight knot around Leona and filed after him.

Gold Mask opened the heavy door, revealing another, smaller candlelit chamber. Leona felt the familiar tingle of energy from the aurora stone. She was careful to keep her expression impassive. The less the members of the Third Circle knew about her ability to work the crystal, the better.

Inside the chamber an old steel chest elaborately decorated with alchemical symbols sat on a carpet. The aurora stone, dull and opaque, rested in an indentation on top.

In spite of the frightening circumstances, a small rush of excitement flashed through Leona. Sybil's strongbox. For generations it had been no more than a legend among the women of her family.

Doing her best to appear calm, she walked across the chamber and examined the strongbox. The thin sheet of gold that covered the lid was etched with a very familiar alchemical code. It was the code in which her mother's journal was written, the code that had been passed down to all of Sybil's daughters for two hundred years.

Silently she translated the warning Sybil had left:

Know ye that the aurora stone is the key. All the mysteries inside will be destroyed if the box is forced by any man's hand.

"Interesting," she said, as though the strongbox was nothing more than an artifact on display in a museum. She looked at Gold Mask. "May I ask why you simply didn't pry open the lid?"

"As it happens, Miss Hewitt, I am something of an expert on the code used by Sybil the Virgin Sorceress. According to the writing on the lid of that strongbox, the aurora stone is the only key that may be safely employed to open it."

Damn. He was able to translate Sybil's code.

"How odd," she said.

"We are waiting, Miss Hewitt." Gold Mask was losing patience. "The instructions are clear. I intend to see that they are followed. It only remains to be seen if you possess the talent to work the stone. If you are not successful, I shall be forced to seek the services of another crystal worker."

"Let me see what I can do for you," she said.

She went to stand on the far side of the table that held the strongbox, facing her audience of five. Slowly, trying to infuse as much drama into the moment as possible, she raised her hands and placed her fingertips on the aurora stone.

Power whispered to her. She channeled a small amount of energy into the heart of the stone.

The crystal pulsed with moonlight.

The men in the cowled robes sucked in their breaths as one and surged closer.

They were riveted, just as she wanted.

"She can work it," one of them said, awed.

"Damnation," another muttered, "will you look at that?"

"You must control your audience, Leona. Never allow your audience to control you."

She opened her senses fully to the power of the crystal.

49

Fog raced through the vaulted doorway and charged down another stone passage, head low to the stone floor. Thaddeus and Caleb followed, pistols in hand. It was all Thaddeus could do to maintain his grip on the leash. The dog had not commenced howling when they had entered the darkened abbey, as Caleb had feared. Instead, as if he understood the need for both haste and silence, he had settled into the hunt.

He had led them through a maze of corridors, the ancient scriptorium and into the ruins of the kitchens. From there he had whined softly until Thaddeus had opened a door. Then he had plunged down a flight of narrow steps, claws scrabbling on stone.

They had not encountered anyone thus far. That worried Thaddeus more than anything else that had happened. Where were Leona's captors?

"There should be guards," he said to Caleb.

"Not necessarily." Caleb raised his lantern to angle the light into the empty chamber they were passing. "They desire secrecy, but they have little reason to fear the police."

"They have reason to fear us."

"True." Caleb's smile was cold. "But they do not yet know that, do they?"

Fog came to a halt in front of another door. Again he whined softly.

"Stand clear," Thaddeus said quietly.

Caleb flattened his back against the wall. Thaddeus opened the door. No shouts or shots rang out but light flared dimly in the chamber.

"This room has been used," Thaddeus said, edging inside. He glanced at the lantern. "And recently."

Fog did not hesitate. He trotted eagerly to a door set with iron bars, tail waving like a banner.

There was a small, choked cry of alarm from the other side of the door. Thaddeus crossed the room and looked through the bars. A figure huddled on a small cot. His stomach knotted. The woman's hair was the wrong color.

Fog had already lost interest in the cell.

"Who are you?" Thaddeus said to the

woman on the cot. The door was old, but the lock was new. He removed the pick from the pocket of his coat. "Where is Leona?"

Hesitantly, the woman got to her feet. "Are you talking about Miss Hewitt?"

"Yes." Thaddeus applied the pick to the lock. "She was here, wasn't she? The dog senses her."

"Dog? I feared it was a wolf." The woman walked forward. "Two men came for Miss Hewitt a short time ago. They took her away. That bastard, Dr. Hulsey, said something about the members of the Third Circle needing her crystal-working talents."

Thaddeus got the cell door open. "Where did they take her?"

"I don't know."

"They're still here in the ruins," Caleb said. He nodded toward the lantern. "They would not have left the lamp if they were not in the vicinity. Too much danger of fire and a fire would draw attention to their secret location."

Thaddeus looked at the woman. "Go through the door we used. The steps lead up to the abbey kitchens. Get clear of the ruins as quickly as possible and hide in the woods. We will look for you after we find Leona. If we do not come out within the next half hour, you must find your own way back into the city. Go to Scotland Yard. Ask for Detective Spellar. Tell him everything that has happened. Tell him The Ghost sent you. Do you understand?"

"Yes. You must find Miss Hewitt. She saved me from the nightmare with her crystal. I intend to repay her with the most beautiful hat any woman ever wore."

"Who are you?" he asked.

"My name is Annie Spence."

He smiled. "I am relieved to know that you are alive, Annie Spence."

"Not nearly as relieved as I am, I'll wager." At the door she paused and looked back, her eyes stark with a mix of exhaustion and wonder. "She said you would come straight down into hell to find us. I did not believe her. But she spoke the truth."

50

"Always give the customers a show, Leona."

Uncle Edward's advice rang in her head, steadying her nerves. Just another audience, she thought. She fed more energy into the heart of the stone. The moonlight grew stronger, gleaming on the cryptic words inscribed on the gold lid.

"It's working," someone breathed. "The key is opening the chest."

The members of the Third Circle watched, rapt with amazement. Leona could feel the intensity of their concentration. They were all focused completely on the stone. Unwittingly they had opened their paranormal senses to her.

An unwholesome lust emanated from each man. It was not the lust associated with sensuality, Leona thought. These five sought Sybil's secrets with a passion that was nothing short of obsession.

"I have awakened the true power of the crystal," she intoned in her best stage accents. Uncle Edward would have been proud.

The silvery glow at the stone's heart began to flare and pulse, darkening and changing hues. She intensified the resonating pattern of the currents. Eerie waves of luminescence appeared around the crystal, radiating outward, enveloping her. There were no words for the bizarre colors that formed and dissolved and reformed. She knew she was bathed in the shifting light.

"An aurora," Gold Mask whispered, astounded.

She had never worked the crystal to this degree. The surging energy aroused all her senses. An exhilarating thrill came upon her. *Think positive?* She wanted to laugh. This sensation went far beyond positive thinking. This was sheer exultation. This was euphoria. This was what it felt like to wield raw power.

The light of the crystal splashed wildly, turning the chamber into a furnace filled with cold, paranormal flames. She cupped the stone in her palms and lifted it out of its cradle. Holding it in front of her face she looked at the circle of masked faces through a flaring veil of brilliant energy.

She smiled, savoring the thrilling fire arc-ing through and around her.

"You all really do look quite ridiculous in those masks, you know," she said.

Perhaps it was her smile or maybe Gold Mask's intuition finally whispered a warning. Whatever the case, he took a sudden, panicky step back and threw up his hands as though warding off a demon.

"No," he shouted. "Put it down."

"I'm afraid it's much too late," Leona said gently. "You wanted Sybil's secrets. This is one of them. It has been passed down to me, generation after generation, for over two hundred years. It comes from the Sorceress, herself. And by the way, she was no virgin."

She sent another surge of energy crashing through the stone. The undulating currents of the brilliant aurora locked on to the energy patterns of the five men, overwhelming them.

The members of the Third Circle began to scream.

They were still screaming a moment later when Thaddeus, Fog and a stranger kicked open the door.

51

The following afternoon, they gathered in the library. Thaddeus was at his customary place behind the desk. He had just come from a meeting with Caleb and Gabriel Jones and he had brought the essence of the day into the house with him. When he had walked into the room a moment ago, deliberately brushing against her skirts, Leona had smelled fresh air and sunshine mingled with his intriguing male scent. The combination had revitalized her as nothing else had since he had brought her out of the abbey last night.

She sat on the sofa with Victoria, waiting to hear the latest news. Fog lounged at her feet, languidly content, as though nothing at all of an exciting nature had occurred in the past twenty-four hours. Leona envied him the canine talent to live in the moment. Dogs did not waste time dwelling on the past, nor did they worry about the future.

One could learn a great deal about positive thinking from them, she reflected.

For her part, although utterly exhausted after working the aurora stone to such a powerful level, she had been able to sleep only fitfully. When she had managed to close her eyes for short periods of time, she had endured dreams of such a strange and bizarre nature that she had been jolted awake. Victoria had provided her with a lotion made of cucumber and milk, which she had applied to her face and eyes before coming downstairs, but she feared she looked quite haggard today.

Thaddeus sat forward and folded his hands on the desk. "Caleb was correct in his initial intuitive suspicion. It appears that a well-organized conspiracy does, indeed, exist within the Arcane Society. He thinks it is controlled by a small cabal of very powerful men at the top. Its members refer to the conspiracy as the Order of the Emerald Tablet."

Leona picked up her teacup. "That is the name of one of the ancient texts of alchemy. It is said that the rules for the successful transmutation of primordial substances were originally inscribed on an emerald tablet by Hermes Trismegistus. The old alchemists believed that if they properly interpreted the code in which they were written, they could understand the secret of life and thereby gain great powers."

"Not to mention pick up a few handy tricks like turning lead into gold," Victoria said, mouth turning downward in disdain.

"The Order must be taken apart," Thaddeus said. "But Gabe and Caleb believe that will be a complicated process. When I left, Caleb was envisioning a network of trusted agents such as myself. It seems my career prospects as a private enquiry agent have just become a good deal brighter."

For the first time in hours, Leona felt some of her natural energy return. "You said he is planning to enlist a number of investigators in this project?"

Thaddeus raised his brows. "Don't get any ideas. You have contributed more than enough to the investigation of this conspiracy. Further efforts on your part would have a disastrous effect on my nerves."

She gave him her best stage smile.

Thaddeus sighed. "I'm doomed."

Victoria tut-tutted. "What on earth do these conspirators hope to achieve?"

"Power," Thaddeus said simply. "It is the greatest lure of all."

"Power of a psychical nature?" Victoria sniffed. "Ridiculous. Why would anyone want more paranormal talent? Until recently I have found my own intuitive abilities extremely frustrating. And look at you, Thaddeus. Your talent has limited not only your friendships but your marital prospects as well. You should have taken a wife and set up your nursery years ago. But women are afraid of your true nature."

Thaddeus's face could have been carved from stone. Leona flushed and leaned down to ruffle Fog's fur. What did Thaddeus think of her own talents now that he knew the full extent of what she could do with a crystal like the aurora stone?

"There are many who would deem great paranormal powers of far more importance than friends, family and a wife," Thaddeus said neutrally. "The founder's formula, if it could be successfully and safely reproduced, holds the potential to greatly enhance and extend the range of an individual's talents. Just consider what I could do if I were not only a parahypnotist but also possessed a hunter's talents and perhaps those of a parascientist as well."

Victoria's eyes widened in shock. "You would be a sort of superman, a superior species of human."

"Not *superior,*" Thaddeus emphasized; "That is a moral and ethical judgment that does not apply. But I would certainly be extremely powerful. And if I happened to be inclined toward criminal activities . . . Well, I'm sure you see the problem."

"Good lord," Victoria whispered, horrified. "I understand. The conspirators must be stopped before they become a menace to us all."

"As it happens, Gabe agrees with you," Thaddeus said. "Furthermore, he is convinced that now that the rumors of the discovery of the founder's formula have begun to spread through the membership, the Arcane Society will be bedeviled indefinitely by those who will seek to get their hands on it. Hence the establishment of a permanent office of enquiries."

"But surely those dreadful men that you and Caleb caught last night will provide the information needed to nip this current conspiracy in the bud," Victoria insisted.

"Unfortunately, it isn't that simple," Thaddeus said. "Last night I put each of them into a trance and questioned them. It was soon obvious that, while they could describe the general structure of the Order and its goals, they did not know the identities of those members in the circles above or below them. They were only acquainted with each other."

"A very clever arrangement," Leona said. "If one Circle is discovered, the members cannot betray the others."

"Right," Thaddeus said. "And the cabal at the top is very well protected. Caleb will have his hands full identifying the people who control the Order."

"What will become of Dr. Hulsey and those dreadful men who kidnapped Leona?" Victoria asked.

"Hulsey vanished in the chaos last night, but we found his laboratory. Caleb is already plotting the hunt for him. As for the five men who were captured, that situation is somewhat complicated."

"I don't see why," Victoria said. "At the very least they should stand trial for kidnapping."

"Unfortunately, there is no way to arrest them without dragging Leona into the middle of a sensational scandal," Thaddeus explained. "Her reputation would be destroyed if it were widely known that five men held her prisoner in that abbey for several hours along with a professional prostitute."

"Good lord, of course," Victoria whispered. "I should have thought of that. The public always blames the woman if there is even a suspicion of rape. It is so grossly unfair."

"As it happens, I've had some experience

recovering from scandal," Leona said dryly. "But I doubt if many in the Arcane Society can make the same claim."

"What do you mean?" Victoria demanded.

Leona patted Fog and looked at Thaddeus. "I suspect the Society has its own reasons for wanting to avoid a public trial, reasons that have nothing to do with me."

Victoria frowned. "I fail to understand."

"Think of the sensation that would be launched if someone were to testify that prominent gentlemen have been secretly engaged in occult practices that involved the kidnapping of women for use in dark ceremonies."

Victoria was incensed. "But it wasn't like that at all. In any event, the study of the paranormal is *not* an occult practice. Members of the Arcane Society do not seek to contact the dead or summon spirits or demons. That sort of deplorable nonsense is the province of the charlatans and frauds who call themselves mediums."

"I know," Leona said. "But I do not think one can count on the ability of the press to distinguish between the paranormal and the occult, do you?"

Victoria bristled, clearly bent on further argument. But after a few seconds of tight-lipped tension, she subsided with a sigh. "No, you are quite right." She turned back to Thaddeus. "Nevertheless, those five villains must not be allowed to go unpunished."

Thaddeus's smile was cold enough to make Leona shiver.

"Rest assured, they are paying for their crimes and will do so for the rest of their lives," he said.

"How?" Victoria demanded.

Leona's hand stilled on Fog's head. "According to my mother's journal, when the aurora stone is used as a weapon in the manner that I employed it last night, there is a great deal of damage inflicted on the nervous system. The five men in that chamber were not driven permanently mad, but virtually all of their paranormal senses have been destroyed. They will suffer from shattered nerves for the rest of their lives."

Victoria's eyes gleamed with satisfaction. "A suitable sentence, indeed."

Leona looked at Thaddeus, the weight of what she had done to the five men falling upon her like a mountain.

"There will be dreams," Thaddeus said, repeating back to her the words she had once spoken to him. "You will come to me when they descend upon you."

It was a promise and a vow.

Something inside her eased.

"Which one of those men murdered Lord Delbridge?" Victoria asked.

"The leader of the Third Circle, Lord Granton," Thaddeus said. "When I put him into a trance he explained that Delbridge had become a serious liability. Dr. Hulsey witnessed the murder and was delighted to offer the leader not only his services but also a crystal worker he was certain could activate the aurora stone."

"Me," Leona said.

"You," Thaddeus agreed.

"Annie Spence will be able to provide a great deal of information about Hulsey," Leona said.

"Caleb has already interviewed her," Thaddeus said.

"Speaking of Annie, I trust the Society will compensate her for what she went through," Leona continued. "After all, if it had not been for the very existence of the founder's formula and the Arcane Society, she would not have been kidnapped and used as a research subject."

"Gabe is very conscious of the Society's responsibility in all this," Thaddeus said. "It appears that Annie's dream is to open her own millinery shop. Gabe has ensured that the funds she needs to achieve her goal will be made available to her immediately."

"I must go and see her today. She suffered greatly because of that madman, Hulsey. I want to make sure she knows to come to me if the hallucinations return."

"I paid a quick visit to her a short time ago to tell her about the money," Thaddeus said. "Her friend, the tavern owner, is taking good care of her. When I left, she was already making plans to search for premises to rent for her shop."

Leona smiled, relieved. "I think Annie will do very well. Hers is a resilient spirit."

"As is yours," Thaddeus said.

Suddenly she felt a good deal more cheerful. *Think positive.*

Victoria frowned. "After all that fuss, what was in Sybil's strongbox?"

"Her journal of experiments and some two-hundred-year-old alchemical apparatus," Leona said. She raised her brows very coolly. "All of which, everyone agrees, belong to me."

Victoria looked troubled. "But, my dear, the journal and the stone are so dangerous."

Leona wrinkled her nose. "In view of that fact I have agreed to allow the Arcane Society to take charge of the aurora stone and the contents of Sybil's strongbox on the condition that I have access to them anytime I wish."

"Excellent decision." Victoria was clearly relieved.

A knock sounded on the door of the library.

"Come in," Thaddeus called.

Gribbs loomed in the opening. "I apologize for the interruption, sir, but the dressmaker has arrived. She says that she has an appointment for the second fitting of Miss Hewitt's gown."

Reality slammed through Leona, jerking her out of her pleasant little fantasy.

"There is no longer any need for me to attend the Spring Ball," she said quickly. "I won't be needing the gown."

Victoria opened her mouth. Leona never discovered what it was she intended to say, however, because Thaddeus was on his feet, circling the desk and giving orders.

"Tell the dressmaker that Miss Hewitt will be ready for her fitting in a few minutes," he said.

"I really don't see any point —" Leona got out. She broke off when Thaddeus arrived in front of her.

He reached down, clamped a hand around her wrist and hauled her unceremoniously to her feet.

"Come with me," he ordered.

He headed for the French doors, half dragging her with him.

She could not be certain because she was feeling decidedly rattled, but she could have sworn that she heard Victoria making a very odd sound behind her. It was the sort of noise one made when one tried to swallow laughter.

52

The conservatory was a very different place by day. The humid, tropical atmosphere was the same and so were the exotic, fragrant scents. But the flood of bright daylight filtering through the overarching glass robbed the miniature paradise of the magical quality of night. Gone was the sense of having been transported to a hidden bower in some other dimension. This was the real world, albeit a very beautiful slice of it. Thaddeus was very real, too. And he was not in a good temper.

He brought her to a halt in the shade of a large palm. "You and I agreed that you would allow me to escort you to that damn ball."

"But that was because we intended to set a trap," she said. "Those plans have been called off, so I assumed there was no reason for me to be present."

"You assumed nothing of the kind. You're

trying to find a way to avoid accompanying me. I think I have a right to know why."

"You know why. My connection to the Arcane Society is of a somewhat strained nature. Now that there is no longer a pressing need for me to attend the ball, I think it would be best for both of us to avoid being seen together in such a public manner."

"You want to continue our affair in secret, is that it?"

She cleared her throat. "Well, it did strike me that might be a more sensible way to proceed, yes."

"When have you and I ever done things in a sensible manner?"

"Surely you can understand that this is all a little awkward for me," she said.

"Because you don't wish to be seen with me?"

It was too much.

"How dare you say that?" she demanded, incensed. "In case you have failed to notice, I've been through a great deal of stress in the past few days. I've encountered two murdered people, been forced to flee my home because of the threat of a killer who proved to be a psychically enhanced lunatic, and was kidnapped by a mad scientist and five conspirators. *To say nothing of losing my virginity right here in this very conservatory.*"

She burst into tears. The sobs welled up out of nowhere, taking her completely by surprise. One moment she was in a towering rage, and the next she was weeping like a waterfall. What on earth was wrong with her? *"Think positive."*

But Uncle Edward's words of advice were useless against the tide of emotion that threatened to consume her. She turned away from Thaddeus, covered her face with both hands and wept.

She cried for the mother she had lost when she was young; for the uncle she had trusted and who had abandoned her; for Carolyn, the friend with whom she had planned to share a house and a life; for the children she might have had if she had married William Trover. Most of all she cried for the nights she had lain awake staring at the ceiling, trying to concentrate on the future, and for all the energy she had put into thinking positive when it was clearly an utter waste of time.

Somewhere in the distance she heard Fog howl, but she could not control her tears long enough to go to him and reassure him. That realization made her weep all the harder.

She felt Thaddeus's hands close around her shoulders. He turned her toward him without a word and wrapped her in his arms.

She collapsed against his chest and sobbed until she was exhausted, until there were no more tears. When she finally fell quiet, her face pressed into his now-damp coat, he kissed the top of her head.

"I'm sorry," he said gently. "About everything."

"Mmm." She did not raise her head.

"Almost everything," he clarified.

She nodded numbly. "Most of it wasn't your fault."

"Except the lost virginity."

"Well, yes, that was your fault."

He tipped her chin up and looked into her drenched eyes. "That is the one thing for which I cannot apologize. I don't feel any regret, you see."

"Why would you?" she said, blotting her eyes on her sleeve. "It was my virginity, not yours."

"The reason I can't feel sorry for my role in the business is because making love with you is the most astonishingly wonderful thing that I have ever done in my life."

"Oh." From out of nowhere, hope returned, just as if it had never been utterly extinguished a moment earlier. "It is that way for me, too."

He frowned. "If that's the case, why did you list losing your virginity as one of the things that had gone wrong during the past few days?"

"I didn't say it was a list of things that had gone wrong. I just put it on the list of things I had found somewhat stressful."

"What the devil is that supposed to mean?"

She glowered at him. "For pity's sake, Thaddeus, just because something is pleasurable, even transcendently so, doesn't mean there is not some stress involved."

"That's ridiculous. Why should there be any stress under such circumstances?"

"Are you going to stand there and quarrel with me about what I felt or did not feel when I lost my virginity?"

"Yes, I am damn well going to quarrel with you about it. I was involved in the process that night, and I didn't feel any stress."

"Maybe that's because you weren't emotionally involved."

"Bloody hell, woman, I told you that first night when you used the aurora stone to save me from the poison drug that some sort of psychical bonds were fused between us."

She drew herself up, straightened her shoulders and prepared to wager her entire future. *Think positive.*

"I wouldn't know about psychical bonds,"

she said politely. "The only bonds I felt that night were the bonds of love."

It was his turn to be dumbfounded. "What did you say?"

"I fell in love with you in the carriage when we fought your demons together and I witnessed the strength and passion of your spirit. I knew then that you were the man I'd been waiting for all of my life."

Exultant satisfaction flared in the atmosphere around her. Thaddeus gave a shout that could surely be heard by everyone inside the house. He fitted his hands to her waist, lifted her straight off the ground and swung her around in a dizzying circle.

"I love you," he roared in his enthralling mesmeric voice. *"I will love you all the days of my life and beyond, Leona Hewitt. Do you hear me?"*

Light, joyous laughter rang from the glass walls of the conservatory. It took her a while to realize that she was the one who was laughing.

"I love you, too, Thaddeus Ware. And I will love you all the days of my life and beyond."

The vows were as binding as any spoken in church. Thaddeus stopped spinning her around, brought her close and kissed her for a very long time.

■ ■ ■ ■

Inside the library Victoria experienced a surge of keen satisfaction. Her talent was frustrating at times, but it was always gratifying when she was proved right.

She looked at Fog, who had stopped howling and now had his nose pressed against the French doors. His ears were pricked, and his gaze was fixed on the conservatory.

"I told you there was no need for all that howling," she said briskly. "They will make each other very happy. Knew it from the first moment I saw them together. I have a talent for sensing that sort of thing, you see. I'm never wrong."

53

There was enough energy in the ballroom to light up the chandeliers. Individually, each of the elite, powerful members of the Arcane Society could move, unnoticed, through a crowd, but put a hundred of them in close quarters like this, and the atmosphere fairly shimmered. The Spring Ball was a glittering affair on both the normal and the paranormal plane.

Leona stood with Thaddeus and Victoria at the edge of the throng. They watched the dancers take the floor. At the heart of the room, the new Master of the Arcane Society swept his wife into the first waltz. The crowd signaled its approval with a round of applause. It was clear, however, that as far as Gabriel and Venetia were concerned there was no one else in the room.

"Born for each other, those two," Victoria announced. She downed a healthy dose of champagne and lowered her glass, looking vastly pleased with herself. "Of course, from now on people will have to pay for that sort of brilliant insight."

"Nevertheless, it's always nice to know that the head of the Society is a happily married man," Leona said diplomatically.

"Right." Thaddeus smiled a little. "Means he'll be able to concentrate better on his job. Got his work cut out for him trying to shove this tradition-bound Society into the modern era."

Victoria frowned. "Word is he intends to make a lot of changes. There's going to be a lot of kicking and screaming."

Caleb Jones materialized from behind Leona. Dourly he surveyed the dancers as though searching for patterns in the swirling turns of the waltz. "The kicking and screaming has already begun."

Thaddeus raised his brows. "The Council objected to the new Office of Enquiries?"

"No," Caleb said, "I did."

"You didn't take the post?" Thaddeus asked, surprised. "Gabe assured me a short time ago that it was all settled."

"It's settled," Caleb said. "But there won't be any Office of Enquiries."

"How very disappointing," Leona said. "I was so looking forward to being a private enquiry agent again."

Thaddeus's eyes narrowed. "You've already got a career as a crystal worker. I'm the one who was going to be a private enquiry agent for the new Office of Enquiries."

She patted his arm. "Of course. I would never give up my crystal work. But it occurred to me that the occasional fling as one of Mr. Jones's agents might prove quite stimulating."

"The issue is now moot," Thaddeus said.

"You know, you sound a lot like Fog when you growl," she observed. "I do hope you won't progress to howling on occasion."

"Actually, it's not moot," Caleb said. His attention was still on the dancers. "I'll need the help of both of you and others within the Society, as well. I require people I can trust absolutely, and there aren't a lot of them around. This damned conspiracy we uncovered is more dangerous than anyone on the Council realizes. It must be stopped."

Leona tilted her head a little to the side. "But you just said you had turned down the position as head of an enquiries office."

"I told Gabe that I would not put myself into the position of taking orders from the Council," Caleb explained. "Half of those doddering old fools are still playing at alchemy. The other half are obsessed with their own status and power. I don't trust any of them to have the future of the Society as a high priority. Gabe agrees with me."

Thaddeus looked intrigued. "You have our attention, Caleb. What are you planning?"

"I am going to establish my own private enquiry business," Caleb said. "Gabe and the Council will be my most important clients. Protecting the Society's secrets will be my firm's principal objective. But Jones and Company will be independent. I and my agents will be free to conduct investigations as I see fit and free to take private clients."

Cool satisfaction gleamed in Thaddeus's eyes. "I like the sound of that arrangement."

"So do I," Leona said.

Victoria looked at Caleb. "I don't suppose you will have some use for a matchmaker?"

Caleb looked briefly startled. Then he frowned in thought, his eyes still on the dancers. "I can certainly envision situations in which it would be extraordinarily useful to have your sort of intuitive sight into an individual or individuals. Yes, I think I can offer you some employment, madam."

Victoria glowed. "How thrilling."

Caleb abruptly turned away from the dance floor. He appeared distracted.

"If you will all excuse me, I must be off," he said.

Leona examined his humorless expression. "Are you ill, Mr. Jones?"

"What?" He seemed baffled by the question. Then his face cleared. "No, I'm well, thank you, Miss Hewitt. I'm leaving because I have work to do. I promised Gabe I would put in an appearance here tonight, but now I must get back to my laboratory. I am working on Hulsey's notes. There is something about the manner in which he organized his experiments that may provide a clue to the way he thinks. If I can comprehend the pattern, I will be able to devise a plan to locate him." He nodded brusquely. "Good night."

Victoria watched him leave. "Odd, even for a Jones."

"I believe Caleb is sinking deeper into his obsession with patterns," Thaddeus said quietly.

Leona smiled. "About my part-time career in the enquiry business."

Thaddeus held up both hands, palms out, and smiled. "Enough, my love, no more arguing about the matter. I refuse to ruin the evening worrying about all the things that might possibly go wrong if you were to get involved in another investigation. I will take your advice; I am going to think positive."

"I am delighted to hear that."

"For tonight, at least. One step at a time."

He took her arm, mesmeric eyes heating. "Dance with me, my love. It will go far to ensure that I maintain my new optimistic outlook."

She laughed, happiness effervescing through her as light and intoxicating as champagne. "Anything to assist you in your goal to think positive."

He responded to her laughter with his wolfish smile and drew her into the glittering pool of dancers.

"I love you, my beautiful sorceress," he whispered.

"I love you, Thaddeus. You are the man I have waited —"

She stopped midsentence, aware that Thaddeus was not listening. His attention was fixed on the far side of the room.

"What in blazes?" He brought her to a halt in the middle of the floor.

Annoyed at the interruption of what had been one of the most romantic nights of her entire life, she turned to follow his gaze.

A visible ripple of awareness accompanied by murmurs and whispers was sweeping through the crowd. Heads turned. At the center of the moving wave was a tall, distinguished-looking gentleman elegantly attired in black-and-white evening clothes. The light of the chandeliers gleamed on his silver hair and sparkled on his diamond stickpin.

The room seemed to waver and shift around her. For the first and only time in her life, Leona wondered if she might faint.

The silver-haired man reached the edge of the dance floor and looked around expectantly, searching for someone. The last waltzing couple stopped midturn. The musicians fell silent. A hush gripped the crowd.

Leona seized fistfuls of her skirts in both hands and flew toward the newcomer, weaving a path through the maze of dancers.

"Uncle Edward," she shouted. *"You're alive."*

54

It was nearly dawn. Through the glass walls of the conservatory Leona could see the first faint blush of morning light. She was still in her spectacular ball gown, its satins and silks turned to warm amber gold in the gaslight.

Thaddeus had removed his black evening coat, unknotted his tie and opened the collar of his pleated shirt. Lounging against the edge of a workbench, he picked up the brandy bottle he had brought from the library, filled two glasses and handed one to Leona.

"To good old Uncle Edward," he said. He raised the glass in a small toast. "And to his amazing powers of positive thinking."

"I knew he would come back someday." Leona sipped her brandy, savoring all the joys, large and small, that the night had brought. "But to be perfectly honest, I wasn't entirely certain that he would ever be able to repay the investors."

Thaddeus laughed. "Thought the crowd was going to turn into a mob when they realized who had walked into their midst. I swear, if Gabe hadn't taken command of the situation, the first Spring Ball of the Arcane Society would have turned into a full-blown riot. But tomorrow I suspect that everyone who was in that room tonight will be standing in line begging to invest in your uncle's next investment scheme."

Once the excitement had died down and the news that the mining investment had finally, if somewhat belatedly, paid off, it seemed everyone had wanted to talk to Edward. He had spent the evening regaling the attentive crowd around him with stories of the profits to be made in American investments.

Leona gave a tiny shudder. "Between you and me, I can't help thinking that it was luck, not positive thinking, that saved Uncle Edward this time. It sounds as if everything that could go wrong in America did, indeed, go wrong. It was a *disaster.*"

Being the positive thinker that he was, Edward had not dwelt on the unpleasant details, but it was clear that the past two years had been fraught with hardship and peril. There was a brief mention of a deceptive banker and an extraordinarily beautiful and charming woman who had turned out to be somewhat less than trustworthy. Finding himself accused of fraud and embezzlement in San Francisco, Edward had been forced to fake his own death, change his name and lie low for some time while he crafted another investment scheme. The second project had proved spectacularly successful, making more than enough money to pay off the original investors.

"All's well that ends well, as we who think positive like to say." Thaddeus set aside his glass and drew her into his arms. "Really, my love, you must learn to take a more optimistic view of life. Where's the good in dwelling on the negative?"

She laughed and went into his arms. "You're right. I don't know what came over me."

She raised her face for his kiss.

Love flared, an invisible aura that she knew would warm their hearts for the rest of their lives.

ABOUT THE AUTHOR

Amanda Quick is a pseudonym for Jayne Ann Krentz, the author — under various pen names — of more than forty *New York Times* bestsellers. There are more than 25 million copies of her books in print.

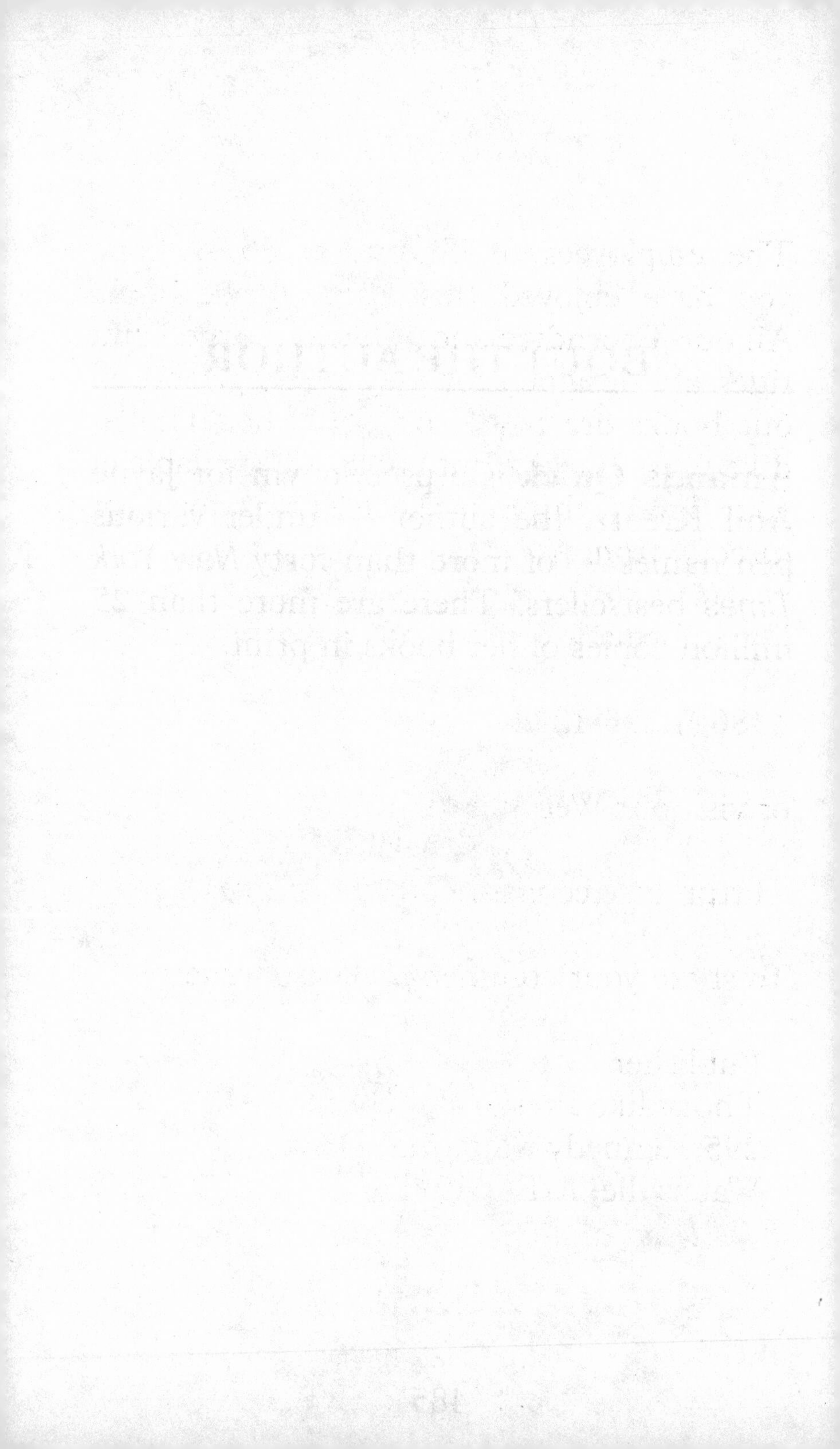

The employees of Thorndike Press hope you have enjoyed this Large Print book. All our Thorndike and Wheeler Large Print titles are designed for easy reading, and all our books are made to last. Other Thorndike Press Large Print books are available at your library, through selected bookstores, or directly from us.

For information about titles, please call:

(800) 223-1244

or visit our Web site at:

http://gale.cengage.com/thorndike

To share your comments, please write:

Publisher
Thorndike Press
295 Kennedy Memorial Drive
Waterville, ME 04901